ANDREW MAYNE

A THRILLER

D0034341

SEA STORM

PRAISE FOR ANDREW MAYNE

BLACK CORAL

"A relentless nail-biter whether below or above the waterline. Even the setbacks are suspenseful."

—*Kirkus Reviews* (starred review)

"Mayne's portrayal of the Everglades ecosystem and its inhabitants serves as a fascinating backdrop for the detective work. Readers will hope the spunky Sloan returns soon."

—*Publishers Weekly*

"Andrew Mayne has more than a few tricks up his sleeve—he's an accomplished magician, deep-sea diver, and consultant, not to mention skilled in computer coding, developing educational tools, and of course, writing award-nominated bestselling fiction. They are impressive skills on their own, but when they combine? Abracadabra! It's magic . . . Such is the case in Mayne's latest series featuring Sloan McPherson, a Florida police diver with the Underwater Investigation Unit."

—*The Big Thrill*

"Andrew Mayne has dazzled readers across the globe with his thrillers featuring lead characters with fascinating backgrounds in crime forensics. The plots are complex, with meticulous attention to scientific and investigative detail—a tribute to the level of research and study Mayne puts into every novel. A world-renowned illusionist with thousands of passionate fans (who call themselves 'Mayniacs'), Mayne applies his skill with sleight of hand and visual distraction to his storytelling, thereby creating shocking twists and stunning denouements."

—Authorlink

Mar 2022

"As I said before, a solid follow-up with thrilling action, especially the undersea scenes and the threat of Big Bill. Here's to more underwater adventures with the UIU."

—*Red Carpet Crash*

"As with the series debut, this book moved along well and never lost its momentum. With a great plot and strong narrative, Mayne pulls the reader in from the opening pages and never lets up. He develops the plot well with his strong dialogue and uses shorter chapters to keep the flow throughout. While I know little about diving, Mayne bridged that gap effectively for me and kept things easy to comprehend for the layperson. I am eager to see what is to come, as the third novel in the series was just announced. It's sure to be just as captivating as this one!"

—*Mystery & Suspense Magazine*

"Mayne creates a thrilling plot with likable yet flawed characters . . . Fans of detective series will enjoy seeing where the next episodes take us."

—Bookreporter

"Former illusionist and now bestselling author Andrew Mayne used to have a cable series entitled *Don't Trust Andrew Mayne*. If you take that same recommendation and apply it to his writing, you will have some idea of the games you are in for with his latest novel, titled *Black Coral*. Just when you think you might have things figured out, Andrew Mayne pulls the rug out from under you and leaves you reeling in fits of delight."

—Criminal Element

"The pages are packed with colorful characters . . . its shenanigans, dark humor, and low view of human foibles should appeal to fans of Carl Hiaasen and John D. MacDonald."

—*Star News*

THE GIRL BENEATH THE SEA

"Distinctive characters and a genuinely thrilling finale . . . Readers will look forward to Sloan's further adventures."

—*Publishers Weekly*

"Mayne writes with a clipped narrative style that gives the story rapid-fire propulsion, and he populates the narrative with a rogue's gallery of engaging characters . . . [A] winning new series with a complicated female protagonist that combines police procedural with adventure story and mixes the styles of Lee Child and Clive Cussler."

—*Library Journal*

"Sloan McPherson is a great, gutsy, and resourceful character."

—Authorlink

"Sloan McPherson is one heck of a woman . . . *The Girl Beneath the Sea* is an action-packed mystery that takes you all over Florida in search of answers."

—*Long and Short Reviews*

"The female lead is a resourceful, powerful woman, and we're already looking forward to hearing more about her in the future Underwater Investigation Unit novels."

—Yahoo!

"*The Girl Beneath the Sea* continuously dives deeper and deeper until you no longer know whom Sloan can trust. This is a terrific entry in a new and unique series."

—Criminal Element

THE NATURALIST

"[A] smoothly written suspense novel from Thriller Award finalist Mayne . . . The action builds to [an] . . . exciting confrontation between Cray and his foe, and scientific detail lends verisimilitude."

—*Publishers Weekly*

"With a strong sense of place and palpable suspense that builds to a violent confrontation and resolution, Mayne's (*Angel Killer*) series debut will satisfy devotees of outdoors mysteries and intriguing characters."

—*Library Journal*

"*The Naturalist* is a suspenseful, tense, and wholly entertaining story . . . Compliments to Andrew Mayne for the brilliant first entry in a fascinating new series."

—*New York Journal of Books*

"An engrossing mix of science, speculation, and suspense, *The Naturalist* will suck you in."

—*Omnivoracious*

"A tour de force of a thriller."

—*Gumshoe Review*

"Mayne is a natural storyteller, and once you start this one, you may find yourself staying up late to finish it . . . It employs everything that makes good thrillers really good . . . The creep factor is high, and the killer, once revealed, will make your skin crawl."

—Criminal Element

"If you enjoy the TV channel Investigation Discovery or shows like *Forensic Files*, then Andrew Mayne's *The Naturalist* is the perfect read for you!"

—*The Suspense Is Thrilling Me*

SEA
STORM

Other Titles by Andrew Mayne

Underwater Investigation Unit Series

The Girl Beneath the Sea
Black Coral

Theo Cray and Jessica Blackwood Series

Mastermind

Theo Cray Series

The Naturalist
Looking Glass
Murder Theory
Dark Pattern

Jessica Blackwood Series

Angel Killer
Fire in the Sky
Name of the Devil
Black Fall

The Chronological Man Series

The Monster in the Mist
The Martian Emperor

SEA STORM

A THRILLER

ANDREW MAYNE

THOMAS & MERCER

Text copyright © 2022 by Andrew Mayne
All rights reserved.

Published by Thomas & Mercer, Seattle

www.apub.com

Amazon, the Amazon logo, and Thomas & Mercer are trademarks of Amazon.com, Inc., or its affiliates.

ISBN-13: 9781542032230
ISBN-10: 1542032237

Cover design by Shasti O'Leary Soudant

Cover photo: Brian Daniel / Gallery Stock

Printed in the United States of America

SEA
STORM

CHAPTER 1
SEA OF FIRE

The bow of our boat bounces across the crashing waves, sending spray and foam into the night sky. Scott Hughes, my partner on the Underwater Investigation Unit, has his eyes trained on the ocean in front of us, trying to avoid hitting debris or, much worse, hitting someone . . .

We had been wrapping up work at our office, getting ready to head home to our families, when the call came in from the coast guard asking for assistance. A cruise ship, *The Sea of Dreams*, carrying four thousand passengers and crew, was having mechanical problems and might be forced to abandon ship.

The thought of trying to evacuate that many people was a nightmare from both a logistical and safety perspective. When the *Costa Concordia* sank off the coast of Isola del Giglio, more than thirty people died in what should have been a safe and orderly evacuation within swimming distance of the Italian resort town. The fact that the captain had been one of the first people to climb aboard a life raft didn't help.

The US Coast Guard trains for these situations, and the coast guard's 7th District more than most. Besides having to worry about drug runners, pleasure boaters, and wayward spring breakers on water scooters, the coast guard watches hundreds of thousands of passengers enter and leave the ports here each year aboard massive cruise ships that are virtual floating cities—cities that sometimes catch on fire, sink, or become hotbeds of infectious disease.

As one of several agencies that work Florida's waterways, we're on the list of who to call when you need an assist. While we've trained with the coast guard and meet on a regular basis, this was one call I'd never expected to get. The fact that they did call us has me concerned.

"There!" says Officer Ava Crozier, a Fort Lauderdale Police Department Marine Unit member on loan to our unit. She points to where her night-vision goggles have caught sight of something.

In the distance, I can make out a faint line of lights. They're closer to the water than I'd expect and look different from what I've seen a thousand times off the beach of Fort Lauderdale.

She hands the goggles to me. "Something's wrong."

I strap on the night-vision goggles and see rows of deck lights, but something does seem off about them. They're fading in and out of view. My first thought is that it's being caused by the up-and-down movement of the waves; then I realize what I'm really seeing, and it's not good.

"Smoke," I shout over the roar of the engines. "Lots of smoke. Coming out the portholes."

"Damn," says Hughes. "Are there any lifeboats in the water?"

"Not yet." I scan the area around the ship and spot a vessel two miles off the aft side. "I think the *Webber's* approaching."

The USCGC *Bernard C. Webber* is one of the coast guard's Sentinel-class cutters based out of Miami. It must have been closest when the cruise ship sent out its SOS.

"Good," says my partner. "The other ships are hours away."

Suddenly, a roaring sound louder than our own marine diesel engines comes from overhead. We glance up at a coast guard helicopter racing to the scene. Its powerful searchlight shines down onto the ocean, turning everything below it to daylight.

When the beam hits *The Sea of Dreams*, the smoke coming out of the aft portholes is even worse than it looked with night vision. Black clouds continue to billow out of the ship.

With the smoke, the situation has gone from critical to nightmare, the potential evacuation now a certainty. I scan the ship again and realize why else the ship's lights looked so weird.

The cruise ship is listing.

"It's sinking!" I yell.

"Fuck."

Scott Hughes is the most straitlaced person I know. Simply hearing him say the word makes the severity of the situation seem so much worse.

I pull out my phone and dial the number for my coast guard contact, the chief of staff for the district.

"McPherson? Are you on the scene?" asks Captain Thomas Plaint.

"We're five minutes out. It looks like it might capsize."

"That's what the crew is telling us. They're loading people into boats now."

"I can get civilian support if you need it," I offer.

"Yes. Yes to anything. Use your judgment, and make sure they have their radio channels open and keep their distance until we give them instructions."

Telling me to use my own judgment is code for "We could use the help, but if you make things worse, we're blaming you." A perfectly understandable point of view.

Our boat bounces over a wave, and *The Sea of Dreams* comes fully into view. Its list is pronounced enough that it's causing problems for the crew trying to lower lifeboats into the water. What had been a straight vertical drop is now a sloping angle. As the boats are lowered, they bash into the hull of the vessel. Trying to lower passengers without dropping or crushing them is posing a serious challenge for the crew running the lift mechanism.

From our boat, we can hear the sound of crew members on megaphones pleading with passengers to stay back and remain calm.

Weirdly enough, the passengers look less panicked than I would expect. As we move closer, I see why. Half of them have their cell phones out and are documenting the disaster, as if they're witnesses, not victims. Someone could get a PhD in psychology writing a paper about that.

The black smoke aft implies there's been some kind of engine trouble. That the ship has lost propulsion also suggests that it's listing for some reason other than a broken rudder.

The most likely explanation is a ruptured hull. But how? The nearest shallow-water reef is miles away. A ship this size could plow through a dozen boats like ours and not even notice.

"I'm going to bring us starboard," says Hughes.

I get on the radio. "*Sea of Dreams*, this is the *Cobia Kai* offering assistance. Over." The name of our boat, which had been a playful pun when we thought it up, now sounds stupid in the face of what we're seeing.

There's no response from the cruise ship. I repeat the message. Nothing.

I switch to a channel for onboard radio and hear multiple voices shouting. The crew's still trying to figure out how to corral people into the lifeboats. It's chaos.

Three words in particular stand out, and ice fills my veins.

People. Trapped. Underwater.

"Ava, take the wheel! Hughes, suit up!"

My partner doesn't question me. He's already opening the locker with our dive gear and laying it out on the deck.

I make one more phone call, to my father.

"Dad, no time to talk. We're approaching a cruise ship that's about to capsize. We need to get boats out looking for people and a barge here as quickly as possible. Call Mom and have her talk to hotels. We're going to have a few thousand people on the beach in less than an hour."

"Got it," he replies.

Dad has seen more maritime disasters than anyone I know. He's probably caused half of them, but there's nobody you'd rather have in a situation like this than an old pirate like him.

We hear a loud BOOM. The cruise ship shudders and passengers scream. I don't know what caused it, but it's not good. We need to get everyone off that ship fast.

CHAPTER 2
ANGLE OF ATTACK

The old joke about how someone went bankrupt—"Slowly at first, then all at once"—echoes in my head as I strap on my vest and tank over my shorts and shirt. There's no time to put on a wet suit. We also won't be using fins because we'll be doing more walking and climbing than swimming.

Hughes opens a case and hands me a portable carbon monoxide detector. Besides running out of air, we also have to be cautious about breathing the smoke and gases from the fire. However, neither will be a problem for us if we can't get aboard the vessel.

On a ship the size of *The Sea of Dreams*, the distance from the waterline to the first deck is several stories. That's why we need what's in the other case that Hughes is unpacking: a grappling hook and ladder developed for the UK's Special Boat Service, the unit that recaptures hijacked oil tankers.

Ava Crozier pilots us under the bow of the ship and around the starboard side. Half the lifeboats are in the water—which is good, assuming they're mostly full. The remaining passengers are leaning out over the railings above us, which is not so good. Not that I can blame them.

When they practiced the lifeboat drills, the ship wasn't listing like it is now.

"What's going on?" a man shouts from above.

All I can do is look up and shrug. As I do so, my eye catches something fifty feet overhead. "Hughes!" I point to the bridge of the ship. Or rather the gaping hole on the starboard side that had once been part of the bridge.

He glances up and sees what I'm looking at. There must have been some kind of explosion. Wait . . . an explosion on the *bridge*? Caused by what? I take a photo with my phone.

Hughes grabs our spotlight and aims it at the waterline of the ship, aft from us. "There!"

Jagged metal edges reveal another apparent site of an explosion. While the bridge explosion was damaging enough, it's the hull damage that's threatening to capsize the cruise ship.

Ava guides us along the side of the ship, weaving past lifeboats that are drifting away. Hughes aims the air rifle with the grappling hook at a deck railing immediately above us and fires.

The hook shoots through the gap, clangs against the metal deck, then pulls back and clings to the rail. Hughes pulls tight on the attached ladder to make sure it's not going anywhere, then uses his weight to hold the base of the flexible ladder down so I can go first. It's not chivalry or cowardice; it's physics. He weighs more than I do, so he's better as the ballast.

I start climbing. Despite Hughes holding the bottom, the ladder twists and swings back and forth. It would have been easier to board via a helicopter—which is what the coast guard divers will do when they arrive.

I learned how to climb up shaky ladders before I ever wore a badge. It's how I earned the tag "Sea Monkey" in my family. One of many nicknames.

Hughes is right below me. Paradoxically, the more people on the ladder, the more stable it becomes—up to the breaking point. But this ladder is rated for a few thousand pounds.

I reach the deck railing and pull myself over, thankful that I didn't skip upper-body-workout days even when I didn't feel like it. It's one thing to climb up a ladder like this at sea; it's another to do it with scuba gear strapped to your back. I move to the side and help Hughes over the rail.

"Thanks," he says as he climbs over.

We have to push ourselves away from the railing because of the list. Our footwear, special booties designed for slick surfaces, makes it a little easier to keep our balance.

We go through an open doorway and into a passage that leads to an impossibly long corridor lined with cabins. Because the lights are still on, other than the list, everything appears normal. A calm voice on the speakers repeats the instruction for everyone to proceed safely to their lifeboat station.

On the first day at sea of every cruise, passengers are put through a drill so they know exactly what to do and where to go. Disasters like the *Costa Concordia* happen when the crew doesn't know what to tell them to do next. In that case, as the ship took on water and sank, crew were telling people to go back to their cabins.

Hughes and I run down the corridor past endless rows of identical cabin doors, some open, some closed, and make our way to the aft section, where the smoke is coming from.

As we pass by open doors, we peer inside, making sure nobody remains.

We reach the end of the corridor and find ourselves at an ornate staircase. A man in a waiter's uniform and life vest is standing guard at the stairs.

"You're not supposed to be here!" he shouts. "Go to your lifeboat station now!"

"We're not passengers," I tell him. "We're a rescue team. We heard on the radio there are people trapped underwater."

His eyes light up. "Yes! Follow me!"

The waiter has no breathing gear, so I stop him. "Just tell us where to go." He motions to a metal door behind him. "Through there. Down three levels."

We push through the doors and into the stark white section of the crew area. Unlike the passenger section, which was furnished like a five-star resort, this area resembles a hospital made of metal.

On a ship this size, there are several levels the passengers never see or even think about during their cruise. There's the deck where cargo is loaded and stored, and food is prepared in the kitchens. There are crew quarters, compartments of cramped bunks; the crew's mess; a gym; a bar; and other sites for employee recreation. Below lie the engines that drive the generators that power the ship and provide propulsion.

Because the engines have stopped, the ship must be running on some kind of backup power, which won't last long. After that, the emergency lighting will kick on until the batteries run down.

At the end of the corridor, we hear the sound of yelling coming from a stairwell below us. We pick up our pace and rush down the steps.

Two decks below, we find a group of men in overalls holding on to a rope leading down a stairwell below them. The sound of splashing water makes it apparent that we're standing above a flooded compartment.

"What's going on?" asks Hughes.

One of the men holding the rope turns and sees our dive gear. "We've got people stuck in a compartment. The fire door's shut at one end, and this part is flooded."

As he says this, water splashes over the edge of the stairs in a huge gush. We're still sinking.

"Which compartment?" asks Hughes.

"The backup power control room," the man replies.

While that clearly makes sense to the crewman, it does nothing for us.

"Go stand directly above where they are," I tell the man.

He understands the problem immediately and runs twenty yards down the corridor, then shouts back, "Here! There's a passage to my right. Directly below."

Hughes nods to me, and I make a mental map and adjust our gear. He steps into the flooded stairwell first; then I follow.

There could be any number of hazards below, from electrical cable or sharp debris to the pounding waves of the incoming ocean. It doesn't matter. We don't even pause to ask the man if he's certain his crewmates are alive. The longer we take, the greater the chance the answer will be no.

"If this compartment gets flooded, leave," I tell the man.

"What about the others?"

"They're our problem now."

I press my hand to my mask to hold it in place and follow Hughes into the water.

CHAPTER 3
CLEARING THE DECKS

The water pushes me against a bulkhead the moment I reach the end of the stairs. I anchor myself, grabbing the railing, then look around me. The corridor lights, sealed inside watertight housings, are still on, but the water's murky and streaked with what looks like oil.

God help us if the fuel tanks rupture and we get a hundred thousand gallons of diesel fuel spilled into our ecosystem. Part of me wants to go back to the surface and call my dad to make sure his friends who specialize in oil cleanup are coming.

I take a breath and calm myself. One emergency at a time. These newer ships are designed to minimize the possibility of such a scenario. No cruise line or their insurer wants to risk the chance of a multibillion-dollar cleanup bill.

Of course, no cruise line or shipbuilder anticipated whatever happened to this vessel. *The Sea of Dreams* looks like it's been through a war.

Focus, Sloan. Find the crew members. Get them to safety. Control what you can control and leave the rest to Neptune.

The current rushing through the corridor is shifting back and forth, forcing Hughes and me to pull ourselves along instead of swim. Inch by inch, we make our way to the compartment the crew member said his friends were trapped in.

Hughes stops at a metal door and looks through a small window. He turns to me and points. We've found the trapped crew.

I pull myself closer. A man is staring back at us from a control room. There are four other people inside with him. That's five people we have to figure out how to get from inside there to the deck above.

They look terrified, but they're not panicking, even though water is filling the space from a ruptured bulkhead. The man is trying to tell us something. He keeps saying it over and over.

One of the others pushes him aside and places the screen of his cell phone to the glass.

A typed message reads: door wont open.

Hughes tries turning the lever. It won't budge. It could be that mechanisms above and below are locking the door in place. They must have been triggered by whatever happened, then malfunctioned.

I lower myself to the bottom of the door to inspect it more closely and see the real reason the door can't be opened the way it's supposed to. The floor plate below has somehow become warped and bent the frame. Probably a structural side effect of the explosion. You see weird things like that. Half a house gets demolished, and antique china still hangs from hooks on the other side.

I use my mask radio to talk to Hughes. "We got a problem. The doorframe is bent. No way it's moving."

He swims down next to me and almost drifts away in the current before grabbing hold of the lever above. His hand runs across the warped metal, and he shakes his head.

I start doing the math in my head for how much air those men have before we can acquire proper rescue gear. I curse myself for not having an underwater cutting torch on our boat and add it to my mental list of things we *should* have but that will do absolutely nothing for the trapped men right now.

I've dived for innumerable automobiles that ended up submerged in canals. In those cases, I can easily pop open a car door with my mini-crowbar or break through a back window. Just about any auto-related disaster, I'm all set for. Cruise ship disasters are something else entirely.

"Would there be a cutting torch somewhere on the ship?" I ask. "Maybe the machine shop. But I wouldn't bet on it."

Trying to cut through the door has its own problems. Cutting torches create a ton of hydrogen gas that can build up inside a compartment and explode. I've known people who have died that way, and they were experts. And while I've used an underwater cutting torch, I'm certainly no expert.

The ship shudders, and we're both propelled toward the far wall. *The Sea of Dreams* is leaning at an even greater angle now. I check my pressure gauge. We're also sinking.

I should have taken more readings to get an estimate of how fast the ship is sinking. In theory, if the damaged areas are contained, the ship should stop sinking at some point before full submergence. In theory.

Maritime disasters have a habit of testing theories.

I've been on several sinking boats. All sank for different reasons. Chief among them, my family's slapdash way of fixing things because we're a little too used to living life on the edge.

Our boats were mostly small craft, in which an exit never lay more than a few yards away, and all the passengers were strong swimmers who could hold their breath for minutes at a time.

This is like being in a tunnel collapse under a city in an earthquake. Getting the door open is only the start of things. We're still underwater with five people who have no dive gear.

I pull myself up to look through the window. The water is rising. The man with the phone has a new message: gonna be okay?

It's not looking good for these men. Time is running out, and real help is still far away. We need a miracle.

Unsure what to say, I instinctively give him the okay sign. Then I pull the wax pencil and tablet from my belt and write a message:

WE'LL GET YOU OUT.

I also add a smiley face.

It's the only thing I can do in this situation: lie my ass off. I can't tell him this is the part in the movie where you have to tell the person on the other side they're screwed and nothing can be done.

The man smiles back, calmer now. He thinks we have it under control. He closes the notepad on his phone, and I see his wallpaper: two dark-haired boys younger than my daughter in soccer uniforms, smiling at the camera.

This is the photo the man takes with him everywhere. It's probably why he works long hours in a claustrophobic environment. He does it for them.

And right now, thousands of miles away, his kids have no idea their dad is about to die.

I can't let that happen.

"I'm going to go find an underwater torch," I tell Hughes over the radio. I start to swim away, but he grabs my ankle and pulls me back.

"Hold on. Tell them to get to the back of the compartment."

I'm about to ask how that'll help, but then I see what he's holding in his hand.

I'm staring at a miracle.

CHAPTER 4
BLAST DOOR

Before Scott Hughes came to the UIU, and before he was a Fort Lauderdale police officer, he was in the navy. Specifically, he was in an underwater demolition unit. Which is a long way of explaining why he's holding a thumb-size container of a C-4-like plastic explosive.

It's a shaped charge used to blast hinges off doors and disable locks. He's wedging it into the gap at the base of the door near the buckle that's blocking it from opening. The device has only a small charge, but it might be enough to dislodge the hatch.

This creates another problem. While the crew in the flooding compartment should be safe enough from the blast at the back of the room with their heads well above water, Hughes and I . . . not so much. The blast's underwater pressure wave could knock out our hearing or worse if we don't get far enough away.

I write a note to the crew members, telling them to move back because we're going to blow the door. They waste no time retreating to the far side.

The one good thing about the ship listing is that it has created an air pocket at the back of the compartment. Still, if the door cracks open, and if Hughes and I aren't knocked unconscious, we'll have only a few minutes at most to get the men out before the compartment floods completely.

"Seventy seconds," Hughes tells me over the radio. "Start moving."

He's still pushing the shaped charge into the gap. I don't want to leave him in the middle of this, but I also know that when someone handling explosives tells you to run, you run.

We need to get our heads above water if we don't want punctured eardrums, so I pull myself back down the corridor toward the stairwell. Halfway there, I turn back to see how Hughes is doing.

He's five yards away now, still working at it. I keep pulling myself along the railing and using my legs to kick toward safety. Fins would be really helpful right now.

Everything abruptly goes dark, and the emergency lights turn on. For a half a second, I think the explosive has gone off prematurely. But, no, this was something else.

The current shifts, pushing me back. I reach out and grab the railing and start to pull myself up the stairs. I glance back again and see that Hughes hasn't moved, so I stop and wait at the bottom of the stairs, ready to lend him a hand.

"Go!" he yells over the radio.

I pull myself up the stairs and keep moving until my head's above water. When I emerge, the flood's already at knee level in this section. I see two crew members still waiting.

"Get back!" I warn them, even though Hughes's charge will at most create a popping sound up here.

I turn back around and look into the water for Hughes. I see his hand grab the railing and his body follow onto the stairs.

KRUNK. The explosive goes off, making a louder sound than I expected. It's like a giant soda can being crushed. I feel a concussion wave around my legs. Not big, but enough to do damage to Hughes, who's still underwater.

His body begins slowly drifting backward.

Damn. The blast must have knocked him out. I scramble down the stairwell and grab him by the wrist before the current carries him away.

As I near the top of the stairs, the two crewmen join me and help pull Hughes out of the water. We pull him to a bulkhead and sit him up so his head and shoulders are above the flooding. I yank off his mask and regulator and check his pulse.

Before I get a reading, Hughes opens his eyes and gives his head a shake. "I'll be fine," he says, a little louder than usual.

"Are you okay?"

He points to an ear. "Ringing."

"Keep an eye on him," I tell the crewmen.

The others trapped in the compartment are on a short clock now. I dive back into the stairwell and swim as fast as I can.

Hughes's charge worked even better than I'd hoped. The door's already ajar, and I pull it open, the water rushing inside assisting in my effort. I swim through and see the lower bodies of the men standing in the air pocket.

When I poke my head above the rising water, the men are lined up, waiting for me to execute my plan—which I'm making up on the spot.

"I'm going to take you one at a time to the stairs." I hold up the backup regulator mouthpiece attached to my tank. "Hold on to my belt with one hand, put this into your mouth, and hold on to it with your other hand. When we get to the stairwell, just keep going up until you reach air."

I see new fear in their eyes and realize I need to reassure them so they don't panic. "Hold tight. If we get separated, just grab hold of anything and wait in place. I will not leave without you. Understand? *I will* not *leave without you.* Okay?"

"Where's your partner?" asks one of them.

"Helping the others," I lie. "Okay, let's go."

The crew members start to push one another toward me, each arguing that another should go first. Noble, but now is not the time.

17

"You," I say, grabbing the man closest to me. "Put this in your mouth. Take slow, deep breaths. Got it?"

He nods and clenches the mouthpiece between his teeth. I grab his upper arm and pull him underwater.

The current has shifted, and we have it at our backs as we make our way to the stairwell.

The man doesn't panic, and our journey down the corridor is textbook underwater rescue.

I return for the others, and while I'm guiding the third man to safety, Hughes swims past me, giving me the okay sign.

Within minutes we have all the men in the upper chamber with the two crew members who waited for them.

Hughes is bent at the waist, catching his breath. "Now what?" he asks, still speaking loudly, but not as loud as before.

One of the crew has a radio.

"Who isn't accounted for?" I ask him.

"All the passengers are on lifeboats. But we still have missing crew."

"Do you know their stations?"

"My friend Danny went to inspect damage on passenger deck two, port side. I haven't heard from him. He was supposed to come back here."

That's two decks above us.

"Okay. We'll go look for him. You need to get to the boats. All right?" I spot his name tag. "Alfred?"

"They'll go. I'll come with you," says Alfred.

I'd argue but I doubt he'll abandon his friend, and there's a fair chance that Hughes and I alone would get lost trying to navigate this massive vessel.

The ship shudders again, and we're all knocked off balance.

"What the hell was that?" yells Hughes.

"Too soon for a rescue tug. Feels like we drifted into a sandbar."

That could make things better or much, much worse. If the ship turns onto its side, we'll need mountaineering equipment to make our way through it.

"Let's find Danny and get off this thing," I say as I start up the stairs to the next deck.

Alfred, not burdened by scuba gear, moves ahead and leads us down a corridor toward the passenger section. The hall's full of linens, luggage, and housekeeping carts, all illuminated by pools of light from the emergency lighting. Running is next to impossible because of the steep lateral angle. Instead, we are forced to move awkwardly, using the starboard bulkhead to balance ourselves and jumping over open doorways as we reach them.

Midway down the passage, I look through a doorway and see that it opens into a small, closet-like compartment instead of a cabin. A panel in the back of the compartment has been removed, and it looks like someone cut into the bulkhead behind it. From the scorched smell, quite recently.

Hughes glances where I'm looking and shakes his head. Maybe the crew was trying to repair something before the incident? Seems unlikely . . .

"Danny!" shouts Alfred.

I glance ahead and see Alfred kneeling over the body of what I thought was a rumpled blanket. Hughes reaches him before I do and takes a pulse.

"Alive."

The man is bleeding from a serious head wound. I take a bandage roll from a plastic bag and start to wrap it to stop the flow of blood.

Normally you'd wait for paramedics in a situation like this, but this is far from normal. Hughes strips off his scuba tank and hoists Danny over his shoulder in a fireman's carry.

I scoop up his tank in case we need it, and we follow Alfred down the corridor toward the exit.

CHAPTER 5
BEACH PARTY

We moved Danny to a coast guard vessel transporting the injured to the shore and spent the next two hours patrolling the ocean downstream from the ship, looking for any passengers who may have ended up in the water. We didn't find anyone and turned the boat back toward the beach where the lifeboats landed.

The orange lifeboats are minor technical marvels unto themselves. On a normal cruise, you'd do the drill, find your lifeboat station once, and never think about it again. In a well-handled emergency, boarding the lifeboat is about as eventful as waiting your turn to get on a ride at Disneyland. You line up in your section with your life jacket, wait for crew members to tell you to proceed, then carefully enter the interior of the craft, where you and your fellow castaways are packed together like sardines. When the boat is full, the doors are closed and you're lowered to the ocean. Once you hit the water, the crew member in charge of the lifeboat takes control of the vessel from a standing cockpit and guides it to shore—if you're lucky enough to be near a shore. Otherwise, you have to settle in and hope the people you're surrounded by are good company.

The passengers and crew of *The Sea of Dreams* were lucky that they were close to not only a shore, but one accustomed to influxes of thousands of tourists.

Unfortunately, as we beached our boat, it was apparent that the bars and restaurants lining Fort Lauderdale Beach Boulevard were making it impossible for the crew to keep all the passengers together, much less get an accurate head count.

The coast guard teams back on *The Sea of Dreams* won't know when to stop looking for passengers if they don't know how many are still aboard.

From the sound of the rescue efforts on our radio, it seemed like everyone was accounted for, including some injured people they found on the bridge. There is still no word on casualties, but it would surprise me if there were none.

"How's your hearing?" I ask Hughes as I drop the anchor into shallow water.

"What?" he says reflexively, then realizes what I asked after processing it. "Coming back."

"I'm going to check in to see what's going on," says Ava after spotting a Fort Lauderdale Police Department SUV parked on the beach. She jumps down and sloshes her way to shore.

My phone rings. It's George Solar, our boss.

"Are you calling to book a cruise?" I reply.

Solar ignores my quip. "Where are you?"

"On the beach directly across from the Island Brewery."

"Hold on. I'll be there in a minute."

I turn to Hughes. "Before he gets here, anything I shouldn't mention?"

I trust Solar and I trust Hughes. And I also know that Solar trusts me to trust whatever Hughes asks me to keep confidential. Like using a thumb-size stick of plastic explosive . . .

"We're good," says Hughes. "I'm licensed, and our friends at ATF won't be a problem."

"Good enough." We might hear some whining from the FBI forensic team about contaminating the scene, but that's manageable.

George Solar finds us on the beach. He's wearing a blazer over his polo shirt, which during the day means that he had to go ask some politician for a favor, and at night means he took his girlfriend, Cynthia Trenton, a well-known local journalist, out to dinner. The two of them are in their late fifties and have quite a history.

"What happened?" Solar asks.

I explain about us getting the call and our part in the rescue operation, then show him the photos I took of the damage to the bridge and hull. He nods as I speak, asking for details only occasionally. When I get to the part about Hughes's little explosion, Solar interrupts.

"Were both of you out of the water?"

I accidentally glance at Hughes.

Solar doesn't miss this. "How's your hearing?"

"Getting better," says Hughes after a moment.

Solar turns to me. "Why isn't he getting checked for a concussion right now?"

"I—"

"I told her I'm fine," says Hughes.

"You're not the judge of that," replies Solar. He turns back to me. "And neither are you. We'll get Crozier to take the boat back." He hands me the keys to his truck. "After we're done here, take him to the ER while I find out if anyone knows anything."

He's not wrong. I should have taken Hughes to a paramedic, at the very least. In addition to the loss of hearing, my partner was out cold for a few seconds.

Solar stares out across the water toward *The Sea of Dreams*, which drifted closer to shore before hitting a sandbar. Two coast guard cutters are anchored close by while other rescue ships, including two tugs, are making their way to the scene. In the distance, a barge is being moved into position to support the rescue and salvage efforts.

"This is . . . weird," says Solar. "Forward me the photos of the external damage."

It's the bridge pic that's most confounding. The other damage could have been caused by any number of things, from chemicals in a storeroom accidentally exploding to the ship hitting something especially hard.

He shakes his head. "I don't like it."

There's a word we're all afraid to say because, if it's true, it could mean that this is only just beginning.

"I'm going to call Rodrigo over at Homeland Security, show him your photos. I'm sure he's on this, but I don't know if he has the full picture yet. They need to get down here sooner rather than later. We're about to have the crime scene flooded with salvage teams, and who knows what evidence we might lose." Solar thinks for a moment. "McPherson, after you get Hughes to the hospital, call any of your friends at the cruise companies and tell them to look for anything suspicious on their fleets. But be discreet. We don't want to raise any alarms just yet."

What he's telling me is to put them on alert but not say the word "terrorism."

CHAPTER 6
AGROUND

Less than twenty-four hours later, we're sitting at long tables formed into a U shape in the Beachside Resort hotel conference room, which is almost even with *The Sea of Dreams'* resting place. Captain Sija of the coast guard and FBI Special Agent in Charge Susan Rowan are at the head table. In the corner, three people, one in uniform, are trying to get a coffee machine to work. I'm already having my doubts about this task force.

On the positive side, it took the FBI all of a second to recognize the damage to the ship was caused not by an accidental explosion but by two *external* blasts. Something hit the ship in at least two places on its exterior.

Forensics hasn't determined whether they were missiles or something else, but clearly this wasn't a mechanical malfunction. The FBI and coast guard haven't formally made a statement to the media yet, but the reports from the passengers and crew have already spread like wildfire.

While the stock market is closed, calls for shorting cruise ship stocks are at a record high.

Nobody knows anything . . . but everyone suspects the same thing.

The navy has been asked to reassign ships toward other cities with cruise ports, and the coast guard is performing inspections of every vessel they can track that was near *The Sea of Dreams*. Nobody wants to wait for this to happen again.

Complicating matters is the fact that the cruise line's insurers want to get their salvage teams on the vessel to repair and refloat it as soon as possible. From the FBI's perspective, the beached ship is a crime scene, and evidence for who caused this might still be found there.

There's also the fact that there are several thousand potential witnesses scattered around Fort Lauderdale hotels, some already booking flights back home. The crew members are in a weird kind of limbo because many don't have authorization to come ashore and are in temporary holding centers.

"Just give me a simple body in a canal," I mumble to myself.

Hughes turns to me.

I can't tell if he could hear what I said, so I text him instead: I'd prefer a body in a canal to all this.

He texts back: Dark, but true.

Solar is at the back of the room, conferring with some of the other chiefs. The UIU is a tiny state agency, but George Solar's reputation is massive. To be fair, ours is growing as well. We've played a critical part in several recent investigations, and other agencies have been asking Solar for the secret to our success. When he tells them the secret's to have fewer bosses, hold fewer meetings, and trust your people, they don't seem pleased.

Privately, he's made Hughes and me aware of his actual success theory: dumb luck and two hardheaded investigators taking too many chances.

Captain Sija stands and starts the meeting. "Everything we're saying here is confidential. This includes not sharing information with the cruise line, their insurer, or the salvage teams. Because this looks like a potential criminal investigation, we have to keep a lid on everything.

"Right now, we're trying to stabilize the vessel so we can conduct our investigation. As it stands, the ship was hit by three explosions: one on the bridge; one aft, near the propulsion system; and another at the waterline near the bow.

"The bridge impact appears to have been designed to take out the command crew. All six people who were on the bridge are in the hospital, two critical. Fortunately for them, the explosion was blunted by the instrumentation panels and the angle of attack.

"The lower decks have compartmentalized flooding. Naval architects are trying to figure out the best way to repair the vessel and move it to port. If you've checked the weather report, you know that we have an approaching tropical storm that's going to complicate matters. I'll now turn it over to FBI Special Agent in Charge Susan Rowan to cover the criminal investigation."

Rowan remains seated but scans all our faces for a moment. She's in her early fifties and has dark-blonde hair pulled back into a bun. She reminds me of a high school principal I had who knew every student's name and what their parents did for a living. As head of the FBI field office, she has to keep track of hundreds of agents and cases. The fact that she's speaking says a lot about the severity of the situation.

"While Captain Sija and the coast guard are focused on the safety of the vessel and others like it, our concern here is quickly identifying who did this, discovering how they did it, and then apprehending them as quickly as possible.

"This appears to be an act of terrorism, but we haven't heard from any terrorist organizations taking responsibility. It could also be corporate sabotage. We saw movement in the markets shortly after this happened. It could also be some kind of bizarre accident or mechanical failure, but at this point I see that as being unlikely.

"At present our investigation needs help with talking to witnesses and, for agencies with maritime operations, assistance in searching for physical evidence.

"We want to search the seafloor for the mechanisms that delivered the explosives. Finding those could put us well on our way to finding out who's responsible."

She looks at Hughes and me. "You're the Underwater Dive Unit? We could use your help with the FBI dive team."

I nod and don't bother to clarify that we're an *investigative* unit. Diving sounds far better than doing hundreds of interviews with irate passengers demanding to know when they're going to get their luggage back and the status of their refund.

The meeting continues, and different agencies are tasked with helping the FBI in various ways. Most jobs sound routine and boring, like going through passenger records and checking shipping manifests, but you never know where a lead might surface.

Afterward, Solar waits for us in the hallway. "You two okay with the assignment?" he asks.

"Fine by me. But our mad bomber should stay out of the water for another few days," I reply.

Hughes gives me a look.

"Doctor's orders," I add. He can scowl all he wants, but I'd rather deal with a thousand angry Hugheses than one pissed-off George Solar.

"Be careful." Suddenly, Solar looks a little distant. Clearly something's on his mind.

"What is it?"

Solar lowers his voice. "The explosions . . . they're weird. They were targeted, but all wrong."

"How wrong? They took out a cruise ship," I point out.

"That's the problem. They were enough to disable a ship. But they're not what you do to sink it. For starters, you'd attack farther out to sea. Second, you'd concentrate on the part of the hull where you could reach the fuel tanks. I spoke to one of my navy contacts. He said this is similar to how pirates in the Mediterranean take out cargo vessels they want to ransom back to ship owners."

"Do you think that's what this was? An attempt to take the ship hostage?"

"If it was, it was the worst place ever to try to pull it off. You'd be better off near a port in Jamaica or wherever. But even better would be far, far offshore. It doesn't make sense," he concludes.

"I guess we'll see what we find when we dive," I reply hopefully.

"You're not getting it," he says, pointing to a window where *The Sea of Dreams* is visible. "If we can see that boat out there, chances are the people who did this can too. They're here. Hell, they could be sitting in the hotel lobby waiting to see what we do next." He looks to me, then Hughes. "What I'm saying is, be suspicious . . . of everyone."

CHAPTER 7

MALLET

Run cracks open a lobster claw on the restaurant table with a mallet and pulls the shell apart so our daughter, Jackie, can yank out the morsel of white meat and dip it into butter. She hands the opened claw to me, and the two of them repeat the operation with mechanical precision. It's adorable to watch my thirteen-year-old and the man I love wordlessly cooperate like this. It also pains me a little because I haven't been spending enough time with either of them.

They've never commented about my frequent absences. Which only makes it more painful. I'd like to know that I'm missed.

"How's Scott doing?" asks Run.

"You mean Scott 2.0," says Jackie. Ever since she discovered my work partner shares the same first name with Run, she's found it endlessly amusing.

It's funny for sure, but in a less stable relationship could add to the tension of a spouse working long hours with a member of the opposite sex. It should be perfectly fine on a rational level, but then I think about how I'd feel if Run ran his boat-design company from a small office with an extremely attractive woman all day.

The cavewoman part of me says I'd probably deal with it fine after I knocked out a few of her teeth and used my fists to make her a bit less attractive.

Run has never acted jealously or treated Hughes with anything less than utter respect. He's even casually joked about Hughes being my work husband, although he stopped that when Hughes's wife overheard the comment and looked visibly uncomfortable.

Cathy Hughes has it the hardest. Run and I have a weird relationship and have known each other since we were kids. Cathy, on the other hand, has a two-year-old girl at home and all the confidence issues young mothers go through when they're too busy managing their toddler to concern themselves with much else.

Odd as it is to say, I was lucky to have Jackie when I was still a teenager. I was too naive to suffer a crisis of confidence. My friends who are approaching thirty and starting to contemplate having children look at me and my teenage daughter with a bit of jealousy. In their view, Jackie is some kind of magical delivery I received when they weren't paying attention. They forget that I was MIA for years while they were out partying at new nightclubs.

I was on my boat watching *Pinky Dinky Doo* and explaining to Jackie that her application to Hogwarts was probably not going to be accepted. While my friends were trying out new fusion cuisine, I was explaining to my daughter that just because mahi-mahi is sometimes called "dolphin," that doesn't mean it's the sea mammal, and it's totally okay to eat. I wouldn't trade any of those moments for a million of what my friends experienced.

There's no photo, no story in their feeds that could match seeing my baby's gap-toothed smile as she watches her birthday candles light up or witnessing her jubilation the first time she touched the bottom of the pool.

I was also fortunate to have the full support of my family. I met some disapproval, to be sure, but that was outweighed by the fact that my already-large family was excited about having another member. Even Run was forgiven and treated like one of us. He had to endure the family nickname "That Bastard," although it was I who declined his marriage proposal.

"Hughes is doing better," I tell him. "God knows what it sounded like underwater."

Run stares at me for a long moment but says nothing. Jackie, getting smarter by the day, picks up the subtext.

"Do I have to be the one to give Mom the lecture about not taking stupid risks?" she asks.

"One of the men had two little boys half your age," I reply.

"Your attempt to deflect the conversation by manipulating my emotions won't work, Mother."

"Ooh," says Run. "You just got a 'Mother.'"

Jackie's way of showing her disapproval is by calling us "Mother" or "Father." It would sting a little less if she still occasionally called me "Mommy," but those days ended when her teen years began.

Two distinct sides of Jackie are emerging. One side is sweet, always happy to help, protective of her younger cousins, and willing to play with Hughes and Cathy's child, Callie. The other side is extremely intelligent and analytical. Almost coldly so.

Happy Jackie comes from Run, no question about it. Analytical Jackie isn't me. It reminds me a bit of Uncle Karl, my dad's brother. This pains me to admit because Karl's done time in jail. Jackie also resembles her great-grandfather and namesake, Jack. Grandpa Jack was brilliant and reckless. I got the reckless genes. It seems like the brilliant ones were recessive until Jackie inherited them.

When you come from a large family and have a child, you spend a lot of time trying to figure out what pieces from the DNA puzzle box compose your kid. You can only pray it's not the bad ones.

"How's the cleanup going?" I ask Run.

He got together with a group of other South Florida businesses to help the local conservation groups protect the sea turtle hatcheries and fish sanctuaries from any potential fallout from the shipwreck.

"Great. No oil spillage. So that's been good. Ethan Granth just put a half million dollars into local environmental funds. So everyone's happy about that," he tells us.

Granth is a billionaire hedge fund manager who moved from New York City to Miami a few years ago. He's made a big name helping out with different charitable organizations and pushing for more environmental protections. He's rich and politically connected enough to get things done.

"Why don't you ask Cathy if she wants us to look after Callie for a while so she and Hughes can have a break," Run suggests.

This is Run being proactive. He knows Cathy and Scott are still too timid to ask outright. But in the past, when we've offered to look after Callie, they've eagerly accepted the offer. Probably more for Jackie's babysitting skills than ours, to be honest. When I go shopping with Cathy, Jackie takes over stroller duty so we can "Mom out," as she calls it.

"Any new information on your end?" asks Run.

Normally in our relationship it's easy to compartmentalize certain things. This is one of those situations where it's harder. I'm under specific instructions not to talk about what I heard and saw, and god knows half the people in the room are already blabbing to their spouses, but I treat secrets with respect.

I trust Run completely, so not telling him everything is hard. Instead of outright saying that I can't tell him, I've learned to use phrases that convey what I'm dealing with.

"Things are probably going to get more complicated," I reply.

Run nods. This is all he needed to know. To an outsider, I said nothing. Between us, I revealed a lot.

CHAPTER 8

DRIFT

The sun is rising, and I'm on one of the two FBI Underwater Search Evidence Response Team boats that are anchored near where *The Sea of Dreams* suffered its first explosion. The other ship has more gear and carries the team piloting the underwater remotely operated vehicle that will be assisting in the search.

While I use ROVs from time to time, I prefer to dive first and cover as much ground as I can before going remote. I'm probably old fashioned . . . or maybe it's simply that I like to be in the water. In my defense, sometimes you can feel things you can't see with an ROV. Of course, there are situations in which ROVs are an absolute necessity.

When I met the head of the FBI dive team, Alec Rayburn, at the dock, he gave my gear bags a look, then asked me why I had brought them. Grover Caulfield, the owner of a local dive shop who was helping set up their tanks, let out a huge laugh.

"If you have to ask McPherson why she's bringing her dive gear, then maybe you FBI folks shouldn't be running this investigation."

"Only my team's going down," Rayburn clarified.

"Then why the hell did you guys ask me to come?" I asked.

"Backup support."

"For what? To bring you snacks and drink boxes?"

Caulfield was watching this with wry amusement.

"I appreciate the help, but we need experienced recovery divers," said Rayburn.

"Want to see my dive logs? Better yet, care to guess what the 'Underwater' part of Underwater Investigation Unit means?" I was pushing things, but I was also pissed. Fortunately, my inner George Solar took over, and I calmed down. "I'll just stow my gear and help out where I'm needed."

Rayburn was probably trying to figure out why I'd suddenly reversed myself. The answer was that I realized I didn't want my ego getting in the way of the operation. Lives were at stake, and making a scene or calling our respective superiors for a final decision wasn't going to help anyone.

Rayburn thanked me and told me where I could stow my gear. The other divers, all FBI agents, came aboard, and we headed out to the search site. Some of them were from the Miami unit, and I knew them personally. Others, like Rayburn, had flown in for the operation.

The search cycle works like this: two two-man dive crews go down while the other divers decompress and rest on the boat. They're using standard recreational dive tables, which is playing it safe. Hughes and I use the navy tables, which are a bit more lenient because they assume you know what you're doing.

Rayburn has laid out a precise grid for their search, and his divers make regular reports over the radio about where they're at and what they've covered.

I've done this kind of precision search before. It's tedious. But it's also effective in most cases. I have my own way of doing things, but this is still probably how I'd instruct other divers to do it. It's not unlike how I've done archeology digs with my professor. The goal is to be so precise and thorough that it's hard to miss anything important.

The drawback to the method, at least here, is that the divers will have to move slowly to account for undercurrents. I know these waters really well and how they shift as the tide comes in and out. After two hours, I decide to say something.

"Agent Rayburn?"

He looks up from the tablet where he's been checking off search-grid tiles. "McPherson?"

"Do we have plans to search this section here?" I point to an area south of us and east of the jetty.

"Out there? Why?"

"Coastal current. It comes down this way, then pushes out that way." Last night, I made my own chart based on recent tide data and some information from Uncle Karl, who knows better than anyone how to track local currents.

"Our models show that this is the most likely place to find debris," Rayburn explains.

"I don't doubt it, but those models tend to take a narrow view of things. For objects that float or drift along the bottom, they're much less precise. In a narrow body like a river or a canal they can help you figure out where a corpse is located, but they're less accurate if you're looking for something like a shoe."

"We're not looking for shoes, McPherson."

I have to tread carefully. These people are experts at what they do and have done recoveries in situations I can't even imagine. I can't come across as a know-it-all telling them they're doing it wrong.

"Understood. It's just that I have a lot of experience in these waters." I point to the map. "I know the eddies and currents in there like the back of my hand."

"I appreciate that. But with the storm coming and the limited time we have, I need to go with this," he says, tapping the tablet.

It's an awkward situation. I'm telling him to go with my instincts, but he's operating according to past experience. Neither of us is necessarily wrong, but I'm pretty sure they're not going to find anything meaningful.

I back up and keep my ear to the radio, relaying information from the divers. I'm trying hard to be a team player, but as I look at the dark clouds in the distance and think about the storm surges that are going to start tomorrow, I hear the sound of a ticking clock.

A little over an hour later and close to when we'll have to call it quits, one of the divers calls out over the radio, "Found something."

When a trained recovery diver says they found something, they usually don't mean a Coke can or rusted anchor. The ROV pilot sends the robot to his location so we can get a better look.

I step under the canopy where Rayburn and the other divers are staring at the screen. He sees me and angles it in my direction.

The camera catches a diver, then tilts down to reveal a large metal object. The pilot pulls the ROV back to get a wider view.

It's a huge chunk of metal that looks like it was ripped right out of *The Sea of Dreams*. I have little doubt that's what it is. I expect that within a hundred yards we'll find glass from the bridge.

While the dive team high-fives each other, I keep my mouth shut and simply smile. There's no point in raining on their parade. While that metal may have fragments in it that will tell the forensic team a fascinating story, my gut tells me there's much more to be found . . . if you know where to look.

If they're not determined to look any further, so be it. I have a boat, I have dive gear, and I'm willing to dive all night before the storm surge buries whatever else is down here or drags it to where it will never be found again.

CHAPTER 9
Night Dive

Run pilots his forty-foot custom powerboat, *The Finish Line*, toward the area I've mapped out for searching. In the distance, we see the glow of *The Sea of Dreams* and her attending vessels working to keep her afloat. We're still hours from seeing the effects of Tropical Storm Melvin, which is forming in the Southern Caribbean, but the authorities have already sent the barge used for rescue operations back to port. Other than the looming storm, it's a beautiful, calm night with a nearly full moon hanging above the horizon.

Jackie's brown hair blows in the wind as she sits folded up with her arms around her knees—somehow managing to keep her balance without effort as we hit each wave. I've got steady sea legs from growing up on boats, but she's in another league. I was raised on bigger, slower boats, but Jackie's grown up with my slow boats *and* her father's crazy go-fast boats.

Run throttles down the engines as we reach the GPS coordinates I marked on the map. The 3D sonar screen shows the ocean floor underneath and part of the long crescent ridge I want to search.

As currents drift from south to north, pushed by the Gulf Stream, this section of ocean floor acts as a slight barrier to anything drifting along the bottom. When the tides are at their lowest, the currents shift and everything the crescent has collected drifts farther out to sea.

One of the hardest things to understand—at least if your understanding of the ocean is limited to what you can see from the beach—is how dynamic the ocean floor is. Entire sandbars can move, even in mild storms. Waters that appear still can be moving at several miles per hour, which you only appreciate when you swim far away from shore and look back and realize you don't recognize anything. A tropical storm accelerates all this.

In Fort Lauderdale, Hurricane Irma's storm surge moved so much sand you could step outside a restaurant and think you were already on the beach, not realizing there was a highway buried beneath your feet. And that's only what happens above the waves.

We don't have time to follow a proper search grid. My plan is to move from one end of the crescent ridge to the other and use my flashlight to try to catch anything out of the ordinary.

Doing a search at night is basically the dumbest thing you can do, but by tomorrow there may not be anything to search for.

"Are we gonna talk about how we're gonna do this?" asks Run.

"I start here and keep going east a few hundred yards. I'll give you updates." We installed an underwater radio transceiver on the boat as well as a diving platform. While I prefer to dive from my own boat, Run's is faster, and he's made a number of compromises a speedboat normally doesn't make in order to turn this into a family boat.

"This is the part of the plan that's a little hazy," says Run. "You mean you and I go down while Captain Runt manages the boat?"

"You need to stay on the boat," I reply. "If something happens to me, we need someone who can drive the boat."

"I can sort of drive the boat," says Jackie.

"'Sort of' doesn't cut it," Run replies, then realizes he's put himself in a corner. "Never dive alone. Isn't that the rule?"

"Mom breaks it all the time," Jackie points out.

"Thanks, snitch," I shoot back.

"Well, it's settled then," says Jackie. "I go down with Mom." She sees that Run and I are about to object, but she cuts us off. "I've gone on tons of night dives with you guys. Mom and I have even walked in from the beach to do them."

"When was that?" asks Run.

"That's not relevant to the conversation. My point is that while I may not be qualified in your eyes to drive the boat, I am totally qualified to do a night dive with Mother. So logically, I should be the one diving with her."

Run and I are speechless. We're seeing this analytical side of Jackie more and more. It's almost like watching a new person enter the family.

While I love Jackie's capacity for logical thinking, part of me is saddened that it'll come at the expense of the giggly, full-of-wonder Jackie who would laugh hysterically at a silly prank or cute dog meme.

"She gets that from you," says Run.

"Come on," Jackie insists.

Run and I look at each other, willing the other one to say yes or no. While Jackie is technically right, I'm afraid to agree and look like the reckless mother.

"All right, but you check in every ten minutes. I want glowsticks, backup flashlights, and your promise that you'll call it when time's up," says Run.

"Deal," I tell him.

"I wasn't talking to you. Jackie seems to be the one in charge."

"Agreed," says Jackie. She turns to me. "Gear up."

She starts to spread the gear across the deck in neat piles. "Can I use your spare suit?" she asks. "Mine is too short."

"Sure, babe," I reply, trying not to sigh at the thought that she's tall enough for my old suit.

"What have you done?" I whisper to Run as we start pulling tanks from the dive-gear locker.

"I put the most responsible person here in charge." He gives me a sidelong glance. "She's sure growing up fast."

"She's thirteen," I respond.

"I was out here night fishing with my friends when I was thirteen. You were scrubbing barnacles off shipwrecks in bull shark–infested waters. I don't want her to be afraid of the water. Just respectful."

"Are you two done jibber-jabbering?" asks Jackie, standing on the back of the boat in her dive gear.

There's something startling about the way she looks. She's grown taller faster than her cousins and has her swimmer's build, but besides looking grown-up, I can't quite place what's odd about the way she looks.

"She looks like you," Run says under his breath.

Jackie hears the comment. "Okay, but don't be all weird about it and try to tell people we're sisters like Claire's mom does."

"Don't worry about that, hun."

"Seriously, don't be weird," says Run, joining in with Jackie. "You're already weird enough."

"We'll see who's laughing when she starts asking you for advice about boys," I tell him.

Run's tan face blanches. That prospect has him even more worried than us doing this night dive.

"Let's enjoy this while we can," he says.

Somewhere in the back of Run's head, he's realizing that Jackie is only five years younger than I was when I got pregnant. We have only so many moments left with our little girl.

I step onto the platform next to Jackie and see that we stand almost eye to eye. She double-checks my tank and equipment, and I check hers.

She attaches a glowstick to my tank, then says, "Follow my lead and don't get separated. If we drift apart, stay put and I'll come find you."

CHAPTER 10

SHIMMER

We plunge into the water and slowly descend, equalizing the pressure in our ears as we make our way to the bottom. This is second nature for us, so we reach the seafloor quickly.

At this depth, the moonlight doesn't help much, but visibility is fairly clear, so our flashlights cut wide swaths through the darkness.

At the bottom, we finally get a glimpse of what's all around us. The thing to keep in mind during a night dive is that 100 percent of the sea life that's present during the day is also there at night. Some of them may have little nooks and crannies to crawl into, but they're still around.

Jackie pans her light to the right and catches a cuttlefish flapping its translucent ridge fins as it darts about its business. The colors change and shift in the light as its chromatophores try to figure out how to blend.

My flashlight illuminates a rock formation, and I instinctively search for the telltale signs of a hiding octopus. True masters of camouflage, they not only match the color of the environment they're trying to blend into but also adjust their surface texture to appear rock- or coral-like.

I remember why we're down here and start scanning the area ahead. Jackie takes position a yard to my left, and we sweep the ocean bottom with our lights.

She spots a soda can and picks it up and places it in the net bag attached to her waist. It's a habit she learned from me. We try to leave the ocean a littler cleaner than we found it.

Our search is likely a fool's errand. We have way more ground to cover than we have time, but I'm betting on my uncle Karl's tide tables. He's an oceanographic genius and can outsmart most of the predictive models I've seen. Not because they're bad in and of themselves; it's just that the researchers who create them rely too much on spreadsheet data and error bars that are too wide.

Before Uncle Karl realized that his insights could be useful to commercial fishers and environmental groups, he used them to advise people trying to get things into the country illegally. For him, it was a game to outsmart the DEA and coast guard, something he started as a rebellious teenager. Unfortunately, this continued into adulthood. It wasn't an everyday occupation for him, but he liked the occasional challenge. Well, he liked the challenge until one of his friends snitched on him to receive a lighter sentence.

When Uncle Karl's drug-runner days came to a screeching halt, he finally saw what he'd become. Things were tense between us for a while after I went into law enforcement. I also had to deal with the burden of a last name attached to an already-infamous family made more notorious by his actions.

Not long ago, I convinced Karl to assist on a case, and he's been helpful to me and other law enforcement agencies since. When I asked him to chart where debris from *The Sea of Dreams* might be found, he drew me up a detailed map in hours.

The FBI search area occurred directly over the coordinates where *The Sea of Dreams* was crippled. It was a smart and practical place to conduct a search—but only for objects too heavy to be moved by the currents.

Rather than split the dive team into two units to cover more ground, Rayburn concentrated everyone in one area—an area in which they were bound to find *something*, but not necessarily something useful.

I studied photos of shoulder-fired rockets and their impact debris while waiting on the FBI dive boat. We'd need to run the underwater metal detector over every square inch of a few football fields to find pieces that small. Rayburn knew that and focused on finding something big so he could go back to his supervisors and say it was a success.

He didn't want to take the risk of a wider search because his organization doesn't encourage wild bets that don't pay off. It's not his fault; it's the system's.

Working for George Solar in a department that lacks even the coffee budget of the Miami FBI field office, we can afford to take chances. If I strike out, Solar will only want to hear why I thought it would work.

Jackie turns her head to the side and quickly jerks her light into the darkness. We see an eye glow for a moment, followed by the swish of a large tail as something moves away from the light.

"Lemon shark," says Jackie.

I didn't get a good look, but I trust her judgment.

To a novice diver, a lemon shark can appear threatening. They grow to more than ten feet long and have sharp, hooklike teeth that are pretty menacing. Fortunately, there have only been ten unprovoked lemon attacks on humans, and none were fatal. You stand a higher chance of dying on a trip to a petting zoo than being bitten by a lemon.

But they're not the only sharks out here. Florida has its share of ferocious species, but even they prefer to keep their distance. Attacks from bull sharks tend to happen in murky water. But if you don't pay attention, they can be a nuisance when they're around. In other parts of the world, they're much more aggressive, and I'd never do a dive like this with my daughter.

I check my air levels, then Jackie's. She has slightly less than me, but there's more than enough for us to go another fifteen minutes.

I roll over on my back and see the lights of *The Finish Line*. Run has been keeping pace with us so we don't have to swim all the way back to the same spot. This lets us double our distance.

My light hits something shiny, and I swim over to get a better look.

It's a palm-size piece of black plastic. I don't know what it is, but I put it in my bag and mark the coordinates where I found it on my log.

While I'm writing, Jackie calls me over the radio. "Mom, want to take a look at this?"

I swim to a rock bathed in her light. It looks like any other barnacle-encrusted rock you'd find down here, although in rare cases that rock can turn out to be a few hundred thousand dollars' worth of silver coins that corroded together after a shipwreck.

I see that Jackie's actually pointing to something beyond the rock. I get closer and see an object that doesn't have any marine life attached to it and zero signs of corrosion.

I fin closer and see broken carbon fiber, metal, and plastic parts with electrical wiring. Beyond it lies what appears to be a blade of grass that refuses to move in the current. When I pull it out of the sand, I realize what I'm holding. Jackie says what I'm thinking.

"Is that . . . a drone?"

CHAPTER 11
BODY SHOP

Jackie and I located several more pieces scattered within twenty yards of the first one she found. They're all sitting on a table in the middle of the Miami FBI forensic lab with several forensic examiners scrutinizing each part. Dr. Rosa Porquet, the head forensic examiner, joins Hughes and me inside her office, where a glass wall overlooks the lab.

She takes the paper cap off her head and tosses it in a trash can. Porquet is middle-aged, has dark curly hair, and expresses herself with an almost childlike awe.

"What an amazing find! And you said your daughter found it?"

"Yes, she's quite thorough," I reply.

"Wonderful. Maybe she has a career in the FBI?"

"Back off, sister. She's either going to be an astronaut or join the UIU like her mom," I say reflexively.

Porquet laughs and holds up her hands. "Of course! Of course! So can you show me where you found it on this map?"

I lean over her desk and mark the spots on the chart. I'd sent her our logs, but she clearly trusts me to do the mapping. "This area."

Porquet studies the section. "Do you think there's more down there?"

When we entered the building, Tropical Storm Melvin was already starting to pound the area. "Probably not in that spot. Or it might be buried right now. That's why we went out last night."

"So, what is it?" asks Hughes, finally speaking at a normal volume.

"It appears to be part of a drone, like you surmised. It's not a commercial brand. It's built with a lot of custom parts," she replies.

"Military-grade?" asks Hughes.

"There's no clear line. Half the parts are Chinese, but that doesn't mean it was Chinese-made. From the wiring, it looks bespoke, like a one-off, or a three-off. The tie-downs aren't spaced evenly, and some of the wiring is uneven," she explains.

"Like it was built in a hurry?" I ask.

She nods. "Yes. Whoever made it knew what they were doing, but they weren't precise where they didn't have to be. Function over form, as it were."

Special Agent Lewis Olmo pops his head in the door. He's one of the agents working the case for the FBI. In his midforties, he has streaks of gray in his dark hair that seem almost a mandatory requirement for advancement to a senior position in the bureau.

"You the UIU folks?" he asks.

"Guilty," I reply.

"Good catch on that. I can't wait to tell our dive team they got outdone by a twelve-year-old."

"Thirteen," I correct him. "And I'm sure if they had more time before the storm, they would have found it."

"Maybe, but they throw a conniption fit whenever someone else makes a recovery and they don't get the credit. I can't wait to see how they handle this."

"They can have the credit. We just want who did this."

"What have you put together so far?" asks Hughes.

"Our ballistics people were already thinking suicide drones with explosives strapped to them, and this pretty much confirms it. We've had problems with naval vessels getting harassed by drones on the West Coast. We don't know if it's just assholes with spare time or the Chinese trying to test our defenses. Unfortunately, something like this was bound to happen sooner than later. I just hope it's not a trend.

"In this case, we have camera footage and audio from the ship showing the explosions happening almost at the exact same time. We think the one you found hit the bow but didn't explode at the same angle as the others. All the attack points were precise. They knew what they were aiming for."

"Easy enough with onboard image recognition," says Hughes.

"Yeah. Image recognition that could just as easily target a person. We're talking to the Secret Service about the antidrone tech they're using to protect the president. We'd like to get that on our ships as soon as possible."

Olmo's casual mention that the drone could just as easily target a person sends a shiver down my spine. Are we going to need to carry personal antidrone defense devices in the future? Or can I just use my shotgun?

"So, why?" asks Hughes.

"That's the big question. They managed to do a tremendous amount of damage to the ship, but they should have done it amidships to take out the fuel tanks. If they only wanted to disable the ship, the attack on the bridge would have been enough." He pauses. "See, pirates trying to take over a boat need to keep it afloat. Terrorists would blow it up entirely unless they wanted to board and take hostages."

"What's the current theory, then?" I ask.

"Well, since it's just us mice, and this doesn't leave the room, the stock market movement has some of us wondering if this is some kind of money play," says Olmo.

"We heard about the short positions that happened after news broke," I reply.

"Those could just be automatic trades that happen whenever bad news hits an industry. There could be even more bizarre angles. I'll give you an example: we had a bombing in a casino in Puerto Rico two years ago. Someone tossed a grenade into a lobby and shut the place down. By luck we tracked down who did it and why."

We nod and wait for the explanation.

"In Macau, some Taiwanese high roller who'd won big at the card tables was getting onto his private jet to spend a few million dollars at a casino in the Caribbean. When word got out that he was heading to Puerto Rico, a casino owner in Aruba paid off someone to bomb the other casino and shut it down so the whale would come to his tables instead."

"That is a convoluted way to do things," I reply. "Had they considered offering all-you-can-eat shrimp? That's what gets my mother to the casino."

Olmo laughs at that. "If only. But you get my point. Until someone steps forward or we get a big break, anything's fair game."

🦋

As we head back to our SUV in the parking garage, I can see that Hughes is still thinking the case over. He's not talkative on a normal day, but he seems even more tight-lipped than usual.

"What's up?" I ask.

"I don't know. I can't quite put my finger on it. Between the dive team and Olmo, everybody's trying to fit this into something they already understand. Which I guess makes sense, but there's kind of an elephant in the room."

"And that is?"

"We know the ship was attacked deliberately, but nobody knows why. Even Olmo, who seems smart, is assuming the purpose of the attack was simply to attack the ship. Clearly it was for some other reason. Why else go through that much trouble?"

"Want to go back to the ship and look around? I know they got our report, but I'm not sure they followed through on everything. I can tell them we're doing a sweep for more bodies."

"Have you looked at the weather?"

"The worst of it should pass in a few hours. We can get on there before the salvage teams start trampling through the ship. It might be our last chance. They pulled the salvage barge but left the access barge in place. So getting aboard won't require a ladder this time. The lower decks are still flooded because the salvage team hasn't been let on. So . . ."

"Am I ready to dive again?" Hughes asks the question for me. "I was ready to dive when I was taken to the hospital against my will by you."

"Okay. But no firecrackers this time," I reply.

"No promises."

CHAPTER 12
GHOST SHIP

I pull our UIU boat alongside the access barge that's anchored next to *The Sea of Dreams*, and Hughes jumps out to tie us to the davits. Rain still pours from the sky, and it's not the best night to be out on the water. But at least the water is only choppy; the waves are mild.

As we approached, the coast guard vessel watching the ship asked us to identify ourselves. They've been having a problem with sightseers getting too close and, in some cases, people trying to board the crippled ship.

When four thousand people leave everything behind in an emergency, that means millions of dollars' worth of personal belongings still sitting relatively unguarded aboard. It's an attractive prospect for someone with a boat and a disregard for other people's possessions.

Right now, the only easy access point is from the barge. A metal staircase has been lashed down to allow access to the lower deck.

I hand our scuba packs up to Hughes. We're using smaller pony bottles, which are much lighter, since we don't plan on doing any diving unless absolutely necessary.

The Sea of Dreams is completely dark except for hazard lights and some small floods powered by generators at the bow and aft decks. To avoid a fire, everything else was shut down, including the backup electrical system put in place by the coast guard.

On the beach, there's an assembly area for the salvage company waiting to board the vessel. Although we weren't part of it, I heard there was a heated argument between the insurer and the FBI about getting access to *The Sea of Dreams*.

Every day is costing the insurance company hundreds of thousands of dollars. But the FBI is resolute in making sure no civilians go aboard until the task force has concluded this part of the investigation. They're more concerned about an attack like this happening again than getting *The Sea of Dreams* back into service.

We reach the top of the stairs and step on deck. The ship is still listing, so we have to use handrails to move around. I take the lead, using my flashlight to guide us into the dark ship.

"Where to first?" asks Hughes.

"The bridge?" I found a map of the ship online and have a rough idea how to navigate.

"Sounds good."

We travel up a corridor and into the main atrium. I shine my light at the ceiling, and it catches the multicolored glass of the chandelier suspended five stories up.

At first, I'm surprised that it's still in one piece, but then I remember these ships are built to handle rough seas—even the furnishings are tougher than they look.

I use my light to illuminate twin glass elevators at the far end of the atrium. Beneath them is a grand piano that slid into a help desk. At the other end is a grand staircase that winds corkscrew-style all the way to the top with ornate light fixtures attached at regular intervals to the gold-plated railing.

It's a floating palace. A bit tacky for my taste, but still awe-inspiring. God knows what my Viking ancestors would have thought about it.

Hughes and I take the stairs to the upper level. "Ever thought about taking a cruise?" I ask him.

"Not on this ship. I guess I'm curious. And Cathy *has* brought it up. But once you've sailed on an aircraft carrier, it's kind of an ego thing. You?"

"I worked on one for a little while as a dive instructor. It felt like I was trapped in a hotel with the rudest people on the planet. But I guess working on one is different than being one of the people shoving an empty margarita glass in your face and demanding another. Maybe I'd like to be the rude person with the margarita for once."

We reach the top of the stairs, and Hughes aims the beam of his light down a row of high-end stores that resembles a miniature Rodeo Drive. There are boutique versions of CHANEL, Louis Vuitton, and Alexander McQueen, among others. All of them have metal gates locked in place. Rolling them down was probably the first thing the shopkeepers did when they heard the explosions.

"Forget the loot in the passenger quarters, this is where I'd hit," says Hughes. "Hypothetically."

"Yeah, but is it worth committing an act of terror and getting Homeland Security and two branches of the military after you?"

"Heck no. I'd just do a smash-and-grab at the mall," Hughes answers without hesitation.

"So . . . um, is there some dark version of you that plots this kind of thing?" I ask, mildly curious.

"Don't you? Isn't that part of being a cop?"

"Now I'm wondering if it's your primary motivation for being a cop."

"We all have a dark side, McPherson. Some of us are just better at keeping it at a distance."

His words sit with me as we move through the upper decks of the ship. Hughes is good-natured, unflappable, and the most honest person I know. Having him admit that he has his own dark side spooks me a bit. Which is silly. It would be weirder if he were so good-natured all the way through. He'd be a robot.

At the end of a corridor, we reach a taped-off section marking the location of the bridge. We both put on latex gloves and I take the lead, entering the bridge first. It's a wide room, stretching from port to starboard with vast windows looking over the sea. I rest my hand on a console, stopping before I step into the main section because the starboard side is completely blown out. Because of the list, I can see the waves below. Wind blows through the broken glass, making an eerie sound.

If you slip here, it's quite a drop down.

The FBI forensic team must have used climbing gear to work here. Neither of us bothered to bring rope from our boat.

All I can say is, "It was an explosion, all right."

"Case closed. Want to go look somewhere else where we're not as likely to set a high-diving record if we slip?"

"Sounds like a plan. What do you have in mind?"

"Something that has been bothering me ever since our first time on board. Maybe nothing, but I'm curious."

CHAPTER 13

LURKERS

We make our way down the corridor where we found the unconscious crewman during our first time aboard *The Sea of Dreams*, stepping over the same luggage and service carts. Nothing has changed since we were last here, except it's now pitch-black without our flashlights.

There's also a strange quiet to the ship. With no engines and no people, the only sound is the wind through the open doors and rain pattering on cabin portholes.

Hughes is leading as I follow. I stop to look inside the open staterooms and scan them for anything unusual. The problem with a shipwreck and the panic that ensues is that people race to grab whatever's valuable before heading for the lifeboats, leaving every cabin looking like a crime scene.

I just want to make sure we didn't miss any bodies.

"Over here," says Hughes. He's standing in front of the open door and closet-like compartment behind it that I noticed during our earlier trip through the ship.

I stand next to him, leaning on the wall opposite the opening. Our lights probe the interior, panning for something to stand out we didn't see the first time we were aboard.

The hole that was cut into the bulkhead behind the panel measures about a yard square. Roughly a yard behind the hole stands a collection of pipes and conduit. There's nothing else in the space.

"Does this mean anything to you?" asks Hughes.

"No. Maybe they thought there was a fire in there and they had to check?"

"I went through the incident reports and interviews taken from the crew. None of them mention this. I also went through the transcripts of the radio conversations. You can hear them responding to different stations, putting out the engine-room fire and all the other disasters, but nothing about this."

"It might be a repair that was being done before the attack," I suggest.

"That makes sense. I'd like to take a look at some plans for the ship."

"They should have a set on board. Several, in fact. We can probably find one of them belowdecks. It would probably show all the modifications made after the ship left the construction yard."

We head back down the corridor toward the service stairwell. I keep searching the rooms, instinctively looking for any kind of clue. Each cabin is like a historical record for the people who were staying in them: formal gowns spread out on beds; dinner jackets still hanging from hooks; and makeup kits, mini liquor bottles, and suntan lotion containers strewn across the floor.

In one cabin, I see a child's stuffed rabbit lodged under a couch. Were there tears when they reached the beach and its owner realized she might never see her friend again?

While the cruise line has told the passengers that they'll make every effort to return belongings to their owners, that in and of itself is a complicated process with ample opportunity for things to get lost along the way.

We reach the door to the stairwell, and I stop. Something doesn't seem right. I grab Hughes by the elbow before he steps inside.

I point to my ear, telling him to listen. He tilts his head to try to hear what I'm hearing. To be honest, I don't know what I'm hearing, other than something sounds *off.*

It's a clanging sound, coming from somewhere aft. We both freeze. I pull myself against the wall, and Hughes does the same. Half a football field away, at the far end of the corridor where we first entered, the glow of a flashlight appears.

Is it someone from the coast guard patrolling the ship? A forensic team? Looters? Someone else?

Silently, we agree to sit tight and see what happens next. We're not well hidden, only motionless. There's a chance they won't even notice us unless they get close.

The light moves toward us, and I hear at least two distinct voices speaking in low tones. The light beam drifts up from the floor of the corridor and points straight ahead, catching me.

For a split second, nothing happens, then the beam goes out and the sound of running footsteps echoes through the corridor.

I sprint after the intruders, stripping off my pony tank so I can move faster.

"Freeze! Police!" I yell.

I have my gun in a waist holster, but I don't draw it. They could be teenagers exploring the ship, and I don't want to fire absent a threat to myself or Hughes. I also need my hands free to navigate through this tilted corridor.

Hughes is right behind me as we chase the trespassers. One of them starts pushing service carts and luggage into our path, slowing us as we have to navigate around them. They already had a distance advantage; this makes it worse.

We reach the stairwell and hear their steps above us. There's a loud hissing sound, and suddenly Hughes and I are covered in chalky smoke. One of them's spraying a fire extinguisher at us.

"Duck!" I yell to Hughes, afraid of what's going to happen next.

I duck and cover my head with my hands and feel a hard thud as the depleted canister hits my back.

My knees buckle and my spine hurts like hell, but I judge I'm okay and resume climbing the stairs before the fire extinguisher finishes bouncing behind me, Hughes on my heels.

We reach the next level and find the corridor empty. Hughes points to the port side and says, "There!"

We race up and out through an open doorway and onto the deck. Somewhere below I hear the sound of an outboard motor revving up. Twenty yards down, I see a ladder similar to the one we originally used hanging over the railing. I race to the edge and lean over to look. One man is in a raft and two others are climbing down the last rungs of the rope ladder.

"Stop!" I yell.

Hughes grabs my belt and yanks me back from the railing.

I'm about to curse him when I hear the loud BOOM of a shotgun. Lead pellets bounce off the railing and ricochet around the deck.

If my head had been in the way of that, I wouldn't have much of a face left.

I draw my pistol and move a few yards down to another position and pop up, aiming at the boat. The craft is already churning away with no lights. I contemplate taking a shot in the dark, but it's too risky. I could hit the gas tank or someone who wasn't willingly part of their crew and create an even bigger problem.

Hughes is on his phone calling for support from any marine units in the area. Air support seems doubtful, given this weather.

We rush back to our boat, but the rain is coming down even harder than before. Still, we guide our craft in the direction we saw them leaving but soon have to turn back because of the lack of visibility.

From the grappling hook to the shotgun, it's clear that these weren't curious teenage delinquents. They were up to something else entirely.

CHAPTER 14

GUARDIANS

Coast Guard Warrant Officer Kevin Mason, of their Investigative Service division, examines the ladder still dangling from the railing. "They certainly came prepared."

"That's one way of looking at it," says Hughes.

An FBI forensic examiner is dusting it for fingerprints while another is taking photos of where the shotgun pellets chipped the paint of the railing and hull. It's doubtful they'll find anything on the ladder, but you never know. The FBI is also good at tracking purchases, especially for odd items like the hybrid ladder. They have specialists who do nothing except create algorithms that can pore through millions of purchases from hardware stores and other retailers to look for possible matches.

If a bomb goes off in your city and you bought a large amount of fertilizer in the last few months, nobody will necessarily knock on your door, but there's a good chance someone in the FBI looked at the security camera footage of you making the purchase and compared it to what was known about the suspect. With facial-recognition systems and pervasive surveillance, we've all been processed through those systems at one point or another.

As a cop, I like this because it can make my life a little easier, but there are trade-offs. When my uncle was arrested and I came home from school to federal agents serving a search warrant, it made me feel more helpless than ever before. Two agents went through my room and my belongings—searching in drawers and boxes that even my own mother knew were off-limits. The kind of violation that makes you feel small and angry.

The agents were respectful and polite, but that didn't change the fact that at least one of them knew some of my most embarrassing secrets. For a teenage girl, that can feel world-ending.

As this investigation continues, there's the real possibility of collateral damage of the kind I experienced. But as a law enforcement officer, I understand that trying to spare feelings can cost lives. I've helped serve search warrants in places where we found guns and drugs hidden in children's toy boxes and, in one case, several thousand doses of fentanyl stuffed into a crib mattress.

Special Agent Olmo joins us on the deck. "You people don't sit still."

"Isn't that the point of being a cop?" I reply.

"Not if this kind of thing keeps happening."

"Any luck on tracking the boat?" asks Hughes.

"Still looking. We have people searching the canals and checking to see if they tried to sink it," Olmo tells us.

"If they didn't ditch it, they might have docked with another boat and deflated the raft," I suggest.

"We're looking into that too."

Something about the way he says that doesn't make it feel like a high priority. "Need help?" I ask.

"We'll let you know. Actually, just out of curiosity, you don't have specific descriptions of the three men or the boat—other than it was a raft. But you were quite specific about the outboard motor, down to the make and horsepower. How could you see that in the rain?"

Hughes is smirking because he knows the answer.

"How do you think?" I reply.

"You can tell the difference between the different manufacturers by ear?"

"It was a Verado. It's one of the quietest outboards. They're like motorcycles. Similar horsepower to other engines, but they sound different."

Olmo turns to Warrant Officer Mason. "For real?"

Mason nods. "Once you know the difference, it's not hard to tell them apart."

"I think the important part is that they were outfitted with a quiet outboard and they knew how to use that," I say, pointing to the grappling hook.

"It's interesting, but I don't know how much I'd read into that. Thieves can be very motivated," Olmo replies.

"You ever try to climb up or down one of those? It's not like you go pick up a grappling-hook launcher from the army/navy surplus store and start boarding cruise ships the next day. It takes practice to learn how to use one of those, and a lot more practice to climb on a flexible ladder," I explain.

"I get you. But it's not like those skills are all that rare, especially with some of the criminal gangs we have. A few months ago, we busted a ring of Colombians who were hitting jewelry stores. All were special forces back home. They knew how to blast doors and open safes. They had practical experience doing raids on cartel businesses. Anything's possible. All the passenger belongings left on the ship are an attractive nuisance, not to mention the computers and all the other valuable gear on board. Looting attempts are to be expected."

Hughes speaks up. "If they were to be expected, how did they still get aboard?"

"We weren't anticipating an approach from port. Because of the list, it's unreasonably high and impossible for someone to simply board," says Mason.

"Unless they have a grappling hook and know how to climb," Hughes shoots back.

Mason points to a small patrol boat a hundred yards from the ship. "We're not making that mistake again."

"Any idea why that piece of wall is missing?" I ask.

"No. It might be undocumented maintenance. Or the ship's fire crew pulled it out."

"Why wasn't it reported?"

Mason sighs and puts up one finger: "Oversight." Two fingers: "It was done after the explosions, and no one logs stuff during emergencies." Three fingers: "Sometimes they make janky repairs to these vessels that they know won't pass inspection and they try to cover it up. I've checked the blueprints. There was supposed to be a fire suppression system there originally, but it got moved twenty yards toward the bow during construction. They may not have known that and nobody wants to 'fess up."

"And the crewman we found unconscious. Has anyone got his story yet?" I ask.

"What crewman?" asks Olmo.

"Danny something. He had a nasty wound to the head. He was nearby."

"I didn't know about that," he says.

"We reported it," I say, trying not to sound accusatory. "But I know things were hectic."

"Noted. We'll look into that."

I sense a lack of urgency on this as well. It's confusing. As a federal cop, he should be eager to dive into these odd circumstances, but he seems hesitant.

"You've got a big lead on something, don't you?" asks Hughes.

Olmo gives us a sly grin. "All I can say is be sure to be at the afternoon briefing. We may have turned a corner."

CHAPTER 15

ECOTERRORIST

The conference table at the Beachside Resort has expanded to accommodate representatives from almost every law enforcement agency in South Florida. I notice the FBI contingent has grown larger as they've added more of their counterterrorism agents.

Other than Olmo's hint at a breakthrough, we haven't heard anything. To their credit, the bureau's done a good job of keeping a lid on this.

The fact that *The Sea of Dreams* was attacked is general knowledge now, and the already-massive number of onlookers and news crews on the beach has only increased. There was talk about shutting down the entire length of highway, but outrage from shop owners already concerned about the long-term impact on cruise-industry tourism kept that from happening.

The salvage company, Atlas Salvage, has been given limited access to *The Sea of Dreams* to start repairing the hull. Their staging area on the beach is a mini-city of cargo containers, boats, and tents. Environmental officials have been paying close attention to make sure the rescue effort doesn't make the ocean impact worse.

My concern is that there could still be more clues back on the ship that we'll no longer have access to. I understand the need to put the boat back into service, but I don't want it to happen at the expense of catching who caused this. Hopefully the presentation from Olmo, the acting lead for the FBI, will alleviate my concerns.

He stands and addresses the assembled group. "We think we may have had a significant break in this case. We've had multiple tips coming in suggesting this may have been an act of ecoterrorism. Some include specific details about who may be responsible.

"While in a case this size, you're bound to be flooded with tips, some legitimate, some pranks, and others vindictive, we've kept secret one additional piece of information that we feel comfortable releasing now." He clicks a remote, and a letter appears on the screen behind him.

The letter appears to have been composed on an old-school typewriter:

THE FOLLY MUST STOP. WE CAN'T KEEP POLLUTING THE SEAS WITH OUR HUMAN GARBAGE. THE SEA OF DREAMS WAS JUST A WARNING. WATCH THE STARS.

"At least five copies of this letter were sent to different addresses, including the cruise line's headquarters, the local newspapers, and the Miami field office. They were placed in different mail drops on the day of the attack. It took us some time, but we were able to confirm that at least one of them was sent before the ship was hit."

A murmur in the room rises, then quiets.

"We consider it highly likely this is authentic and was sent by the perpetrator or a coconspirator. At first, we were skeptical that this was a genuine act of ecoterrorism and not a red herring to distract from some sort of attempted market manipulation, but other evidence has convinced us that the letter's stated intent is genuine.

"You'll notice the last line, 'Watch the Stars.' As many of you may know, *The Sea of Stars* is the sister ship to *The Sea of Dreams* and ports out of New York City. This may be misdirection, but we're putting extra security around that vessel just in case."

Well, this took an interesting turn. If Olmo is right, the fact that the letter was sent before the ship was attacked is pretty damning. Law enforcement and the media get letters all the time from crazies saying they're going to blow something up or something is going to happen because they had a vision. They're rarely this specific. Or prophetic.

A detective from the Broward sheriff's department raises his hand. "How does blowing up a ship in an environmentally sensitive area protect the environment?"

Olmo nods. "Right. I don't assume these are the most rational folks around. But also, we have to keep in mind that the precision of the attack prevented a massive fuel spill. I think that lends some support to the idea that this was ecoterrorism.

"What we want to do now is concentrate on capturing the person or persons who are responsible. We think it's highly likely they're a South Florida resident who has spent time on or around the water. We're going through past cases looking for suspects who have committed similar crimes, and we'll be conducting interviews with any we find.

"We'd like your help by contributing anything you have. For example, have you ever made an arrest of someone behaving suspiciously around a water-treatment facility? Have you ever pulled someone over who had a drone in their vehicle and acted unusually nervous?"

That list will end up running in the thousands, but that's how these things work: cast a wide net.

Olmo concludes by asking us all to help with background checks to narrow down the list of suspects.

"What do you think?" Hughes asks me during a break in the briefing.

"I think they have some specific people in mind and are okay with us spinning our wheels tracking down harmless whack jobs and petty criminals. Which normally I wouldn't have a problem with."

"I hear you. I'd actually been wondering myself if there might be an 'eco' angle to this. So I just did a search through old cases and came up with a couple of interesting prospects."

"Really? Anyone stand out?"

"One does. Maxim Schrulcraft. He's been arrested at a number of protests, including at the Keystone Pipeline. He was also with Sea Shepherd for a while but got kicked out because he was too radical even for them. A fellow crew member found him with pipe bomb parts. Four years ago, he was arrested for sneaking onto a cruise ship in Key West. The charges got dropped for some reason, and there was never an explanation for what he was doing there."

"Where is he now?"

"That's the big question. He seems to have gone off the grid after that. No address. No phone number. It's kind of weird." Hughes shrugs.

"Okay. But why him?"

"Schrulcraft has a degree in electrical engineering and also studied aeronautics. Plus, he was a member of the UCF drone club."

This just got interesting. "Have you talked to Olmo about him?"

"I'm about to, but I wanted to brief you first. I have a feeling that Schrulcraft is already on their radar."

"There's only one way to find out."

We walk over to Olmo and pull him aside.

"Will you be able to cover some ground for us on this?" he asks us straightaway.

"Maybe some specific ground," says Hughes. "We were thinking about talking to Maxim Schrulcraft."

Olmo's sly grin makes a return. "You guys *are* thorough. How long has he been on your suspect list?"

"Not until you showed us the letter. That would have helped earlier," Hughes adds.

Scott's not the type to carry a grudge, but he's clearly annoyed that the FBI kept this from us.

"I understand that now," says Olmo. "Schrulcraft's high on our list, but we don't have any leads on him. If you think you have a better chance of locating him, be my guest."

"I don't know if we have a better chance," I tell the agent, "but we might have some resources we can use to make it happen."

Scott and I have deep ties in the local community, not to mention everyone my family knows, from ship captains to the guys who sell bait to the big-box stores with fishing departments.

"Anything that makes a difference. We're already ramping up security in New York because of the threat. We've got people on the ground looking for him there," says Olmo.

We leave him to his work and move to a quiet corner of the conference room. I ask Hughes what he thinks of the indirect reference to *The Sea of Stars*.

He shakes his head. "I'm not sure I buy that. Whoever did this would be stupid to put that kind of attention on their next target."

I agree with him, but I feel like I need to point out the other side. "Unless they *know* they can pull it off. We don't know how or where the drones were deployed from. Either way, if he has roots in South Florida, then we should start looking around here. I can handle the boating community."

"I was thinking I might talk to some of the environmental groups and see what I can find out about the more extreme members of their community," says Hughes.

I look at Hughes's pleated slacks and tucked-in polo shirt. "Square" is too loose a term for him. "You, um, sure they'll talk to you?"

"You'd be surprised by how eager true believers are to talk." He smiles. "And if that doesn't work, I'll tell them I'm trying to catch a guy who punched a baby dolphin."

CHAPTER 16
SEA LIFE

From the run-down look of the place, you'd think Holt Marine Supply got its start selling anchor rope to Juan Ponce de León when he first explored Florida. The business has been in the family for generations and has row after row of dusty shelves holding everything from fishing lures to parts for outboard motors whose manufacturers went out of business while we were still in Vietnam.

As a little girl, I'd come here with my father and brothers and roam the aisles, inspecting each curiosity. Dad would usually be at the counter arguing with the owners, Stephan Holt or his wife, Francine, about the price of something he needed to fix our boat.

It was friendly banter. The Holts were friends of our family until they both passed away a few years ago. Now, their oldest daughter, Gayle, runs the place with her husband, Cliff. He's a grease monkey who does boat repairs in a building next to the store while Gayle minds the cash register.

She's friendly enough, but I get the sense that she feels trapped in this mausoleum of rapidly depreciating marine supplies.

My family has a boom/bust history, and the only thing I inherited was experience. But I'm glad for it. It's much worse to be tied to a legacy you don't want.

Gayle finishes up with a customer and sees me inspecting some ancient weight belts. "Hey, McPherson!"

When you're born into my family, for some reason your surname becomes your only name. I could have had five relatives with me in the store, and Gayle still would have shouted, "McPherson!" at whichever family member she was addressing. The only person who escaped the McPherson tag is my mother, and that was through divorce.

"Hey, Gayle," I reply as I step up to the counter.

"How's Run?" she asks.

Of course she asks about Run. That's what every woman in South Florida from eighteen to eighty asks when they see me.

What she's really asking is whether he's dumped me and is back out on the market.

"We're great. Jackie's getting taller. We can't tell which one of us she takes after most," I say defensively.

"Hopefully the better-looking of you," replies Gayle.

When did *she* get so bitter? All the empathy I was feeling for her quickly drains away . . . until I catch a glimpse of her hand and see a pale band where her wedding ring belongs.

Ah, damn. I get it. If Gayle had been feeling trapped before, it must be even worse now. I take back all my judgments.

As if reading my mind, Gayle holds her hand up to show the missing ring. "Good riddance. I found out his night repair calls were actually trips to the Indian casino. Which wasn't too big a problem until I noticed things were missing from here and showing up over at the Boat Barn. I should have had him arrested."

"I'm sorry to hear that. If you change your mind, let me know."

"Right. I forgot you're a cop now," she says a little derisively.

Is she angry that I got to determine my own destiny? Normally I'd make some snappy comeback, but I've been learning about the concept of punching down. Am I maturing? Am I okay with this?

"I enjoy it," I tell her with a small shrug. "It's rewarding. I get to punch back at all the scumbags now."

"I hear you. So, what brings you in?" she asks, her demeanor improving slightly for the better.

I came here because this is exactly the place a boater looking to keep a low profile and also working from a limited budget would look for parts. The Holts were always willing to work in cash with no receipts. That meant there was a strict no-return policy. It also meant that some of the items they traded in had been liberated from their previous owners without their permission.

The Holts were smart enough to know that if anyone came in here trying to sell something they freely admitted to having stolen, they should call the cops. Which they did on several occasions, putting them into a bit of a gray zone, where the local authorities didn't bother them and the crooks kept coming in.

"I'm trying to find Maxim Schrulcraft. Have you heard of him?" I pull out a photograph and show it to her.

Gayle scrutinizes the image. "I don't know the name, but he's been in here."

"How recently?"

"A few months ago, I'd guess."

I glance up at the security camera by the door. "Is there still footage?"

"Not since 1994, when lightning fried all our electric. Dad took it as a sign that we needed to go back to the old ways, where we just trusted people. Mainly because it wasn't insured and he was too cheap to fix it."

"Do you remember what this fella bought?" I ask, tapping the photo.

"Maybe some bilge pump parts?" She thinks for a moment. "We also had one of those wind meters. It was older and broken. But he bought it anyway. I think some lead-acid batteries too."

"Do you know what the batteries were for?"

"Power, I guess. What did he do?"

"Nothing specific. I'm just going through a backlog of cases." Sometimes it's better to lie than to tell people you can't tell them anything. Fewer hurt feelings that way.

"Do you know where he lived? What kind of car he drove?" I ask.

Gayle shakes her head. "No. I wasn't paying that much attention. He may have gotten out of an Uber once, now that I think about it. Not sure . . . Oh, and he was polite. A little *off,* but polite. I don't know if that means anything."

"Maybe. Is there any way you can remember roughly when he came in here? Was it close to a holiday?" If I can narrow down the dates, I might be able to get a subpoena for his Uber trip records. If Olmo can access the times an Uber or a Lyft dropped a passenger off here, we might find Schrulcraft, along with the origin point of his trip.

For a store like this, it shouldn't be a long list. Dozens at the very most, if he did come within the last three months.

"I honestly don't remember. It may have been further back. And he paid in cash," she replies.

Of course he did. Either way, the fact that we might be able to trace him back to a physical address is a big lead. A little thing like that can break the case—assuming he's our criminal. I've had more than one really promising lead crash and burn because all our evidence was only circumstantial.

"Thank you, Gayle. Please let me know if you remember anything else," I say as I head to the door.

"And let me know if you get bored with Run. Or even if you just want me to take him off your hands," she calls after me.

"Get in line, sister," I reply over my shoulder.

I return to my car and send an email to Olmo about the lead and text Hughes as well. Hopefully Olmo can have his people chase down the Uber and Lyft records. Since our hunt relates to terrorism, the bureau has resources at their disposal that we at UIU can only dream about. Scary resources, but damned useful in a case like this.

Good work, Hughes texts back. I may have a lead on an old girlfriend of his. Looking into it. You?

Instead of going to all the other marine-supply stores, I've decided to give my intuition a chance. The fact that Schrulcraft was buying boat parts semirecently makes me think he still has a boat and there's a good chance it's on the water. If he's the hermit I think he is, then I'm inclined to check out a few spots where people who like the water but don't like people tend to live.

CHAPTER 17

RECLUSE

From Key West to Alligator Bend, Florida has its share of communities of people seeking to escape society at large. Sometimes it's for philosophical reasons, and sometimes it's to engage in criminal activity. Often one leads to the other.

If you look at a map and trace your finger from Miami, south to Key Biscayne, then into the water and to the left a bit, you'll find the word "Stiltsville," the name of a group of houses on stilts in the ocean. Hurricanes and rezoning have taken most of them away, but for a time it was a thriving little community of outlaws and eccentrics.

One of the first inhabitants was "Crawfish" Eddie, who built his house just outside the one-mile zone, which meant that gambling was legal.

Other houses began to pop up for legitimate and not-so-legitimate purposes. One enterprising person intentionally beached his ship on a sandbar and created a floating bordello. The Quarterdeck Club was another venture, complete with yacht slips and a slightly higher-class appeal that even got it featured in *Life* magazine. It was raided for illegal gambling when the laws changed, but no evidence was found. As with many of the other Stiltsville structures, a hurricane ultimately shut it down.

While I don't think Maxim is hiding out in Stiltsville, I have a sneaking suspicion that he'll have connections within whatever remains of that community.

If it weren't for the maritime connection, I'd be looking at RV parks, but something tells me that Schrulcraft's deeply connected to the water. This could mean he's renting a room in a house near a canal or living on a boat.

Since I have no reason to think he has a lot of money, I'm guessing he's living on a boat. For a guy like Maxim, that'd mean a small boat and either renting dock space or anchoring in one of the spots in the Intracoastal Waterway where you can get away with it.

I also have a suspicion about the kind of boat Maxim would be living in—a sailboat. Not a large one, but an older model with a single cabin. If he's the ecoterrorist that we suspect, then I doubt he'd be living aboard a gas-guzzling cabin cruiser. I could be wrong; extremists are often hypocrites, but the serious ones tend to try to live by their words.

There are more than 2,600 miles of canals in South Florida, longer than the distance from Los Angeles to New York City. Not all of them have direct ocean access, and many are used as water control for the Everglades, but that still leaves a lot of territory. There's even a twenty-mile-long canal that was dug to make it easier to transport rocket engines from the Aerojet factory via barge up to Cape Canaveral.

I've marked off a few spots on my map, some from memory and some from looking at aerial images showing places that even I have never noticed before—and I've spent more time going up and down these canals than just about anyone else.

My primary focus is the Intracoastal. Namely, all its bends and pockets, where boats are frequently anchored on a semipermanent basis.

Maxim strikes me as the kind of guy that would want as much distance between himself and suburbia as possible. This makes searching difficult. I have to plot a trip along roads that'll give me a good view of the water. It'd be easier by boat, but that would take much longer. The highways and bridges that crisscross the canals and waterways are a faster way to get around.

After leaving Holt's, I started in North Miami and made my way up A1A, stopping from time to time to inspect the sailboats anchored in places where they're least likely to get harassed by Marine Patrol.

After three hours, I've only covered a fraction of my search area. This is partly because I've been looking up the registrations of any boats that look suspicious. Turns out, I dramatically underestimated the number of sketchy sailboats I'd encounter.

I pull over and look at a gleaming sailboat anchored in a bay across from a high-rise condominium that resembles something out of a utopian science fiction movie. Everything is perfect. The setting sun even gives it a picturesque, golden-hour look.

On the map, this looked like a remote location. From the ground, it's the middle of an oceanic metropolis. A guy like Maxim would hate it here. He wants to be close to nature, not real estate development. This place would anger him.

Anger him . . .

I used to manage a marina. What do angry dudes living on boats do a lot?

Complain.

While any South Floridian who lives on a canal is apt to complain about a boat not observing the speed limit, Maxim would be more bothered by boaters dumping and hurting the environment. As would I. But a guy like Schrulcraft might go looking for violations. He'd see it as his mission. But at the same time, he'd want to be anonymous about it.

I call George Solar.

"McPherson, how's the search going?"

"On a scale of one to meh, pretty meh. Quick question: Do we have a contact at emergency services who has access to call logs?"

"Yeah. I got someone. What do you need?"

"I'm thinking the suspect might be the kind of person to make a lot of calls about dirty boats, dumping, and that kind of thing on the waterways."

"Huh. Interesting. If his calls were anonymous, we can't get the phone numbers without a warrant . . ." Solar pauses to think.

"But we could get the cell tower location," I tell him. "And if our suspect's the type of person to use a burner phone, the number might not even make a difference."

"Yeah. I think that it won't be too hard. Let me call you back."

It takes less than fifteen minutes.

"My friend came up with some cell towers. Three of them have unusually high call volume to emergency numbers for marine-related calls. I'm texting you the coordinates now. Hughes asked for my help to go talk to one of Schrulcraft's former friends. Guy served time for manslaughter, and he might not be cooperative. So I might not be available for a while. Don't do anything stupid."

I quickly plot the coordinates that Solar gives me on my map and see that one of them matches an area I'd marked to search. No big highrises, nothing but a few houses to one side and mangroves on the other. My Sloan-sense starts to tingle.

"Got it," I tell my boss. "Nothing stupid."

CHAPTER 18

STEALTH

Boca Verde Lake is a body of water on the Intracoastal that has a state park on one side and a nature center on the other. Although there's a high-rise condo to the north, it's one of the most isolated places on my map. It's also where the second-largest number of calls came from—the first place being a marina south of here.

As I pull up to the park, a maintenance worker in a golf cart is pulling a gate closed for the night. I roll down my window and show my badge.

"I need to get in for a little bit and check something. Is that okay?"

"I'll push it shut, but I got to lock it up in an hour. Is that all right?"

"Perfect."

He waves me through, and I follow the winding, tree-lined road to the far end of the park, where the waterway should be visible. I park my car where the road terminates and walk along a small path until I come to a wooden walkway that follows the shore for ten yards. Twisted mangroves curl around the deck, and in some places their roots shoot through the gaps. Water laps against their trunks, and I can hear the sound of birds climbing through trees, and probably an iguana or two hundred.

But it's not the flora or fauna that has my attention. It's the run-down sailboat anchored a hundred feet away from me. The sail is furled, and based on the stains around the lashings and the barnacles at the waterline, this vessel hasn't been moved in quite some time.

When Ted Kaczynski's lawyers wanted to show jurors that isolation had made him deranged and not responsible for his actions, they had his cabin brought on a flatbed truck from Montana to Sacramento so they could walk jurors through it and hopefully make them sympathetic to his situation.

While a dramatic gesture, it probably had the opposite effect. Instead of making them feel that Ted had been trapped in some kind of prison that warped him, it was hard to escape the fact that he'd chosen to live like that. He wasn't cast from society; he cast society aside. What kind of monster sends bombs to strangers, maiming and sometimes killing them? The kind of monster that would choose to live in a place like that. The defense attorneys would have been better off dragging out Dracula's coffin and pleading for compassion.

While I am not quite getting "Unabomber" or "vampire" vibes looking at the sailboat, I am getting creepy ones. There are several antennas and devices on the roof, including a satellite dish and a wind-speed meter like the one Gayle Holt described: telltale signs of someone living on the boat permanently.

Oh, and there's also the name on the back of the boat: *Gaia's Protector*.

If you asked me what kind of person would live on a boat like this, I'd say it was an eco-nut who was too extreme for an environmental group known for its extreme behavior.

Lest I seem judgmental, I should add that I'm someone who will not only grab the trash thrown in the water by someone else on a boat but also throw it back at them and start a fight. Before I became a cop, Run had to restrain me more than once when I was prepared to techni-cally commit piracy by boarding a boat and attacking a captain.

So I don't call the owner of this boat a nut lightly. I also don't know if I'd call them anything because there's no dinghy, so I'm not sure anybody's even home.

I text Solar, telling him what I found. Then I remember that he's helping Hughes.

How long should I wait?

I could call in Marine Patrol to have them check out the boat. But, technically, if I have probable cause, I can check it out. I have a folding kayak in the back of my truck that takes two minutes to set up . . .

Hmm . . . it's dusk and the sailboat's navigation lights aren't on. Officially, that's a navigation hazard and probable cause for me to board the vessel.

It takes me five minutes to get my little kayak, unfold it, and drop it in the water. If I had planned on diving, I'd have taken out the raft instead, but that takes forever to inflate. The kayak's perfect for this short a trip.

As I paddle to the sailboat, I realize that whoever lives on the boat could also have one of these. Ergo, not seeing a dinghy doesn't mean the sailboat's owner isn't home.

Okay, maybe I was a bit impulsive here. No matter, I'm already at the sailboat's side. I pull up to its stern and throw a line around a cleat.

"Is anyone aboard?" I call out. "I'm a law enforcement officer. Your vessel has no navigation lights. I need to board."

No answer.

I repeat my warning and get no reply. Fair enough.

"I'm coming aboard!"

I pull myself over the gunwale and approach the cockpit. The sun has set now, so I turn on my flashlight to see more clearly.

Wow, it looks like the deck was cleaned recently. And the cockpit's in fine shape. I inspect the wheel and instruments. The black plastic has turned gray from years of direct sunlight. I see no signs that this boat's been used to go anywhere recently.

If this *is* Maxim's boat, and if he's the one who attacked *The Sea of Dreams*, it certainly wasn't from this vessel. He would have had to use another boat and possibly an accomplice.

"Hello? Anyone aboard?"

Still no answer.

I inspect the hatch to the cabin and reach down to turn the door handle, then stop myself before turning it.

What if he's belowdecks and waiting for me with a shotgun? Like the one fired at me the other night?

I need to take a more cautious approach. I move to the side and take off my shoes so I can step more quietly, then set my flashlight down on the captain's chair.

It's hard to move without making a sound on a boat like this, but not impossible. The secret is to step only on the most reinforced parts of the deck. I've played this hide-and-seek game with my cousins since before I can remember. I'm slightly heavier now, but the principle's the same. I hope.

I step onto the deck above the cabin, putting part of my weight on the boom, which is firmly lashed down.

One careful step after another, I make my way to the bow and crouch over the forward hatch. It's already propped open to enable air flow. This should be directly over the forward berth.

If I wanted to drop in and surprise him from behind, assuming Maxim is aboard—or whoever it is who owns this boat—this would be the spot. I'd have to be quick, though . . .

The impulsive part of my brain decides that's my cue to flip open the hatch and jump down, getting the upper hand.

I land in a crouched position and freeze. All I can see is the glow of my flashlight from where I left it above. The scatter from its beam is backlighting something . . .

Something shaped like a person.

My eyes adjust, and I see the back of someone's head. They're sitting on a chair, wearing a life vest and facing the cabin door, completely motionless.

Are they sleeping?

I take a deep breath and smell something I didn't notice before. It's a mildly pungent reek. The smell of death.

I take my penlight from my pocket and shine it at the body. I can't tell if it's Maxim, but the hair color and build appear correct.

"Maxim?"

No response.

I ease forward to inspect him more closely, moving carefully in case this is a trap.

I reach him, lean around in front of him, and see his face. His eyes are open, and there's bruising around his temple. Saliva has crusted around his mouth.

I check his neck for a pulse but can't find one.

His hands are slack at his sides, and there's no gun to be found anywhere on the floor, but an empty pill bottle lies nearby.

I search his body with my light and realize that it's not a life vest he's wearing. It's a bomb vest.

Twelve bricks of explosives are strapped to his torso. There's also a thin wire leading from a box on his chest to the cabin door handle.

Oh damn.

It's rigged to explode if someone opens it.

I almost opened it.

I notice several other wires running from the vest and along the floor and walls, where more bricks of explosives have been taped to the hull. There's also a wire running from them along the hull and up to the hinge on the hatch that I ripped open.

I yanked it so hard I pulled it off the hinge and the trip wire, preventing it from exploding. What are the chances of that?

But the trigger wire is now dangling across the space I came through. And at the far front of the bow, I see another box like the one on Maxim's chest. Only this one has a blinking red light.

Was it blinking before?

I don't know.

All I do know is that I'm trapped.

CHAPTER 19

TRIGGERED

"Marzal speaking," says the voice on the other end of the phone.

"Hey . . . it's Sloan. Sloan McPherson," I reply nervously from the explosive-wired cabin.

"Hey, McPherson. How are you doing? I heard you were one of the first people aboard the cruise ship. What was that like?"

"Can I give you the details later? I need you to look at something. I'm sending you the photos right now."

I hear the alert from Freddy Marzal's text message app.

"Huh. That's one hell of a setup. That black box is a bit of a nightmare. God knows what's inside there. I'd hate to be the poor SOB who has to dismantle that."

"Well, I got bad news for you."

"Oh shit. This is an active situation? Isn't Wilkinson already there? He should be on shift now."

"Nobody's here but me, Freddy. Me and the bomb."

"Oh shit," he says, even more gravely than before.

"I was doing a search on a sailboat. I was already inside before I realized the owner had booby-trapped it. I called you because you're the only one I trust with this."

"All right, give me your location and I'll get the squad and we'll get you outta there. Just don't touch anything," he warns.

"I think I may have triggered it. I'm not sure if there's time."

"Can you FaceTime me or whatever and show me what we're looking at?"

I call him back on video, terrified that it'll somehow cause the bomb to go off.

"Okay, it's great that I can see your face, but I need to see what we're looking at here, kiddo. Flip the camera around."

"Oh, right." Being called "kiddo" feels strangely comforting instead of condescending.

I adjust my phone and use my penlight to highlight where the explosives are mounted. Freddy has me move closer, then zoom in on the box at the point of the bow.

"Okay, that's what has me nervous. If it were my call, I'd have a robot try to dismantle it. But getting that onto the boat's a problem. Also, there's the fact that you're in there."

I aim my phone at the trigger on the hatch that I miraculously managed not to set off.

"It's your call," I tell him. "What would you do in my situation?"

"Jeez, kid. Honest truth? And this is going against everything we're told . . . I'd try to find my way around that wire and jump for it. You have the water. If there's a half-second delay, and there's a good chance that's how long it'll take the capacitor to build up, then I'd just fly like the fucking wind."

"Is that what you're telling me to do?"

"McPherson . . ."

"Sorry." I realize the horrible position I've put him in. It's not fair, especially since I'm the one who stupidly put herself into this situation.

"Look, I can be there in twenty minutes. I can try to take it apart by hand. I'll have my gear on, so I'll be protected."

No, he won't. And he knows that. I really have put him in a horrible situation. I only know Freddy Marzal from work. I've never met his family. I don't even know the name of his wife. I can't have him come here alone and try to take this apart hastily for my benefit. That would be selfish.

"Nah, I'm going to jump for it. I'll call you back."

"Wait, McPher—"

I cut the call.

I take another moment to photograph everything inside and email it to Hughes and Solar in case I don't make it out before the boat explodes.

Freddy tries calling me back. I set my phone on "do not disturb."

God knows what's going through his head at the moment, but I can apologize later . . . or not.

All I really want is to see my baby and tell her I love her. Everything comes down to that right now. It's the only thing I care about. That and wishing I could go back in time to when Run proposed to me on the beach when we were teenagers and I told him I wasn't ready. Sure, I already had his baby on the way, but I wasn't ready for something serious like marriage.

If only.

If my life were a time-travel movie, I'd go back to that moment and say yes. I'd say yes because that would have meant I could spend more time with the people I loved. I'd say yes because Jackie was a certainty. There's no time-travel loop to undo her. I'd have had her and Run. Forever.

The blinking red light is staring me down, telling me I might have only seconds left.

Easy, Sloan. Everyone knows you don't put blinking red lights on a bomb. That's a movie thing. You only do it when you want to fuck with somebody.

It worked.

Okay, focus.

That inner voice starts giving me directions.

It's less than three feet from the V-berth to the hatch.

Crawl onto the berth, put yourself under the opening. Avoid the wire and the hinge. Jump as high as you can. Think of it as a ring of fire. Don't hit either side, and try to make it all the way over the bow and into the water. Go as deep as you can and swim. Keep swimming. Don't stop until your lungs ache.

The voice is comforting. It's telling me everything's going to be okay.

It's Jackie's voice, but not quite. It's an older Jackie. Wiser and more mature than me. She's telling me how I'm going to survive this.

Maybe one day I'll hear her tell this story to her kids.

Maybe.

Blink.

Blink.

Blink.

I jump hard. My quads explode, and I leap out of the hatch. My toes touch the railing, and I kick off and dive into the water.

I go so deep I can feel the muck on the bottom. I keep swimming. I kick as hard as I can and keep kicking.

It's pitch-black and I can't see anything, but I keep going. I've got good lungs, so I'm able to keep kicking without surfacing.

I lose track of my kicks, which I never do. But I keep going. My lungs are starting to tell me I need air.

I angle for the surface, which is farther above me than I realized. The lights from the condo complex come into view, and I burst into the night air and fill my lungs.

When I spin around, I can't see the sailboat. Then I realize it's the small one in the distance. I swam farther than I realized. A lot farther.

My fear starts to subside. I'm safely away. In the distance I can hear sirens and see the flashing lights of police vehicles. A helicopter's approaching.

This is what *safe* feels like.

First, I'll hug Jackie and Run for as long as possible.

Then I'll—

BOOM.

The night turns into a giant fireball, and a blast of hot air hits me in the face. Windows shatter, and I feel the concussion wave hit my chest and steal my breath.

Pieces of the sailboat—and of Maxim Schrulcraft—begin raining down. I dive back underwater to avoid the debris.

There must have been more explosives than I realized. I didn't check the head or the cupboards. No, I simply stumbled on board and triggered an explosion that wiped away all the evidence.

My joy at being alive is quickly replaced by my guilt for having made a ruin of things. I pray to god that nobody else was near the boat.

It's bad enough that I destroyed key evidence in our case, but the unforgivable part is that I could have gotten somebody killed.

CHAPTER 20
DEBRIEF

Olmo can't hide his anger as he sits at the other side of the table. I don't know how much of it is directed at me versus George Solar's insistence that we meet in our UIU office—which is little more than a warehouse in a marina. Sitting next to Olmo are two other FBI agents who have been working the case. I'm getting disapproving looks from the woman, who looks a few years older than me.

Is it professional anger? Personal? Does she think my bumbling made all female law enforcement professionals look bad? *Did* it?

When I got home last night, the explosion was already in the news. The helicopters and broken condominium windows were a sight made for television. I had to explain my involvement to Run and Jackie— which from their perspective only made the blast more horrifying.

By the time I made it to shore, police and fire trucks were pulling into the park. Parts of the sailboat were still on fire and spread every-where. As fire crews rushed to put out the blaze, paramedics, seeing me soaking wet, ran to my aid. Other than having the wind knocked out of me, I was fine. Solar and Hughes arrived a half hour later, and I gave them the full details before speaking to anyone else. This pissed off the sheriff's department captain who responded, but I knew I needed to go through Solar on this.

When Olmo found out, he demanded a meeting as soon as possible. I could have played the "still recovering" card, but I didn't want to delay things any further. The sooner we deal with the repercussions of my screwup, the better.

"McPherson, would you mind explaining the sequence of events that led to the incident last night?" asks Solar.

I recount the clues I followed to the sailboat and my reasons for being suspicious when I found it.

Olmo interrupts me midway. "So, you decided to board this vessel without a warrant? Knowing that could make anything you found inadmissible? And possibly jeopardizing the case?"

I've worked with George Solar long enough to know that this is where I pause and give him a chance to reply. Instead, he simply nods for me to continue.

This exchange isn't lost on Olmo. "What? Are you acting as her lawyer?"

"No. Her supervisor. She's answering your questions because I've made her available to you to do so," explains Solar. "McPherson, would you explain why you boarded the boat?"

I quote the Florida statute back to him verbatim: "'All vessels, when not underway, are required to display a white light visible in all directions whenever they are moored or anchored away from docks between sunset and sunrise and/or during periods of restricted visibility.'

"This boat had neither a white light nor running lights. It was a navigational hazard. Upon pulling alongside the boat, I hailed the owner and received no response. I then decided it was prudent to board and see if they were on board or incapacitated."

"By dropping through a hatch?" asks Olmo.

"I didn't want to damage the cabin door," I reply, leaving out my fear of getting a face full of shotgun pellets.

The door opens, and a man in a Florida Marine Patrol uniform enters. I don't recognize him, but Solar directs him to a seat at the end of the table.

"This is thin, McPherson. Real thin," says Olmo. "Our best evidence was on that boat, and now we're picking up pieces all around the canal—including pieces of a main suspect. Our chance of quickly closing this case blew up with that boat."

"Do we have a DNA match yet?" asks Solar.

"We're working on it. Right now, we're trying to track down family members for a match. And then there's the evidence from the boat. We'd love to have that right now. But we don't."

"I took video and photos," I say defensively.

"A box of drone parts isn't enough to pin him to *The Sea of Dreams*," he replies.

"Drone parts?" I ask.

"We did enhancements on the photos you took. He had rotors, controllers, and other drone parts on that boat. Now we have fragments in the water."

At least Rayburn and his dive crew have something to do, I think to myself.

"We'd have a lot more if you'd stayed in your lane," growls Olmo, truly pissed.

"I was just doing my job. Chasing down leads."

"Well, as it turns out, we knew about that boat. That was on our list of suspect vessels to be investigated. Had you stuck to doing background interviews, everything in it would still be in one piece and in our forensic lab."

"May I speak?" asks the Marine Patrol officer. He's fresh-faced and late twenties at most.

"Yes, Officer Davenant," says Solar.

Davenant reaches into his pocket and pulls out a photo and sets it on the table. It's an image of a smiling girl no more than two years old.

Oh, dear god. Please don't tell me someone was hurt when the condominium windows shattered . . .

My chest starts to clench and my skin burns.

"I was the one who was asked to inspect that boat. My supervisor sent me the order, along with a list of twenty other vessels," he explains.

"And how would you have proceeded?" asks Olmo.

"Pretty much exactly like Investigator McPherson, with one exception." He pauses and wipes at the corner of his eye. "That little girl in the photo wouldn't have a daddy anymore." He turns to Olmo. "I'd stopped at eleven vessels on the list already. Three of them were missing decals or had some other reason for probable cause. On every single one of them I tried to open the hatch. If what I've heard is true, then if I'd done that on this boat, I'd be a dead man and you'd be picking DNA out of the water for two people." Davenant looks to me. "I don't know if it was dumb luck or smarts, but I'm here because she did things differently. And if y'all'd rather it went another way, then I wouldn't be here to talk about it."

"Thanks for your—" Olmo begins but is cut off by Davenant.

"One more thing: I read the request to conduct searches on those vessels. There was no mention of any connection to the attack on *The Sea of Dreams*—"

Olmo's turn to interrupt. "That's because we couldn't risk a leak to the press."

"Fine. But there was also no mention of the possibility of a booby trap. Had we known that, I would have proceeded differently on all the boats," the young officer fires back.

"We had no way to tell," Olmo says.

"Exactly. And neither did I and neither did she. And you managed to tell *us* even less," says Davenant.

Solar speaks up. "I think we've all reached the conclusion that although this outcome was not the one we wanted, it's probably the best outcome we could have hoped for, given the circumstances."

"Fair enough. Let's move on to looking for coconspirators," says Olmo.

"One more thing." Solar slides his phone from his pocket. "I understand you made a statement to the press regarding last night. Something to the effect of, 'The FBI was not directly involved in the explosion and is looking into seeing if any other agencies may have acted inappropriately.' Does this sound correct?"

Olmo's face tightens. "Someone may have made that statement based upon what we knew at the time."

"Would that other agency be *my* agency? Is this the story you want to go with?" Solar checks his watch. "I think you still have time to replace that statement with something along the lines of, 'Thanks to the quick thinking of our law enforcement partners, no lives were lost.'"

"All of that has to go through headquarters. I'm not sure—" Olmo begins before getting cut off by Solar.

"How would they feel about the headline, 'FBI's Botched Operation Almost Killed Florida Marine Patrol Officer'?"

"Hell, I'll go on the record," says Davenant.

Watching this escalate in my favor doesn't change how badly I feel. Maybe Davenant would have been killed. But maybe I could have called Hughes and Solar to the boat and gotten their opinion. There had to have been a smarter approach.

"Fine. We'll make the statement," says Olmo.

"I think it would mean more coming from you," says Solar.

"Fuck you, Solar. Fine. Whatever it takes to close this case and move on." He turns to me and asks, "Ever wonder why you keep getting into these kinds of situations?"

Yes. Lots of times.

"I'm sure some guys on the bench wonder why the quarterback is always getting tackled," says Solar. "There's a difference between being in the game and watching it."

Olmo's face turns red and he lets loose. "And what happens when one of your investigators cuts it too close? Hughes nearly lost his hearing and McPherson almost got her face blown off by a shotgun *and* nearly got blown up by a bomb all in the same week. I'd consider retiring if that were me. But, hey, what do I know? I'm just the guy on the bench."

Solar says nothing. No comeback. No put-down. Silence. After a long pause, he finally replies, "You might be right."

CHAPTER 21

POSTMORTEM

After the others leave, it's Solar, Hughes, and me sitting at the conference room table. I don't even know where to begin. Olmo's last tirade hit close to home. It was a harsh thing to say to Solar, but it wasn't all wrong. We do take more punches than other agencies, and I find myself in more dangerous situations than a sensible person should.

"We're taking too many chances," says Solar, as if reading my mind. "How do we prevent something else like what happened from happening?"

"I should have waited for backup," I reply. "I could have held off until I had support."

"So Officer Davenant could go through the door?" says Hughes. "If it had been me on the boat with you, I would have kicked in the door. Then we'd both be splattered all over the Intracoastal, and Jackie and Callie would be missing parents. My take?" he tells Solar. "McPherson has good reflexes—amazing instincts, to be honest. She may not think things through before she leaps, but she knows what to do in the moment."

"Um, thanks?" I reply.

"You know what I mean. It's been instilled in you since you were a kid. Another name for a diver who panics is 'a dead diver.' You don't panic. You react."

I sure feel like I panic. "But to George's point, we do find ourselves in these situations a lot."

"So did my friends in special operations. Solar said it. You're either on the field or you're on the bench."

"There has to be a smarter way," says Solar. "I thought adding you to the team would . . . temper McPherson a bit. Instead, it's like the two of you are multipliers."

"What are you saying?" I ask.

"Nothing. Just observing. That's all."

But he's clearly doing more than observing. I feel like he's wrestling with a decision.

"Here's something to observe," says Hughes. "We get things done. I came over from the police department because things moved too cautiously. Maybe we're first in the room and the first to take fire, but often someone has to do it. If we didn't exist, Davenant would be dead. Sleazy Steve would still be on the prowl. Bonaventure's cocaine ring would still be running, and we'd have a handful of renegade DIA operatives controlling drug trafficking in South Florida." Hughes lets that sink in for a second. "*That's* what no UIU means. If there's a way to be smarter and take fewer risks while being just as effective, I'm all ears."

I've never heard Hughes make such a passionate statement. Obviously, he's been thinking a lot about this.

"Noted," says Solar. "So, what are our options?"

"More people," replies Hughes. "We're spread thin. We can grow slowly, but we need more hands. I don't know if that would have prevented what happened last night, but it would help for other things."

"How was working with Ava?" asks Solar, referring to the Fort Lauderdale police officer who initially sailed to *The Sea of Dreams* with Hughes and me.

"She was nice," I reply. "She did everything we asked."

"She's a clock-puncher," says Hughes. "She's what I wanted to get away from at the department. She'll do what she's asked but little more. Once she saw her buddies on the beach after we boarded *The Sea of Dreams*, she was gone. She didn't like our unit."

Wow, Hughes is on a tear. I've never seen him lit up like this.

"Noted. Now do you see the problem?" asks Solar. "The kind of people we need are too smart to go anywhere near us."

"What does that say about Hughes and me?"

"I think that's self-explanatory. Look, we can expand, but we have to figure out how. And . . . there's something else," says Solar.

Uh-oh. He's ready to say whatever's he's been holding back, just as I feared. Something's been off about Solar lately. I've had a sneaking suspicion that he might be looking to retire or that it could be health-related. Both scare me. Either could lead to the dissolution of the UIU.

"The governor has asked me if I'd be interested in running the Florida Department of Law Enforcement," says Solar.

"Holy crap," I blurt.

"My feelings exactly, McPherson," says Solar.

Suddenly I feel like I did when my parents told us they were getting a divorce. Of course, in that instance, anyone within a mile radius of our house who heard the arguing knew that was coming.

"Congratulations," says Hughes. "That's incredible."

"Yeah, that's amazing. You'd be great there," I reply, following Hughes's cue.

"*We'd* be great there," says Solar. "I'd bring you two along in important roles. *If* I took the job."

Huh. This isn't a divorce; this is, "The family moves to a new city." I'm not sure how I feel. The FDLE is a big agency. It employs more than two thousand people. Solar could do a lot of good with those resources. I'm not sure how I'd fit in.

"And . . . I'm also getting pressure to run for sheriff," says Solar.

Before I can say anything, I have to step back and be happy for Solar. This is a man who's been through a lot. A cop who let people believe he was crooked in order to complete an undercover assignment that landed him in jail. He endured it all, being called a crook, then a snitch. He persevered, and now he's being sought for the top law enforcement job in the state.

"You can forget the sheriff thing. That's too political for me," he tells us.

"But the FDLE?" asks Hughes.

"That's still up in the air. It really comes down to two things." He glances from Hughes then to me.

"Us?" I ask, incredulous.

"Yes. I want you to think about it. We can keep doing things here or go try to shake up things at the FDLE. I pulled you into this. I'll take you along."

"What do *you* want?" I ask.

Solar hesitates for a long moment. "I don't want to see either of you get hurt. I don't want to have to make a phone call and tell your spouse that you're not coming home. I don't want to have your children growing up without you."

"Well, I guarantee I'll be just as stupid and reckless at the FDLE as I am here," I say, only half-jokingly.

Solar lets out a sigh.

"We'll think about it," replies Hughes. "We'll also think about ways we can expand the UIU. The FDLE offer sounds interesting, but we've got something unique here."

"Fair enough. Let's move on to discussing plans to wrap up our involvement in *The Sea of Dreams* case," says Solar.

"Wrap up? That seems a little premature," I reply. "Sure, the main suspect managed to blow up and implicate himself even further, but we still have no idea what really happened."

"Elaborate," Solar tells me.

"I saw a dead guy strapped in with explosives and a pill bottle on the floor. He never confessed to me or anyone. I know what it looks like, but I don't know what it really is. We still have a lot of questions. If Maxim was on his boat ready to go dead-man suicide bomber, who shot at us on *The Sea of Dreams*?"

"You think they were more than looters?" asks Solar.

"Yes? Maybe? I don't know. We have no idea yet."

"Hughes?" asks Solar.

"It looks pretty open-and-shut to me. But I've been fooled before. I still have some lingering questions."

"Okay. Keep on it . . . carefully. And keep your distance from Olmo, but if there are any developments, let me know as soon as possible. I'll figure out how to tell him."

CHAPTER 22
FAMILY NIGHT

I'm squished into the massive couch with Jackie curled up next to me. My nephews, some of their friends, and the rest of the family are either similarly seated or at the bar in the back of Run's giant living room. Dad is even talking to Hank, Mom's boyfriend, and the two are laughing.

Dad is in a great mood because he got hired to help supervise part of the environmental cleanup. He now has a mini flotilla of boats picking debris from the reefs, thanks mainly to the can-do billionaire Ethan Granth twisting the arm of the cruise line to be more proactive in helping pick up the mess.

We try to have a family night like this at least once a month. This one was put together by Run on a moment's notice. His mansion was built for parties, and I suspect part of his initial attraction to me was that it took only a phone call to fill the place with my relatives, if there was free beer and seafood.

Ostensibly, the reason for the get-together is because we forgot to do last month's. But the real reason is because Run felt this is what I needed most. It's strange that being surrounded by the people you've spent the most time arguing with and yelling at can make you feel so relaxed.

They all know about the bomb blast, but none of them have mentioned it. I simply got warm hugs and "I love yous" from everyone. Even Donovan, my older brother's youngest child, all of two years old, hugged my neck and said, "I wuv you, Aunt Sea Monkey."

When Jackie curled up next to me, she mocked me with, "I wuv you too."

Family night means seafood, barbecue, and beer. There's no formal seating arrangement, and you're just as likely to see my dad sitting at the kids' table telling jokes as by the bar talking football. Right now, everyone is debating what movie we're going to watch on the big-screen television.

"Meg," shouts Robbie Jr. In the McPherson clan, we have no concept of age-appropriate material.

"That's fake," says Cedric, a friend of one of the cousins.

From the bar, my father's voice bellows out, "Did I hear someone say the megalodon isn't real?"

Here we go . . .

"It's extinct," says Cedric, who has a reputation of explaining things to adults he suspects of being dumb.

"And why is that?" asks Dad.

"Because it disappeared from the fossil record, and it's too big not to be noticed," the boy replies.

Dad takes the center of the living room. He's not a tall man, but that makes him no less imposing. He strokes his white beard, which stands out against his tan skin, and contemplates this in dramatic fashion. "Let's think about this for a moment."

The thing to understand about my father: when he's not out on expeditions chasing sunken treasure, he's telling compelling stories to rich people who can give him money to fund his ventures. I think half of those folks do it because he's such a character, and being around him is part of the experience.

"Let's talk about the fossil part first. Have you ever heard of the coelacanth? It was a big fish, as tall as a man and as heavy. They once swam in every ocean, then vanished from the fossil record sixty million years ago. Scientists were convinced it was extinct. But nobody bothered to tell the coelacanth. He kept swimming along, doing his thing, until some fishermen in South Africa caught one and brought it to market. There, a scientist, one of the people who'd decided the coelacanth was no more, came face-to-face with one and had to throw out everything he thought he knew.

"Now I know what you're about to say next. The megalodon was *huge*. The size of a city bus. There's no way it could still be chomping at whales and nobody would notice. Surely somebody would have seen something with a bite mark that huge. But you'd be making an assumption.

"You ever hear of a place called Wrangel Island? It's north, way north. All the way on the edge of the East Siberian Sea. Do you know what makes it special?" Dad leans in with his finger pointed at the child.

Cedric shakes his head.

"That, my skeptical friend, is where the last woolly mammoths died out four thousand years ago. Stonehenge was already a thousand years old by then. The first pyramids were ancient relics. And yet it took that long for the mammoth to go extinct. But here's the curious thing: the mammoths on that island, while definitely mammoths, were hardly deserving of the name. Trapped on that island, they did what large animals often do on a small patch of land: they shrank. And quickly too! All it took was a few generations, and the runts took over. No offense, Jackie." That gets giggles from the audience.

"So you're saying the megalodon could have shrunk?" asks Cedric's mother from the back of the room.

"Or just not have grown much larger when they're born. When the whales they ate out-evolved them and got too big, maybe they got smaller. A juvenile megalodon would be the same length as a coelacanth and half the size of a fully grown great white," explains my dad. "Do you know the difference between the tooth of a pygmy megalodon and a great white shark? It takes an expert to know and another to disagree with him."

"That's a lot of would, could," says Cedric's mother.

Here we go.

"Would, could, ma'am?" Dad walks to the bar, taking everyone's attention along with him. "What would or could you tell a young man who was deep-sea diving six hundred feet below the Indian Ocean, welding a stanchion for an oil rig, who came face-to-face with a creature with a body like a great white, only stockier, with thick fins and deep-set eyes like a pig's? He'd seen a thousand whites, but never anything like this. Tell him what he saw?" Dad leans in, his nose almost touching hers.

"You saw this?" she asks.

He holds up his empty hand. "If I didn't have my welding torch to scare it off, I wouldn't be here to tell the story."

"I call bullshit," Jackie whispers into my ear.

Dad somehow hears this and gives her a sly wink.

I've heard versions of Dad's story a hundred times. Sometimes it's giant squid, other times mosasaurs or a mythical, deep-diving whale. When he's not putting on a show, he freely admits that he doesn't actually know what he saw, but it was nothing he'd ever seen before or since. Still, the story has a wonderful way of adapting to whatever point he's trying to make.

For me, the moral of Dad's tall tale is that we *never* get the full story. And sometimes the details we can't see are the important ones.

Details like the unconscious crewman we found on *The Sea of Dreams*. The armed "looters." And the compartment we found cut open. They don't fit the simple narrative that Maxim was a nut who built some drones to attack a cruise ship. They complicate the big picture, much like pygmy mammoths or a fish that didn't know it was supposed to go extinct with the dinosaurs.

The movie *Meg* starts, and Dad tells everyone that Jason Statham's character was based on him and that the only inaccuracy in the entire film is that Statham is nowhere near as good-looking.

Dad's story has me thinking about the empty compartment and what could have been inside there. Drugs? People? Nuclear weapons? Hard drives filled with Bitcoin?

"What would be the most valuable thing you could find inside of a box?" I ask Jackie in a whisper.

"Like, a Forever 21 gift card?"

"Not a present, but any valuable thing."

"Maybe a magic lamp that could grant me wishes. But keep granting them? Then I could get the Forever 21 gift card," she says with a smile.

"Okay, hint taken."

Run hands me a drink, then gives me and Jackie a kiss before sitting back on his barstool. I try to forget terrifying things like shotgun blasts, exploding sailboats, and crippled cruise ships and focus on more relaxing things, like a giant prehistoric shark on a rampage.

CHAPTER 23

TWINS

Kirsten Gonzalez, hotel engineer for *The Sea of Wonders*, a sister ship to *The Sea of Dreams*, guides us down a corridor.

Four hours ago, I had no idea *The Sea of Dreams* had another sister ship other than *The Sea of Stars*, let alone one docked only twenty miles away in the Port of Miami. Hughes found this out while going through the security reports for the different ports.

The Sea of Wonders has been docked for several weeks, undergoing maintenance. We were able to get ahold of the cruise line and arrange a tour on short notice. Gonzalez met us at the gangplank and let us board after double-checking our identification.

Despite the fact that *The Sea of Wonders* has no passengers and isn't due to set sail for another two weeks, the port has heightened its security, and a coast guard cutter's patrolling the harbor.

I don't know how much of this prep is truly preventive versus a public show that something's being done. Olmo and his team have been under intense pressure to close the case quickly because the longer it remains open, the more doubts grow about the safety of taking a cruise.

"Is there something you wanted to see in particular?" asks Gonzalez once we're aboard.

Hughes pulls a printout from his pocket. "This section here." He points to the location where we found the cut-open section on *The Sea of Dreams*.

"Follow me," she says, and leads us up a flight of stairs and down another corridor.

This part of the ship is a mirror image of *The Sea of Dreams*, except this one isn't tilting at an extreme angle and all the lights are on. My brain's making me feel like I'm back on the original ship.

"Here we go," says Gonzalez as she leads us to a solid wall.

"What's on the other side?" I ask.

"Conduit and plumbing."

"On *The Sea of Dreams*, there was a one-yard-deep compartment behind a panel. How much space does the conduit take up?" Hughes asks.

"On the plans it takes up the full space. But you're saying on the other vessel there's a gap?"

"Yes." I take out my phone and show her the photos.

"Interesting." She takes a socket wrench from her toolbelt and unfastens four bolts holding the outer panel in place.

We help her set it aside and are left staring at a solid steel bulkhead. Solid except for a one-yard-square section that looks like it's been cut and then welded back in place.

"That's odd," says Gonzalez. "Now I want to know what's on the other side of there." She takes out her radio. "Aditya, can you meet me mid–passenger deck two with a drill and a cutting torch?"

"Are there any other people that have access to this section to do repairs?" I ask.

"Lots. We have a number of different contractors that do repairs. Including people who work for the builder. All of that should go through our office. There's also another hotel engineer that I alternate with every three months. He might know more. I can also check the records. There'd have to be something in there if a crew was cutting through the bulkhead."

Aditya, dressed in a blue jumpsuit, joins us, pulling a cart filled with tools.

"I need you to drill a hole in this wall," Gonzalez tells him.

"Sure thing." He begins to set up a power drill on the cart.

Gonzalez speaks into her radio and tells the safety officer that she's drilling into the wall, in the event we trip a fire alarm or cause a minor catastrophe.

Aditya positions the power drill and slowly pushes the turning bit into the wall. Metal shavings fall to the mat he placed below. He pulls away when the hole is finished.

Gonzalez takes a tool from his cart—a camera on the end of a flexible neck and a monitor at the other end—and inserts it into the gap.

The monitor shows only darkness at first, but then she flips a switch and a light turns on, showing us the interior of the compartment. It's empty, just like the other one.

She cranes it all around, getting a full view, then turns the camera upward. Some of the pipes appear to have been bent to make room for the hidden compartment.

"This is weird," she says. "Really weird. It's not on any of the plans. And this is what you saw on the other ship?"

"Yes," I reply.

"Aditya, get Bellot up here and cut away the panel where the welds are. You two, let's go to my office."

We follow her belowdecks to the crew section and enter a compartment with three desks and a row of filing cabinets.

"Have a seat," she says as she takes a chair behind a computer. "I'm pulling up the logs for before I was here to see when requests were made to the safety office to cut into the ship."

Her fingers tap away at the keyboard. She scrolls and scrolls, then stands and walks over to a file cabinet.

"This is very peculiar. There's a log entry for replacing a UV air handler in that section. But there is no UV air handler there. We have them fore and aft, next to air cyclers at either end." She pulls out a sheet of paper. "Yet here's a work order to do the replacement. And there's Laggard's signature. He's my alternate. I need to call him and ask what's up."

"Don't," I say, a little too forcefully. "We need to figure out what's going on first. Let's take this step by step. May I see the work order?"

Gonzalez hands it over to me. The company on the work order is Sea Breeze Environmental Systems and has an address in Miami.

"Thank you. Can you tell your guys to hold off on cutting through the wall until we get someone here?"

"Of course," she replies.

"I got it." Hughes steps into the hallway to call Solar.

Gonzalez probably suspects what's going on, but I don't want to ring any alarm bells. Especially because I have no idea who aboard right now might be involved. The right course of action is to get someone from DEA to oversee the removal of the panel. We couldn't see anything, but a drug dog might have another story to tell.

"Solar has someone at the port who can be here in twenty minutes," says Hughes as he enters the room.

"What can I do?" asks Gonzalez.

"Just sit tight until they get here," I tell her.

While Hughes and I pay a visit to Sea Breeze Environmental in Miami.

CHAPTER 24

FRONT

The address for Sea Breeze Environmental Systems takes us to a donut shop in Miami. Just to be on the safe side, I ran a background check from my laptop in our SUV while Hughes went inside and talked to the Thai couple who run the place.

According to the records I could find, the Tasty King Donut Shop has been here for eight years, and no business by the name of Sea Breeze Environmental Systems has ever had an address anywhere in Florida.

When I ran a search on the phone number on the invoice, it led to a burner account. However, that same number had been used on a website for Aquatech Marine Maintenance. A search for Aquatech resulted in a registration form with a mailing address less than half a mile away from here.

Hughes returns from his visit with a box of donuts.

"Any luck?" I eye the donuts as he climbs into the passenger seat.

"No. Nice people, though. They insisted I take this when they found out I was law enforcement. If they're behind all this, I'm kind of okay with it," he jokes.

"We all have our price," I reply. "And thanks for reinforcing the stereotype about cops and donuts."

"What about you?" he asks. "Anything to explain this?"

I open the box on his lap and select a donut. It's delicious.

"Yeah," I say with my mouth full. "I found an address near here that matches up with the phone number on the work order. Burner account, but still . . ."

"Oh, good. You drive while I call it in to Solar."

I hand over the laptop, doing my best to not get cream from my Boston cream donut on it, and mostly succeed. Hughes once remarked that he could calculate my caloric intake entirely from the smudges on my computer and phone. He's probably not wrong.

As I drive away, I realize something: since our talk with Solar, Hughes has been going out of his way to keep our boss informed about what we're doing.

Smart man. I should be doing the same.

The address for Aquatech takes us to a modest, pale-yellow house with a white tile roof. There's an old work van parked out front with its back end positioned a few feet away from the garage. All the blinds are drawn, hiding the home's interior from the street.

Hughes and I get out and knock on the door. There's no answer. We knock again and wait, but nobody answers.

"I'm going to talk to the neighbors," says Hughes.

"Okay, I'll look around."

"When you say 'look around,' it makes me nervous."

He's not out of line. I had a complaint a year ago from a potential suspect after I was a little too inquisitive. Also, considering the fact that I just blew up the home of the last suspect I went to talk to, I get why Hughes wanted me to stay in the car at the donut shop.

Scott's right, I tell myself. *Be careful. Don't snoop* too *much.*

Hughes walks away, and I take a look around the front of the house. As I head for the side to peek over the fence, I notice something on the concrete behind the van. I kneel for a closer look.

Yep. That would be blood spatter.

"Hughes!"

He comes running back up the driveway and kneels to see what I'm looking at. "Did that come from the garage?"

I notice more blood leading to the gate to the backyard. When I take a look over the top, I see even more blood on the tile walkway. Smudges make it look like someone was dragged.

Hughes and I both have our guns out.

"I'll call Miami-Dade Police," he says.

"Law enforcement officers!" I call out. "We're stepping into the backyard."

I open the gate and make my way slowly to the back patio, careful to stay clear of the bloodstains, while Hughes stays in place to watch the front entrance.

The sliding glass door is partially open, and I can see a knocked-over chair in the kitchen and more blood spatter on the tiles.

"Is anyone hurt?" I shout into the house.

There's no answer.

I push the door open with my elbow and step inside. Halfway in, I freeze when I see a bloody footprint.

From where I'm standing, it looks like the owner of the blood was sitting in the chair when he was struck and then dragged out back. The assailant or the assailants appeared to be in a hurry, not bothering to cover anything up.

Neither the front door nor the sliding glass door shows any sign of forced entry. Normally this indicates the victim knew his assailants well enough to let them in, or did so at gunpoint.

Since they didn't bother cleaning up, and because they clearly dragged the victim, it suggests that the bleeder was still alive when they left. Which implies they *needed* him.

I step out of the kitchen and join Hughes out front. In the distance, I can hear the sound of sirens.

"What's going on?" asks Hughes.

"Looks like they hit him hard in the kitchen and then dragged him out. From the condition of the blood, I don't think the assailants have been here for a while. I figure we wait for Miami-Dade PD before searching the rest of the house."

"Good call." Hughes is already texting an update to Solar.

"Be sure to tell George to put that on my report card."

He finishes the text and looks up at me. "I will. But for extra credit, can you tell me why a group of smugglers would go through the extra steps of blowing up a cruise ship? That seems a little extreme. Especially if the plan was to go back aboard and try to get their payload off the ship during the distraction. Why not cut and run?"

"Well, it worked? Didn't it? Somehow someone managed to get what was behind that panel and inside the compartment off the boat. Dumb plan? Maybe. But . . ." I stop talking as I consider the looters we encountered.

Hughes picks up on what I'm thinking. "They didn't get everything."

"Hopefully not yet. We need to put extra security on that ship. I don't care if Olmo thinks it's wrapped up. We also need to talk to DEA directly and explain what we've found. I mean, there are about to be dozens of salvage workers on that ship and god knows who else."

"So it's drugs?" asks Hughes.

"Could be kangaroos for all I know. What I do know is that we got someone connected to those compartments who went MIA about the same time our main suspect was overdosing in a bomb vest."

"Or made to look like he overdosed," replies Hughes. "That whole thing smells."

"Agreed. First step is we need to know who was living here. Hell, maybe he's still alive and can tell us something. We also need to find out what happened to the crewman we found unconscious. Olmo's been sitting on that for too long."

CHAPTER 25

SAWGRASS

Robert Howell, the owner of Aquatech Marine Maintenance and the man who was renting the house where we found the blood and the signs of a struggle, hasn't been seen by his neighbors in at least two days. Around that time, his cell phone stopped transmitting. While this is bad news in general, it gives us a starting point to search for Howell.

Phone companies keep logs of when a number is near a specific cell tower. Subpoenaing those records in a missing-persons case takes about an hour if you can get a judge to sign off on it. Thanks to Solar's connections, doing that wasn't difficult.

As we take the highway west to the point where civilization starts to give way to the Everglades, the difficult part begins.

It's Hughes's turn to drive while I study the map on the laptop. I've passed through this area a few times but never paid much attention to the scattered gas stations and farms. Although not long ago, twenty miles north of here, I spent considerable time trekking through the sawgrass marshland looking for victims of a serial killer.

Only two towers picked up Howell's phone before it went dead, which actually makes it harder to pinpoint his location than if we had three towers and could triangulate him to a specific spot.

This part of Florida is wide and flat. Signal attenuation can be affected more by weather conditions and how close one stands to a tree or a building than by urban landscape features. We have software that tries to adjust for that, but it hasn't been much help here.

I watch our progress on the GPS and tell Hughes once we're at the exact point between the two towers that last registered Howell's cell signal. Which puts us on a stretch of highway where there's a canal and endless sawgrass to our left and another canal and scattered farms to our right. The probability of Howell still being alive isn't quite zero, but I wouldn't bet against it.

There's also the complicating factor that we found a lot more of his blood in the back of the parked van, which makes us consider that his abductors may have used the van to take him somewhere else, then dump his body before returning the vehicle to his driveway.

Why bother returning the van? Perhaps because it would receive less attention in his driveway than abandoned in a parking lot where it would soon stand out.

If we hadn't been searching for Howell, he might not have been reported missing for weeks.

I look out across the rows of tilled farm soil, then to the canal and sawgrass.

"If you wanted to drop a body, which side would it be?" I ask.

"If I wanted to be helpful, I'd put him on the side of the road in an orange vest with a sign that said 'Dead Guy Here.' But I don't think these people are the helpful types."

I climb out of our SUV and walk over to the other side of the road. The canal is about twenty feet across and stretches uninterrupted for miles in either direction. Algae and water lilies form green clusters haphazardly on the dark water. I spot bubbles from submerged turtles and hear the splashing of fish in the distance.

It would be hard to spot a body if it were below the surface—and even harder if they went through the trouble of taking it across the water to dump it in the sawgrass.

"Well, McPherson, ready to dive in?" asks Hughes.

"Not on your life. I was thinking we walk the edge and see if we notice anything," I reply.

"I've got a better idea." Hughes holds up a large case he's been holding on to. This would be the quadcopter he requisitioned for UIU a few months back.

"How long have you been waiting to use your toy?"

He opens the back of the SUV and starts to set up the drone. "All our investigations have been underwater, so I haven't had a chance."

"You do know you signed up for the *Underwater* Investigation Unit . . ."

He sets the drone on the ground, flips a switch on the remote, and it jumps into the sky. "At least with this you don't have to swim across the canal to search the sawgrass."

He flies the drone up and over the wetland, making it easier to see what's in the brush while giving us a clear, aerial view of the canal.

As much as I hate to admit it, this makes it a lot easier to see what's in the water. I'm starting to rethink how I'll handle search dives in the future.

Other departments have been using drones for years, but I always considered them more of a time-wasting toy than a practical tool. I am obviously biased, as I prefer to do my searching firsthand.

Ironic, maybe, because I have an underwater ROV in the back of my truck that I use from time to time. Especially in situations where the water looks too sketchy even for me. Watching Hughes cover vast areas of ground with his drone convinces me that I need to be a bit more adaptable.

As the drone flies down the canal, the buzzing of the propellers scares away a few birds and causes an alligator that had been lounging just out of view of the road to scurry deeper into the sawgrass and slide into a pond on the other side.

I pay close attention to the water and adjacent vegetation, looking for signs of a dumped body. Enough time has probably passed that the decomposing gases would cause the corpse to float to the surface if not weighted down. There's also the chance that the large reptile I spotted took a few bites.

If they wrapped the legs in chains or anything else readily available in the back of the van, like a tire iron or jack, then the back and head might be visible from above.

However, since we found the tire iron and jack still in the van, it's likely that they dumped the body in a hurry. But in how much of a hurry?

Simply leaving it in the canal could be problematic because it would potentially be visible from the road. A trucker passing by on this route could see clearly down into the canal.

This suggests they found another way to weight the body . . . or dragged him into the brush . . . or only tossed his phone here, and there's no corpse—at least not here.

As Hughes brings the drone back for another pass, the tossed-phone theory is starting to build credibility. We should have seen a body in the sawgrass unless they went to the extra trouble of concealing him from an aerial search. Which seems unlikely.

"I'm going to take it over the other side," says Hughes as he flies the drone across the road to search the farm side of the canal.

He does several more passes, going slower with each one, even bringing the drone just a few feet over the water, skimming the surface. Still no luck.

"Another pass on the sawgrass side?" asks Hughes.

"Why not."

He flies the drone down the canal, close to the water like last time. Nothing stands out.

"That's frustrating," he replies, then pulls the thumb stick back, sending the drone high into the air, giving us a god's-eye view. "Well, it was worth a shot."

"Yeah. You saved me from trekking across the sawgrass," I agree.

Hughes flies the drone back toward us, this time with the camera aimed at the bank of the canal by the highway.

Something stands out.

"Wait. Go back," I ask.

Hughes flies the drone back a dozen yards. "Here?" He trains the camera on the water.

"No, aim it at the road."

He pivots the camera to the grassy slope alongside the highway. The grass is too short to hide anyone, so we didn't pay much attention before. And that's why we missed it.

"Huh," says Hughes as he sees what I'm looking at.

Although we passed over it a dozen times, neither of us thought to inspect the drainage culvert running under the highway.

He brings the drone down so we can get a look inside. It's just over two feet in diameter. Big enough to shove a body into. And if I'm not mistaken, the object wrapped in garbage bags that's wedged inside looks an awful lot like a body.

"I'll call the sheriff's office," says Hughes.

I check the highway marker. "I think we're on or close to Big Cypress Reservation," I tell him. "Let me call the Seminole Police Department too."

A moment later, Detective Cathleen Sharp answers. "McPherson? Speak of the devil. I'd been meaning to call you. What's up?"

"I've got a body in a culvert at the edge of Big Cypress Reservation."

"Hendry or Broward side?" she asks.

"Broward," I reply.

"Okay. I'll join you there. Also, you can help me with something."

"What's that?"

"Nothing like a body. But when I saw it, I thought about you. We found a bunch of dive gear dumped out in the middle of nowhere. It's kind of curious."

I'll say.

CHAPTER 26

OCTOPUS

Detective Sharp leads Hughes and me to the back corner of an industrial park where the chain-link fence is holding back the overgrowth of an undeveloped lot.

The body from the culvert was hauled to the medical examiner for an autopsy. An on-scene inspection indicated it was Howell. From the head wounds, he appeared to have been beaten severely, then shot in the back of the skull.

Detective Sharp's mention of scuba gear got us curious, so after the body was taken away, we followed her to another Seminole reservation in Broward County where the industrial park is located.

"We had a patrol officer parked down the road looking for speeders," she explains. "We have a problem with tourists getting drunk at the casinos and then drag racing down this section. Anyway, he saw a car pull in at night, then pull out fast a little while later with another vehicle. He tried to follow but lost both cars once they got on the highway." Sharp points at the lot. "He drove back here and did a search on foot and found the dive gear in the photos I sent you. There was a dry paper bag underneath the tanks. Since it rained that afternoon, we assume the tanks and gear were left that night by one of the vehicles."

The dive gear consisted of four sets of air tanks, vests, and regulators. What's even more curious is that night was the same night as the attack on *The Sea of Dreams*.

"Is there a chance I could see the gear?" I ask.

"Let me make a call and find out where it ended up," says Sharp, stepping away.

"So, what's our theory?" Hughes asks as he leans on the hood of the SUV.

"The easy one is Olmo's theory that Maxim really hated cruise ships, launched a one-man attack on one, and then killed himself after setting up a giant booby trap. Everything else is just the random stuff you find when you start poking your nose around.

"However, somebody was using the ships to smuggle contraband. Howell was involved in moving contraband off the ship and somehow pissed off the others enough to get himself killed, or they were afraid that what happened on *The Sea of Dreams* might link back to him, so they killed him."

"So the attack wasn't connected? It just exposed what was going on?" asks Hughes.

"Maybe. We have to consider it. The Calabrian mafia apparently lost a large shipment of cocaine when the *Costa Concordia* sank."

"I see a flaw in that theory," says Hughes.

"Yeah. A hole the size of that missing panel. If they were on that ship and wanted to recover what was in there, then they got there pretty fast. Faster than us. Which doesn't make sense, unless it was coordinated *with* the attack."

"Think Maxim was involved in the smuggling operation?" asks Hughes.

"I don't know. Blowing himself up seems odd."

"Unless he didn't blow himself up," says Hughes.

"I saw the body. I saw the explosion. He's blown up all right."

"Yes and . . . ," says Hughes.

"I know. I've been thinking about that. The idea that somebody staged it to look like he killed himself is a bit elaborate, though."

"Elaborate, yes. Elaborate enough to work? Just ask Olmo. He's convinced," Hughes responds.

"I know. I know. But that feels like committing homicide to cover up a speeding ticket. Unless . . . there's something in your trunk you really don't want to get caught with. But that still leaves the problem of why they staged the attack on *The Sea of Dreams* in the first place. Why not just wait for the ship to get to port?"

"Maybe they couldn't," says Hughes.

I think this over for a moment. "So, our smugglers got wind that they couldn't wait for the ship to get to port. Maybe because they were afraid someone had tipped off the authorities. But they knew about this early enough to concoct a way to cripple the ship, get aboard, and retrieve what they need while it's still out at sea."

"Maybe they thought Howell was the one who tipped off the police," Hughes speculates.

"It almost connects all the dots. However, if Howell talked to DEA or Customs, then they would have been all over the secret compartment and searching the rest of the ship. Nobody I know at either agency has said anything."

"Maybe Howell never tipped them off. Maybe he threatened it, and they couldn't take the chance. Of course, that doesn't explain why we were shot at," says Hughes.

"Maybe it does." I glance over to the spot where the diving gear was left. "We're assuming that there was only one secret compartment on *The Sea of Dreams*. Maybe there's a second one, and they were coming back for *it*."

"I'm going to call Solar and tell him he needs to make real sure that Olmo and the coast guard keep that ship locked down," says Hughes.

"Tell them to pay extra attention to salvage crews cutting into bulkheads in unusual places. They should also be photographing and fingerprinting everyone going aboard. That might slow 'em down."

Sharp walks back over from her police cruiser. "We've got the gear in a locker at the station. I also sent you some more photos."

"Thanks," I reply, then take out my phone to look at the images.

These provide a clearer view of each tank from all sides. All the cylinders are the same dull, unpainted aluminum. There's a lot of scuffing on them, and the inspection stickers have been scraped away. Somebody wanted to make sure that they wouldn't be easily traceable. Still, I'm sure a good forensic lab could tell plenty from grit, corrosion, and other details the eye misses.

I zoom into the upper section of a tank and notice that part of a sticker is still attached. I make out a partial word, "Aval," and four numbers, "0704."

"Okay, I've got Solar on it. He's also checking with the different tip lines to see if Howell made a call," says Hughes.

"How likely do you think it is these tanks are connected to *The Sea of Dreams?*" I ask.

"Highly suspect. Why?" he replies.

"I think I know where one or more of the divers came from. We need to talk to Solar about a field trip."

"A field trip where?" asks Hughes.

"Catalina Island."

CHAPTER 27
ROLL CALL

George Solar sits with his hands folded and listens while we fill him in with what's happened so far. When I get to the part about the dive tanks, he raises a skeptical eyebrow. "Why were they dumped there?"

"I don't know. There are five businesses nearby: a printing shop, two car mechanics, a company that builds pool cleaners, and a vending machine company. We've run background checks on them all, and nothing has come up. Seminole PD asked the business owners, and none of them knew anything about the tanks or who would have been there."

"Curious."

"The vending machine company has cameras on the front and back. They said they'll try to get the footage for us."

"Okay. Explain to me what you *think* may have happened."

"The way it all fits together? Someone knew about, or maybe caused to happen, the design change in the cruise ships. A gang then used the compartment to ship contraband to or from the United States. We also learned that you can close the fire doors on either end of that corridor, and passengers and crew can still use the elevators and stairs at either end without disrupting boarding."

Solar nods for me to continue.

"So a local vendor or a crew member seals the contraband inside while the ship is at port in some place like Curacao. When it gets to Miami, where security is tighter, Howell or some other 'maintenance' person would come aboard and cut that section open after Customs and DEA did their inspections. Because it's behind a steel bulkhead and not mentioned anywhere on the plans, it's unlikely it would ever be detected," I explain.

"That's a lot of cutting and welding. Not to mention getting everything off the ship," replies Solar.

"Getting it off the boat might not be that hard if they're moving machinery and whatnot off the ship. As for the cutting, it'd take less than a half hour with an angle grinder or a plasma cutter in the hands of someone who knows what they're doing. But there's no way a contractor could board a ship and do that without help from someone on the crew. They'd need someone senior enough to authorize it."

"That might explain what happened to Danny Ribé," says Solar. The unconscious crewman. "We finally interviewed him. He said he saw someone in a coast guard uniform removing the panel. When he went to call it in, he was struck from behind."

"That seems significant," says Hughes. "What's Olmo's reaction?"

"He's trying to disregard that. It doesn't fit into the open-and-shut case he's looking for. Unfortunately for him, his forensic people have some issues with the explosion on the sailboat. They found more of Maxim Schrulcraft than was expected."

Hughes raises his eyebrows and looks at me.

"It seems when McPherson triggered the first explosion on the bow," says Solar, "it blew his body through the cabin door. The vest went off an instant later, sending enough of him into the water to get a toxicology report as well as more forensic data. He had a head fracture before the bomb went off. If the cabin-door explosives had triggered first, he would have been caught in the middle and blown into small pieces. Instead of larger chunks," Solar explains in graphic detail.

I was planning on skipping lunch anyway.

"Good job, McPherson," jokes Hughes.

I glare at him.

"So, the question with Maxim Schrulcraft is: Why him?" asks Solar.

"Is he a patsy?" asks Hughes.

"Maybe."

"I almost feel sorry for the guy," I say, "but he might have been the source of the drones and a way to conveniently clean things up."

"Weird way to clean things up," murmurs Hughes.

"You know what I mean. He might have been involved in some other way or known one of the people well," I explain.

"Which brings us to the next question: Who *are* these people?" asks Solar.

"There were at least three the night we got shot at. Cutting the compartment open fast is a two-man job. So there had to have been two when Danny Ribé was knocked unconscious. One of them may have been a passenger crossing with the cargo or a crew member, because there was probably at least one crew person involved. Although, if all of this happens in port, it could be a repair person from the cruise line. We should check that."

"Or a contractor," adds Hughes.

Solar nods.

"One thing's for sure: this team has had some training. One or more of them had to be able to get on the boat in the middle of the panic."

"Did they?" asks Hughes. "They could have boarded at the last port of call."

"I doubt it. For one, it would have been easier to pull this off there, so it sounds like the plan was set after the ship had already set sail. Second, if they thought DEA and Customs were suspicious, they might not have wanted to try to board the ship under tight security."

"What else?" asks Solar.

"They're divers."

"Because of the dive gear you found?"

"Not directly. Remember the ladder the three guys used to escape? It was tied to the railing. Either someone was already on board and tied that there, or they brought it with them to use as an escape route. Which means they snuck aboard the access barge and used the same stairs we did to get on the ship. And since the coast guard was only watching for boats on that side, that means they may have used scuba gear to swim around the ship and to the barge.

"They may also have escaped on the night of the attack by diving. If another boat came too close to *The Sea of Dreams,* it would have looked suspicious."

"So, we have a highly trained team of scuba divers with demolitions experience working with an organization that's smuggling contraband. Which still leaves the question: Who and what?" says Solar.

"It had to have been worth a lot to go through this much trouble," Hughes says. "And why the return trip? Another compartment? Did they miss whatever it was the first time?"

"Maybe, or maybe they got it and came back for something in another compartment because they didn't have enough time before. As far as who," I tell them, "I have an idea where we might look. The ditched tanks had inspection stickers from a dive shop in Catalina. That might be their base of operations. Or at least where one of them lives. I think they ditched the tanks because they were heading to the airport and didn't want to risk taking them with them. They might have even driven them all the way here from California to begin with."

"That's a long way to go," says Solar.

"If they bought or rented tanks here, they'd have to show their certification, or at the very least, run the risk of someone in a local dive shop being able to identify them. A paper trail. Bringing all their gear in by car from California saves them the risk," I explain.

"What exactly are you suggesting?" asks Solar.

"Actually," I reply, "I was thinking I might go to Catalina and look around. I know the diving community, and I know what to look for."

Solar presses his temples. "I was afraid you were going to say that."

"I could go too," offers Hughes.

"We need you here. We need you both here, to be honest." He shakes his head. "I know I'm going to regret this . . . I need you back in three days, McPherson. And no going rogue. You stick with whoever we get as your liaison. Understand? No craziness?"

"Of course. I promise."

I don't tell him that I have a very poor sense of what crazy looks like until after I've done it.

CHAPTER 28
AVALON

Less than twenty-four hours later, FBI Special Agent Jane Noyes is standing on the pier, waiting for me as I get off the giant catamaran that ferried me from Long Beach to Catalina Island. I recognize her from the photo she sent me; otherwise I'd easily confuse her for the other tourists on the island. She's dressed in shorts and a track jacket with a small backpack over her shoulder.

Nothing about her screams "FBI," which is good. We're not exactly working undercover, but the less attention we attract the better.

When I spoke to her by phone, she explained that normally they work with the local police, the Avalon Sheriff's Department, which is actually run by the Los Angeles Sheriff's Department, but she decided in this situation that we should scope things out ourselves first.

There's a nonzero chance that the people we're looking for might have some law enforcement or military connection, so word could get out. Our concern wasn't that someone might out us, but that if the FBI and another agency were investigating something on an island that's practically crime-free, it might get us a little too much assistance and attention.

"You ever been to Catalina before?" asks Noyes as we walk down the pier toward the main part of Avalon, which is to say the main part of Catalina.

Almost all the inhabitants live on this small patch of the island, which is shaped like a giant seashell facing the ocean toward Los Angeles.

I point to a spot out beyond the north side of the bay. "We moored our boat out there when I was a little girl for a few weeks. Before that, we were in Guadalupe."

"I've always wanted to go cage diving there to see the great whites," Noyes says.

"You can see them better without the cage," I point out.

"Huh. I hadn't thought of that," she responds hesitantly, then changes the topic. "So, how do you want to proceed?"

"I want to go to the dive shop where the tanks came from. But there's a good chance they know the person who got them from there, so I don't want to spook them." I thought about this a lot on the flight over. "I'm guessing the man we're looking for has worked professionally as a diver. That could mean anything from an instructor to someone who does underwater construction. My guess is construction and that he's also done underwater welding."

"So, we just walk into a dive shop and ask them if they know any sketchy dudes that happen to know how to weld underwater," says Noyes.

"Just about."

❦

Avalon Undersea Adventures, the dive shop where the inspection sticker came from, is less than five hundred feet from the end of the pier. The outside is lined with golf carts, which both locals and tourists use to explore the island. The inside is filled with racks of T-shirts, swim gear, towels, and the little gifts and toys that you find in just about any sea-side tourist town.

At the back of the store is a long counter with dive gear. Through an open door behind it, I see a back room with shelves full of tanks and rental equipment. Stacks of fins and wet suits litter the floor like the skins of captured sea creatures. A broad-chested man with a reddish tan is sliding weights onto a belt as we approach the counter.

"How can I help you ladies?" he says warmly.

I point to Noyes. "I'm Sloan; this is Jane. We have another friend joining us and wondered how long it takes to get certified here."

"Nice to meet you. I'm Luke. You mean open-water certification? We can do supervised tours where you dive with an instructor."

"You don't have any quick courses?" I ask.

He shakes his head. "No. I wouldn't recommend that kind of thing. Better to learn the right way than the wrong way."

"Are there people on the island who might offer that?" I ask.

"There are one or two certified instructors that might bend things a bit, but I would steer clear of them. One second." He goes into the back room for a moment and returns with a black wet suit that's been cut to shreds. He sets it on the counter. "We rented this to a tourist that came here with his own private instructor. Turns out the instructor wasn't certified and didn't know what to do when the man started suffering from a seizure. By the time he was dragged back to Casino Point it was too late. The paramedics tried, but nothing could be done. They cut him out of the suit and left it there. I keep it as a reminder that there are no shortcuts."

The man seems sincere. Scuba diving is a self-regulating activity, with various organizations and shops following an agreed-upon set of rules. Someone can offer you a one-day scuba diving course, and it's perfectly legal to take it, but in most situations it's ill advised.

"Do you dive?" Luke asks me.

"A bit," I reply. There's no way to hide it from another diver. If you're tanned and built the way I am, it means I obviously do some kind of physical activity in the sun. The other guess I get is volleyball player, though people never ask if I'm a pro because I'm too short. Time to lie, but not quite lie. "I have a brother who does technical diving on the East Coast. He was thinking about moving out here. Is there much work for that?"

"A bit. Some in the ports, and we've got offshore refineries. I know a few people are based out of Los Angeles and fly out to do that kind of work around the world. I've got a couple guys that come into the shop who live on the island. I think that's what they do. They're always buying the latest gear, but they don't really talk about their work."

Interesting.

Noyes tilts her head a little but otherwise doesn't react. Only I know it's her poker face slipping because we're listening for the same thing.

"Do you think I could ask them about it?"

"I guess you could. I just sold one of them a new dive radio. I suspect he'll be out testing it at Casino Point tomorrow and then back in here tomorrow afternoon to complain to me if he's not satisfied."

"What's he look like?"

"What are you, a cop?" Luke jokes. "Stocky guy. Maybe forty or so. Short-cropped red hair. Kind of looks like a ginger tank. He goes by the name Terrence Copley, but it could be anything. He either pays in cash or uses a prepaid credit card."

My Sloan-sense is screaming. "Thanks, Luke. We'll see if we run into him tomorrow."

"Anything else?"

It takes me a second to think it over. If we're going to Casino Point, the place where you can do a shore dive into the Avalon Underwater Park, then it makes sense to fit in like all the other divers.

"Can you set us up with some suits and gear?" I reply.

"Sure thing. Let me go in the back and put it together. You can rent the tanks at the point so you don't have to lug them all the way down. I'll also need to see a SCUBA certification card from one of you."

"No problem."

As soon as he enters the back room, I turn to Noyes and ask, "Do you dive?"

CHAPTER 29
PING

Noyes is out on the balcony of our duplex hotel room talking to a friend, while I update Solar from my room. We've already run the name "Terrence Copley" through various databases and come up with nothing. It sounds like an alias that he uses only on the island.

If he's been getting his tanks filled and renting equipment here, then chances are either he has a fake ID or a real one with his actual name.

Noyes has offered to have the FBI do a spot-check on the records of any establishments that might have kept a copy of his driver's license. A fake one would give us probable cause to take him in for questioning and charge him with a felony in the hopes that we might use that to get more information from him.

However, something tells me that he might not be the type to readily talk, no matter the pressure, and we should take a wait-and-see approach. If he makes a run for it, we can have people watching the ships and aircraft leaving Catalina to make sure he doesn't slip away.

"Is the dive radio he bought from the shop significant?" asks Solar.

"I don't know. If they're still trying to get something off the ship, then they might want it to coordinate the op between boat and diver.

Also, if he's testing it tomorrow, like the dive shop guy said, then that implies he'll need a partner to test it with," I tell him. "Don't worry, I'll keep a distance. I'm not going to run up and start interrogating him. I just want to see who shows up to talk to him tomorrow."

Solar gives me an exasperated sigh. "I know there's a voice in your head by now that sounds a lot like me. Try to listen to it."

"The problem is that I have another voice in my head that keeps asking, 'What would George Solar *do?*' and he gives me completely different advice than the 'What would George Solar *say?*' voice."

Another sigh. "I've given you my obligatory lecture. Just keep me in the loop and stay close to Noyes."

"Will do. Oh, have we made any more progress on what may have been smuggled?" I ask.

"No. And it's frustrating. The DEA's dogs checked out *The Sea of Wonders*, and it *may* have had cocaine in its compartment, but we've been unable to access the one on *The Sea of Dreams* because of the safety concerns and the flooding."

"Got you."

"Anyway, Olmo wants to do a press conference and effectively say that Maxim Schrulcraft is the main suspect. I've told him that it's premature until we understand what was in the compartment and if it's connected to the attack."

"Isn't it obvious the two are related at this point?"

"Not to him. He's also under a ton of pressure. Cruises are still being suspended, and the companies are losing money. Not to mention all the extra effort of providing coast guard and naval support," explains Solar.

"From my point of view, the threat is only to *The Sea of Dreams*. I doubt any other ships are going to be attacked. Maybe announcing Schrulcraft as the chief suspect isn't the worst idea," I say, thinking out loud.

"The problem's that Olmo is leaning into the idea that Schrulcraft is the *only* suspect, which would hamper the search for anyone else involved. It could be hard for us to get support after that. And there's also the risk that we might be missing something really important, and letting cruise travel go back to normal could be a mistake."

Solar sounds like he's holding something back. "But if this is just about smugglers trying to get something back that was on *The Sea of Dreams*, what difference does a few hundred more kilograms of cocaine mean? That's what, one Ultra Music Festival's worth?"

"*If* it's cocaine," replies Solar.

"Okay, fentanyl. It's bad, but we miss that much coming across our border every day."

"Okay, this is *very* confidential, McPherson. We've got the NRC and the DOE involved too as a precaution."

The Nuclear Regulatory Commission and the Department of Energy? *What the hell?*

"Um . . . and?"

"They took a Geiger counter onto *The Sea of Dreams*, and the compartment came back relatively clean. We don't think it was used for fissile materials. But that doesn't rule out other bomb parts," says Solar.

"This is a rather dramatic discovery, to say the least. What prompted it?"

"Just a precaution. Also, that neither Robert Howell nor Maxim Schrulcraft has any prior history of involvement with narcotics. Howell didn't even have a criminal record."

"Then why all his shady business fronts?"

"Not having a record isn't the same as being clean. He's just never been caught. Howell might be one of those people who were involved but not directly."

I get what Solar is saying. Somebody had to build the secret compartment in the boat for concealing drugs. But as long as you're not caught admitting that you knew the compartment was for cocaine—and not, say, for hiding valuables from pirates instead—then you're not even an accessory.

"What about crew members?" I ask.

"Laggard, the other hotel engineer from *The Sea of Wonders*, is missing. It also turns out he was supposed to do an inspection for *The Sea of Dreams*."

"Ain't that a coincidence."

"Yes, it is. We've got a bulletin out for him. I'd love for our people to talk to him."

"You might need a Ouija board for that," I say. "The condition we found Schrulcraft and Howell in doesn't give me much confidence that Laggard will have much to say."

"Maybe. But on the chance that he's still on the run, we might be able to use that to our advantage. I'll explain more when you get back."

CHAPTER 30
CASINO POINT

As I pull my cart with our dive gear down the walkway to Casino Point under the morning sun, tourists go back and forth on golf carts and bicycles. Agent Noyes and I are carrying on a light conversation while we keep a lookout for anyone matching Terrence Copley's description.

She has a digital SLR camera that she's using to take photos of the buildings and the ocean while also getting a zoomed-in look at all the faces we pass.

I watch as she carefully rests the body of the camera on her arm, lens facing to her left, and photographs two men sitting at a table. She laughs at some imaginary thing I said, then checks the display to see whether either one is our suspect.

"Nope," she whispers under her breath, then takes a photo of the Catalina Casino at the end of the jetty called Casino Point.

The Catalina Casino is a large, round building that's been the home to a movie theater, a live theater, a museum, and even a ballroom on the second floor. Throughout its almost hundred-year history, it's been many things, except an actual casino—much to the frustration of the occasional tourist who arrives on the island and didn't bother to read the travel brochure.

As the heyday of the Catalina Casino faded, the area around the building, known as Casino Point, became one of the most popular diving destinations in Southern California because of the relatively shallow water and the large kelp forest that starts only a few feet from the seawall.

It's a weekday, so it's not nearly as crowded as it would be on a weekend, when tourists flood the island and the water. Still, it's much more crowded than I remember when I first came here as a little girl.

"The first time I fell in love was here," I tell Noyes as I look out across the water.

"What was his name?" she asks.

"I don't know. I was seven. I went snorkeling out there with my brothers. I loved to free dive. I remember swimming deep into the kelp forest, and then I saw him."

"A merman?"

"Close. A baby sea lion came up close and swam alongside me for a while. I didn't have any scuba gear on, so he was surprised to see someone that deep making no sound. I think he thought I might have been another sea lion. He followed me to the surface and then swam away. When I came back a day later, he found me again and followed me on several more dives. He was curious, trying to figure me out.

"On the last day, I tried to find him, but I couldn't. I told myself that he was a boy who'd transformed into a sea lion. Not really, but in that playful fantasy way we look at things as children. Wow . . . I haven't thought about that in years."

Noyes smiles. "It's a cute story. Who knows, maybe we'll see him today."

I do the math in my head. "It's not impossible. But I think we've both moved on with our lives."

Noyes makes an "uh-huh" sound as she focuses her camera on someone on a bench close to the seawall.

Without the benefit of her zoom lens, I see only a dark shape. She snaps a few photos, then shows me the screen.

Red hair: check. Stocky build: check. Expensive dive gear: check. Face like a hit man: check.

"I think we found him," whispers Noyes. "Our suspect, not your sea lion friend."

"I'm just glad they're not the same," I tell her. "Let's find a place where we can keep an eye on him while I set up the gear. We can kill time by me explaining what everything does."

"Just as long as I don't have to go in the water," says Noyes.

"Don't worry. We're only here to see who he talks to. We only have to *look* like divers. Nobody's going diving today."

All the benches are taken, so I spread a large towel near the seawall and begin to lay out my equipment. I let Noyes watch Copley because she seems extremely good at subtle surveillance. I simply check out her photos when she shows them to me and continue setting up like I'm about to give her a dive class.

She keeps nodding and pretending to listen to me while keeping her attention on everyone except me and taking photos.

"This tank is where we keep all the unicorn burps . . . and this mask is to keep the spitting cobras from giving you cooties . . . this weight belt keeps you from floating up into the sky like a balloon . . ."

"Interesting," she says. SNAP. "Okay . . ." SNAP. "Ah, I got it." SNAP.

I place a valve on my tank and glimpse the man who we think is Copley doing a last-minute check on his regulator. There's no one else near him. He's already shoved all his extra gear into a duffel bag.

People here leave their gear on the ground while they dive. There's a high amount of trust in this community, as well as a police officer at the far end of the jetty on a golf cart next to an ambulance. Since it's a small island, word would travel fast if someone were snatching dive gear while the owners were underwater. But Copley's extra precaution doesn't surprise me, given the expensive dive computers and other gear he probably brought with him.

His dive mask covers his full face and has the new radio attached to the side—which brings up a pressing question: Who the hell's he going to talk to with it?

Underwater radio requires an underwater antenna. To talk to someone else underwater, you need them to be close to you. To talk to someone on a boat, you need them to have a really long wire suspended below the hull.

While my back's to the man, I ask Noyes, "Have you seen anyone else near him?"

"No. But I did see him typing on his phone. Maybe he was texting someone."

"Where's his phone now?"

"Inside his vest pocket."

I can remember a time when the idea of taking your phone underwater with you was crazy. With the newer underwater cases, though, phones can go deeper than most people. It would make sense if he brought his phone with him. Not that I would try to get a look at it if he left it in his bag . . .

"He's heading to the stairs," says Noyes.

The stairs are a set of concrete steps that lead right into the ocean. They look like something Aquaman would use to walk home to Atlantis.

"Anyone near him?" I ask.

"Nobody. He hasn't even so much as nodded at another person."

"Then how is he going to test the radio?"

"Maybe he just wants to see if it's watertight?"

"You can do that in the bathtub. I'm sure he'll be talking to someone." I pull my buoyancy compensator on with my tank and yank the straps tight.

"What are you doing?" asks Noyes.

"Going in."

"Is that smart?"

"No. Just let me know once he's gone underwater. If he's testing the radio, then his accomplice must already be underwater—or on a boat in the harbor. It seems suspicious that he doesn't want to be seen talking to them."

"Do you think he knows he's being watched?"

"If he's who we think he is, that means he just helped commit one of the biggest terrorist attacks in recent history. If he's smart, he's going to assume that he's always being watched."

"He just went in the water," Noyes tells me.

"Okay. My turn." I start toward the water.

Noyes fakes a smile as she takes my photograph. "I don't like this situation."

"I've dealt with worse underwater, trust me," I reply before stepping into the ocean.

CHAPTER 31
Dark Forest

The waves are a bit choppy and try to push me back into the steps, but after I move a few yards away and sink below the surface, everything grows calm. I have about twenty feet of visibility before everything turns a murky aquamarine.

The leafy stalks of the kelp forest begin a few yards farther out, so I let the air out of my BC and start to descend into them.

Copley is somewhere ahead of me. The stalks of kelp that stretch from the seafloor to just below the waves create a dense maze that's easy to get lost in. Divers here either use boundary cables or come to the surface and search for the giant Catalina Casino in order to orient themselves.

I'm blessed with a strong sense of direction. I also pay attention to currents subconsciously and count my kicks to keep track of how far I've traveled. Plus I have a compass on my wrist and take frequent note of landmarks.

As I swim through the dark shafts of kelp, a school of silver and blue perch dart ahead of me, trying to get out of my way, then suddenly dart to my right when they realize I'm still headed in their direction. I pass through them without making contact, and they vanish into the underwater jungle.

Five yards below me and to my left, a dive instructor sits on the bottom with two students, communicating with a whiteboard full of written instructions. Copley is nowhere to be seen, but I keep moving forward, assuming he followed a similar path.

Boats aren't allowed directly over this part of the underwater park, but they can come close to the edge or anchor south of here in the harbor, which is only a few hundred yards away.

If Copley is talking to someone on a boat, my guess is they would be in the harbor. While he might want to test the range of the radio, it's likely he'd want to be able to see them when he surfaces.

I move through the forest, trying to keep from the wide-open spaces and doing my best not to collide with groups of divers coming from either direction.

You have to constantly check above and below you because you never know when someone is ascending or descending. For novice divers it takes a while to be able to navigate in this three-dimensional environment. NASA trains astronauts underwater with a mockup of the International Space Station.

Instead of a full-scale replica of a space station, I have shimmering schools of fish and giant sea bass that slowly drift along, watching me like an old man from his lawn.

The kelp begins to thin out, and I drift closer to the bottom to keep a low profile. I don't want Copley to do a Crazy Ivan, spin backward to check if anyone's following him, and see me.

Being an experienced diver, he's bound to do that at some point. Even though this kelp forest is a pretty safe environment and not a place where you're likely to run into a predatory shark, the habit of occasionally checking behind and around you is a wise practice.

I've gone diving numerous times and spun around to see that I was being stalked by a large shark. Not that they were necessarily planning to eat me, but they're always curious to discover what I *am*.

And sharks aren't the only things that like to stalk you underwater. The creepiest encounter I ever had was near a reef not too far from where *The Sea of Dreams* is stuck. In this case it wasn't a shark; it was a mammal—a lobster diver who saw a young woman diving by herself and decided to follow her.

Dive culture is extremely friendly to strangers, and it's not uncommon to find yourself swimming next to another group of divers you've never met and dive together for a while, pointing out fish and other creatures. But there was nothing friendly about this dude. He kept behind reefs and rocks, trying to hide himself. I don't know if he thought he was James Bond or Ted Bundy.

When I'd finally had enough of that clown, I tucked myself behind a rock and held my breath so I wouldn't give off any bubbles. He swam right past me and kept going into the deep ocean, where there were no more reefs or rocks to hide behind.

When I got back to my boat, I could see him out in the distance with his BC vest inflated, waving desperately because he'd run out of air. A small fishing boat eventually pulled him aboard, but even then, he kept staring off into the distance, trying to figure out what had happened. Did I drift out to sea? Was I swallowed by a whale? When the fishing boat passed me, I gave him the finger. The other people aboard laughed at him, obviously having heard his tale of the mysterious vanishing scuba-diving woman.

I hope that I'm following Copley a little more stealthily than that idiot.

As I near the outer edge of the kelp forest, I spot a diver near the surface, facing toward the harbor.

It's him.

Whomever he's talking to is too far away to see from my depth, so I ascend to the surface, taking only the briefest of safety stops to decompress. Technically I don't need to do that for this depth, but it's a habit I learned from my father. If you're going to play a little fast and loose with the dive tables, it's better to take precautions when you can. Which is surprisingly good advice from a family for whom getting the bends is considered a rite of passage, like a Knievel wrecking a motorcycle.

I pop my head to the surface and spot Copley twenty yards away, bobbing in the waves and adjusting something on his helmet. I can't tell which boat, if any, he's talking to. At least a half dozen are anchored nearby, but too far for me to make out their names.

I'm squinting, trying to see if anyone on a boat looks like they're talking to someone on a radio. I don't realize Copley is staring at me until a wave brings me higher and I find that he has spun in my direction.

I try not to flinch and instead stare into the distance, pretending to be fascinated by the beauty and landscape of the Santa Catalina mountain range, which is a totally normal thing for a scuba diver to be doing from this location.

Damn it.

If I'd brought a camera in an underwater housing, I'd at least have an excuse to be away from everyone else in the dive park. Though, admittedly, me trying to take photos above the water would look extremely suspicious to Copley.

I contemplate calling Noyes and telling her I may have been spotted, but I realize that would make me look even more suspicious. From Copley's point of view, it might seem as if I were making a 911 call.

Instead, I dive back down and turn toward the kelp forest. Rather than linger and only make things worse, it's better if I run and hide.

I kick hard and take a path to the north side of the kelp forest, where it's the thickest. In case Copley is following me, I'd rather lose him in there.

As I weave through the forest, something I saw sticks out in my mind. One of the boats had an unusually tall antenna for a vessel that size. While that wouldn't help with talking to someone underwater, it would be vital for ship-to-shore communications—especially if you were using an encrypted band.

Hopefully, I can find out what boat that is when I get back to Casino Point. If so, then this dive wasn't a total loss. It would have been better if Copley didn't know he was being stalked, but at least I may not end up empty-handed.

As I weave my body through the labyrinth, scattering schools of fish and annoying meandering halibut, I glance back to see if I'm being followed.

I can't see anyone behind me, and I'm taking such a random path it would be hard for him to be on my tail, but I have to assume that he's as good an underwater tracker as I am, or better.

I reach the edge of the forest near where the dive stairs are located, and my body is pushed back and forth in the surge. As I'm timing the best moment to crawl up on the first step, I see a shadow above the surface.

I feel my mask crack into my nose, and everything goes black.

CHAPTER 32

FLOATER

There's a bright light in my eye. Someone is yelling at me and has their hand on my face. Reflexively, I swipe it away and put my fists in the air. But everything's so blurry, there's nothing for me to punch at. I wait for the voice again . . .

"Ma'am, can you hear me?"

As I prepare to strike, I realize it's not an aggressive voice. My nose feels like I inhaled a thousand copper pennies, and my face feels like an ax struck the middle of my forehead.

"I think she's conscious," says the voice.

I'm lying on something soft. I can't feel my tank on my back and its absence feels wrong . . . like a shark left to die after her dorsal fin has been cut off so some asshole can eat soup that tastes like hair and piss.

I sit upright and my head spins. Someone tries to push me back down. I resist.

"Where is he?" I yell.

"Your husband?" asks the voice.

"Fuck no! The asshole who did this!"

Best I can figure, Copley was waiting for me on the stairs, and he dropped his air tank on my face. If he wasn't trying to kill me, he came damned close.

I climb off the stretcher. The paramedic tries to pull me back down.

"Let go of me. I'm a cop."

A firm hand grabs me around the bicep. I can feel his fingers on my skin because the top of my wet suit has been cut away.

"Lady, sit back down," says a man in the crowd that's gathered around me.

"Where did he go?" I demand.

It doesn't matter. There are only two paths from here on St. Catherine Way. One leads to a beach club on the right, the other back to Avalon and the harbor. I push my way through the crowd and run in that direction.

"Where's she going?" a woman asks from behind me.

Even though the rough stones of this path weren't meant for running barefoot, I don't care. Run says I have hobbit feet, anyway, from all the time I spend without shoes.

People are walking to and from the point along the narrow path. I search every face I see as I weave through them. Copley can't be that far ahead of me. I was only out for . . . how long *was* I out?

Somebody had to pull me out of the water and take my dive gear off.

And where the hell is Noyes?

I look across the harbor at the boats, trying to spot the one I saw with the antenna. I can't see it from here.

There's a group of people boarding a boat from a dock near the edge of the harbor. Copley isn't any of them. I keep running.

I can hear voices shouting in the distance and heavy footsteps. I don't turn because Copley's somewhere ahead of me.

I have to catch him. I have to.

My blood boils, and I manage to put on even more speed. People stare at me and back away as I pass.

"Stop her!" shouts the paramedic.

Bad advice, man. Bad advice.

A man in flip-flops and a ponytail stretches his arms out to catch me, trying to be a Good Samaritan.

I duck under his elbow and keep going.

"Miss! You're hurt!" yells the paramedic.

Yes, and I'm pissed too.

The near-misses with the shotgun and the exploding boat swell in my mind's eye. I'm running because I'm angry at Copley, but I'm also running because I'm angry that I'm mortal.

"Miss . . ." The EMT's voice fades in the distance.

Somewhere there's a siren. I keep pumping my arms and my legs. My quads are burning and breathing's getting harder.

I let out a cough and spew blood on my chest and the ground. An old woman gasps at the sight of me and backs up, probably fearing this is the first stage of the zombie apocalypse.

I ignore the rasping in my lungs and keep going. I have to . . .

Suddenly I'm dizzy.

I've reached the rotunda where the path to Casino Point starts. Hundreds of people are walking around, sitting at cafés, and buzzing back and forth in those damn golf carts.

Copley's nowhere to be seen.

I stop and put my hands on my knees. The edge of my vision is starting to get dark. I fight back the urge to pass out by slowing my breathing and trying not to clench up.

The siren grows closer.

I breathe, and bubbles of snot and blood trickle down from my nose. When I wipe them away, I notice that my chest is dark red. My eyes are watering.

Now that I've stopped, the world catches up and a crowd starts to gather. A teenage boy with an ice-cream cone hands me a wad of napkins. He's too stunned to say anything. They all are.

Despite my dizziness, everything's becoming clearer. Copley tried to kill me and shattered my nose in the process.

From the way my face hurts, it's not pretty. From the amount of blood on me and the people gawking at me, if I hadn't been pulled out of the water, I would have died.

Real anger begins to surface like lava from a volcano. I'm not alive because of my quick wits. I'm alive because someone else saved me.

As many times as I've cut it close, for every time Solar has given me a lecture or my mother's wagged her finger at me, I've always known my little secret: I'm too smart to die. Too fast. Too many steps ahead. Every close encounter with death has only reinforced that.

I'm furious because I realize that not only am I mortal . . . I'm vulnerable.

"McPherson?" asks a voice from behind me.

I turn around and see a man in a Los Angeles County Sheriff's Department uniform making his way through the crowd.

I pull myself upright and wipe a gob of blood and mucus away from my nose. "That's me."

"Let's go over to the station and get you cleaned up."

The paramedic, panting and wheezing, finally catches up. "We . . . we need to take her . . ."

He passes out before he can finish his sentence.

CHAPTER 33

GHOUL

When I see the face looking back from the mirror in the police station, all I can think about is the sleepover when my cousins and I tried to summon Bloody Mary in the bathroom. This is pretty much what I'd expect her to look like. The blood's cleaned away now, but my eyes look like the face of a raccoon that had a meth addiction before turning into the walking dead. I'm so puffy it's almost comical. The pain reminds me that it's not funny.

"McPherson? You doing okay?"

"I'm fine. Tell your wife she has a future as a mafia enforcer."

Ten minutes ago, Captain Martin's wife, an ER doctor, set my nose back in place as I sat at a desk. I don't remember all the swear words I used, but afterward she complimented me on my colorful way of expressing myself.

It's a family trait. If swearing were a recognized form of poetry, my grandfather would have been a Nobel Laureate. My mom claims that it was listening to my dad after he banged his head on a hatch that made her fall in love. "I thought a man who had such a gift for language must have been deeply romantic."

I step out of the bathroom and find Martin waiting for me with two other deputies, Miko Yates and Alan Abulí.

I'm wearing a tracksuit that Miko had in her locker. "Thank you," I say to her, pulling at the collar. "Any sign of Agent Noyes?"

"She's back at the point with Deputy Rothko, talking to witnesses. They have your belongings too," says Martin. "We're in the process of getting a search warrant," he adds.

"A search warrant?"

"After Agent Noyes saw you'd been pulled out of the water, she chased the suspect and followed him up Whittley Avenue to a house. We think he already left through a back door, but I have two people watching it now," he explains.

"Copley's dangerous," I warn the captain.

"We know. He always struck me as a little odd."

"You've met him?"

"I've seen him around in the bars, but I don't think I've ever talked to him."

"What about acquaintances?"

"I've seen him with other divers. None from here. He dated a bartender for a while. She wasn't from here and went back to the mainland after they broke up."

"We can't let him off the island."

"We've asked every boat captain to be on the lookout, and no ship's leaving the harbor without getting stopped," says Martin.

I start to remember details about my earlier encounter with Copley. "There's a boat, maybe an open fisher, with a really tall antenna. Even taller than a normal long-range VHF antenna. I think he had friends aboard."

"Okay. We'll keep an eye out for that. Alan, you want to call the harbormaster? Miko, could you check in with Rothko?"

The other deputies depart, leaving me alone with Martin. He sits in a swivel chair opposite me. "Care to tell me why you're after this man and why the FBI's on the island?"

"I'm not FBI," I reply. "I'm UIU."

"UI what?"

"Sorry. My head is still pounding. Underwater Investigation Unit. We're a state agency in Florida," I explain.

"I've never heard of it."

"We're small." I don't tell him that a full one-third of the department is sitting in his office. "I was following a lead on a case, and Special Agent Noyes was helping us."

"Can you tell me about the case and what I should be concerned about?"

It's a fair question. Captain Martin is responsible for everyone on the island and needs to know what he's dealing with.

"I'll put you in touch with my supervisor, and he can explain. As far as *how* concerned, you need to treat Copley and his associates as extremely dangerous. If you haven't already called for coast guard support, I suggest you get them to put a cutter in the harbor as quickly as possible and get whatever backup you can. These are dangerous men who'll shoot their way out of a situation if they have to. How soon can you get a SWAT team here?"

"Two hours."

"Do it. Tell your deputies watching the house to keep a careful distance 'til then."

"What the hell have you brought to my island?"

"It was already here. It just came home to recalibrate."

"For what?" he asks.

"That, I honestly don't know. Maybe when your warrant and your SWAT team get here, we can find out."

"I'm not sure we want to wait for them to arrive."

I get up, immediately regret it, and walk over to a map of the island on the wall. There are several smaller communities around the island and dozens of roads going to and from them. "Have you talked to the other parts of the island?"

"I already sent out a bulletin. I've also talked to the airfield and the helicopter charters. It would help me if I knew more. Is he a bank robber? Do I need to worry about a hostage situation?"

"Right now, he's only concerned about getting off this island. I doubt he'll try to take out civilians. As it stands, we don't even have much on him other than maybe a false ID and an assault charge he would probably claim was an accident. My guess is that he's trying to figure out the smartest way out of this situation."

"And what do you think that is?" asks Martin.

I search the coastline of Catalina on the map, examining every harbor and place where he could get on a boat. There are more than a half dozen small communities with ocean access around the island. "Either wait things out or make a run for it at the first possible moment."

CHAPTER 34
WATCHERS

Noyes and I are on the deck of a rental house high up on a hill at the north end of Avalon, which affords us a wide view of the city and the roads leading in and out of town.

The house Noyes followed Copley to is a small blue bungalow at the upper end of the town. Martin's deputies have taken up positions around the house, quietly evacuated the neighbors, and closed traffic on the block.

Through my binoculars I spot Captain Martin down the street, putting on a bulletproof vest.

"It looks like he's going to serve the warrant himself," I tell Noyes.

We have a police radio on the balcony, but it's silent. Captain Martin and his deputies are operating under the assumption that Copley might have a police scanner—possibly one with access to their encrypted channels.

"I doubt Copley will come out all guns a-blazing," says Noyes.

"I hope not."

Noyes was standing by my gear when Copley came out of the water. From that position, she didn't have a clear view of the bottom of the stairs and never saw him hit me with his tank.

After he did that, he calmly walked over to the table where he kept his duffel bag, shoved his fins inside, got onto a moped, and left Casino Point.

Seeing our suspect leave the scene, Noyes raced over to the stairs and saw me floating in the water. Thankfully my BC vest had air and I wasn't facedown.

She had to call for help to get me out of the water. Fortunately, that ambulance was already at Casino Point. Once she saw that I was being looked after, she chased after Copley, who had been slowed by a throng of arriving tourists flooding the streets.

Captain Martin walks up the steps of the blue bungalow and knocks on the door, careful to keep his body to the side of the entrance. I can't hear what he's saying from here, but it's not hard to figure it out.

Apparently, there's no answer because Martin knocks again.

From his body language, he seems like a patient man. His gun is still in his holster. He's trying to make his approach as unaggressive as possible.

Still no answer.

Martin looks toward someone I can't see and nods.

A minute later someone says, "All clear" over the radio, and a deputy in tactical gear emerges from the front door. Martin steps inside.

"He's not here," Martin says over the radio. "Tell Two Harbors to be on the lookout."

Two Harbors is the location of the other police station on the island. It gets its name from its location at a point where Catalina narrows like an hourglass with harbors on either side.

"Damn," says Noyes. "I was really hoping this was going to be easy." She looks over and sees my black eyes and taped-up nose. "Well, easy from here."

"It never is." I can see the rest of the town with my binoculars. Copley has to be somewhere out there. There wasn't enough time for him to make it to one of the smaller Catalina harbors.

Nobody's spotted the boat with the really tall antenna, but Harbor Patrol has the bay covered and is doing inspections, ensuring that Copley can't slip away from there.

If I were him, I'd be counting on the fact that this level of security can't be maintained forever. Boats have to be able to come and go freely, ships have to load passengers, and deputies need to sleep. Nor can this level of manhunt last long, especially when our evidence against Copley is so slim.

The search has only gone this far based on Noyes's insistence. Eventually, there will be a phone call between Martin, someone higher up at the Los Angeles Sheriff's Department, and the FBI field office, and the hunt will largely end, except for assurances that they'll keep an eye on the harbors.

This is what Copley is waiting for, if he's smart. In a day or two, his friends will bring their boat to some unwatched part of the island, and he'll be able to swim out to it and get away.

"We're going to proceed with a house-to-house search," Martin says over the radio.

It's better than nothing. There's a good chance someone saw something, but with several thousand tourists wandering around, I worry the number of false leads might only make things more complicated.

"Don't worry. We'll get him," says Noyes, probably noticing the dour look on my face.

"Copley is smart," I reply. "He's been engaged in high-level criminal activity for a while and hasn't been caught."

"They all screw up at some point."

"Maybe. But what I'm getting at is that he's probably thought about this exact situation. Living on an island like this comes with risk if suddenly you're a wanted man. Given that he's still committing crimes, he has to have planned for contingencies."

Noyes shrugs but seems to get it.

"I grew up in South Florida," I tell her. "Whenever there was a hurricane approaching, we had to decide whether to take to the sea or go inland."

"Why would anyone go to sea during a hurricane?" asks Noyes.

"Sometimes it's the only way to save your boat. If the storm is going to cut west across the state to the Gulf, then you take the Intracoastal north. If you think you can outsmart the storm by going east or south, then you do that."

"This sounds really dumb," replies Noyes.

"Oh, it is. But this is my family we're talking about. The smart choice is always to go inland. Forget the boat. Save yourselves and ride out the storm. At sea, you have fewer options."

I gesture to the ocean beyond the bay. "If Copley makes a run for it now, he runs the risk of the coast guard stopping him. He knows they track vessels and which direction they're heading. If he's on a boat with friends and they decide to fake it like they're headed to Long Beach and instead turn north for Santa Barbara, that'll tend to get noticed. Even though there are thousands of boats between here and the coast, it's literally the coast guard's job to keep track of them. Not perfectly, but well enough that it might not be a risk Copley wants to take right now."

"All right, so what's his inland plan? Hide up in the mountains? I don't know if you've seen the island, but it's mostly knee-high brush and cacti. You could spot him for miles."

I shake my head. "He's not some drifter turned fugitive. Copley's a mercenary. He has money."

"Okay, so we call up the hotels and find out who's running really huge room service tabs."

"No, not that."

"I was joking. Does he try to bribe his way out?" She points to a ferry in the distance. "Pay off a captain to smuggle him on board?"

"Interesting idea, but I don't think he trusts anyone that much. It would also back him into a corner."

"So, what?"

"I don't know." I rest my hands on the balcony and stare down at the city. That bastard is somewhere out there. Somewhere he feels safe . . .

"A safe house," I say suddenly.

"You mean a backup house?"

"Yes. But owned under another name. Maybe a company."

"Okay . . . so one of the several thousand houses here that fit that description. That's all we need to look for. Got it. Captain Martin and company already have their hands full doing house-to-house searches in a town where half the homes are empty timeshares or vacation homes."

"Good point. There has to be a way to narrow it down quickly. Maybe something about him . . . ," I think out loud.

"He's a redhead."

"Well, yes. That's how we spotted him from Luke's description back at the dive shop."

"He's cheap," says Noyes.

"What?"

"Luke said that Copley complained about tiny things and argued over the prices. I have a friend like that. She's got money, but she's the cheapest person I know."

"Wait a sec . . . Copley's cheap. So, would he really go to all the expense and effort of securing a safe house in case things went bad? I doubt it. He might, however, already have a place where he keeps his 'work' stuff."

"All right. So tell me which of those houses it is." She makes a sweeping gesture over our panoramic view of Avalon. "Maybe we should throw a rock over our shoulders and start there?"

A sudden realization hits me like a scuba tank to the face, except it feels good this time. "I got it." I start to grin but wince when my face hurts.

"You okay?" asks Noyes.

"Yeah. I have this stupid grinning problem when I think I've done something clever. Only now it *really* hurts to smile."

"Maybe you should just tell me, and I'll decide if it's clever or not and save you the pain," Noyes jokes.

"Okay. Back at the police station, after Martin's sadist wife reset my nose, he mentioned that Copley dated a woman who was a bartender here. She went back to the mainland when they broke up."

"Should we talk to *her*?" asks Noyes.

"Definitely, if we knew who she was. But that's not what I'm getting at."

I reach for the radio, then pull out my phone instead. I call Captain Martin.

"Martin here. What's up?"

"I think I know where Copley is."

CHAPTER 35

BREAKUP

Noyes and I are ducked down behind a police cruiser. Martin and his deputies have fanned out through the neighborhood and are approaching the white house on the corner from all sides.

The house is two stories tall, with the lower one being a basement garage set into a steep hill. The driveway is dug into the hill, and a walkway from it leads up an incline to a set of stairs at the front door.

A helicopter is hovering in the distance, keeping watch in case Copley makes a run for it and breaks the perimeter. It's already dusk, and visibility is getting worse, increasing his chances of escaping.

Noyes's remark about Copley being cheap and Martin's comment about his girlfriend are what led us here. He met his ex-girlfriend on the mainland, and she came here but left when the two broke up. I put the two together and realized that maybe the reason she left so quickly after they split is that he evicted her.

Martin contacted the bar where the ex-girlfriend worked and got her old island address. It was different from the blue house where Copley was living but owned by the same company in Delaware.

So, Copley moved her into this house and, when things didn't work out between them, sent her packing, like the class act that he is.

"They're about to go in," says Noyes. She has an earpiece connected to the police's encrypted radio channel.

I remove the ice pack from the bridge of my nose and turn my ear toward the house.

Martin's voice calls out on the megaphone, "Police! We have a search warrant!"

There's a loud bang as a deputy knocks the door in with a large piece of welded tubing called a "door knocker."

Police flood into the house and someone yells, "Down on the ground! Down on the ground!"

My heart races as I anticipate the sound of gunfire.

"Hands behind your back!" yells another voice.

There's a long moment of silence. For the first time in hours, I don't feel the searing pain of my cracked nose.

I watch Noyes as she concentrates on the radio. Her eyes light up, and she clasps me on the shoulder.

"They got him. They got the fucker."

I stand up, hands clenched, and start striding toward the house.

"McPherson! Hold up!" shouts Noyes. "They haven't given us the all clear."

I reach the front gate, and Deputy Abulí raises his arm. "Wait a second."

I glare at the doorway, then at him, but I don't push past. Captain Martin steps out of the house and spots me.

"Let her in."

"Don't do anything rash," Abulí whispers.

Rash? Me?

I walk up the steps and into the house. Two deputies in body armor part to let me into the living room.

Copley is sprawled out on the floor with his hands cuffed behind his back. He's barefoot in a T-shirt and shorts. Clearly, he thought he wasn't going to have to make a run for it tonight. We caught him by surprise.

"Is this the man who assaulted you?" asks Martin.

I kneel so I can get a better look at his face. In reality, I know it's him. I just want him to see mine.

"Have him look at me."

"Would you look at Investigator McPherson?" Martin asks Copley.

Copley doesn't move. He's defiant and angry he got caught. He's also trying to run through his options. He may not know why I'm here or why he was being followed.

"Deputy Yates, would you and Deputy Rothko assist the suspect so McPherson can get a better look?" asks Martin.

The two deputies lift him by the elbows, causing discomfort, and twist him to face me.

He stares at me, a hint of a grin at the corner of his mouth when he sees my black eyes and broken nose.

"Do you know who I am?" I ask.

"You look like you need to watch where you're going," he replies.

Miko pushes on his shoulder, making him wince. I motion for her to stop.

"That night on *The Sea of Dreams*? Maxim Schrulcraft's boat? Today . . . ?" I lower my voice so only he can hear me. "I'm the bitch you can't kill."

He searches my face, trying to recognize me, then finally makes the connection. His grin fades. Now he looks like he wants to throw up.

He won't be facing a simple assault charge with extenuating circumstances that a competent lawyer could get bargained down to a misdemeanor. He may well face murder charges for Schrulcraft and Howell and attempted murder for me—assuming we can tie him to all those. But right now, he doesn't know what we know. And that's our advantage.

I stand. Miko and Rothko push Copley back to the floor. Martin and the other deputies begin searching the house.

"You can't do that," says Copley.

Martin doesn't even bother turning around as he opens drawers in a cabinet. "You're welcome to have a look at the search warrant."

"Call the USC research center and ask if they have a ground-penetrating radar system you can use," I say loudly enough for Copley to hear. "This guy has a penchant for secret compartments."

Through an open door, I see a deputy with a screwdriver has unfastened the plate of a wall socket in the bedroom.

"I found something."

I follow Captain Martin into the room. The deputy holds up a plastic bag with a cell phone.

"Does the warrant cover phones like that?" I ask.

"Physically, yes. But if he's put an encrypted password on it, that could be a problem."

The deputy inspects the phone. "Virtual SIM card. That'll be a problem."

"I'll see what we can do," says Noyes, who is now standing at the door with two other FBI agents.

"Great," says Martin. "In the meantime, let's get Mr. Copley to the station and see if he's willing to talk."

CHAPTER 36

LIABILITY

"Has he said anything?" asks Solar from the other end of the line.

Right now, Terrence Copley is being grilled in a break room inside the Avalon police station because they don't have an interrogation room. Jail cells, yes. But on an island this small, most interrogations happen at the desk of the arresting deputy.

For now, the break room will have to suffice. The FBI agents are here; they've even brought their own cameras and recorders.

I'm in the gated yard behind the police station, catching Solar up on what happened and still trying to process it myself.

"No. Nothing other than he wants to talk to his lawyer. Two agents from the Los Angeles FBI office are in there. They seem to know what they're doing."

"Olmo and I spoke to them on the way over. They're smart. But he isn't going to say anything," says Solar.

I think he's right, but I'm curious to hear his thinking. "What about a plea?"

"Right now, time is working in his favor and not ours. He knows we're worried about a repeat of *The Sea of Dreams*. The longer he keeps his mouth shut, the more desperate we are and potentially the better deal we offer."

"Deal? We don't even know what's at stake here. How can we negotiate with the man if we don't even know what he was involved with?"

"That's another factor working in his favor. As well as whomever he's working with. And that's the real risk. We have no idea who they are. Is this a cartel? Domestic terrorists? Extortionists?" Solar sounds a bit exasperated.

"He knows," I reply.

"Yes, well, unfortunately or fortunately, depending upon how you look at it, we can't go in there with a rubber hose and beat it out of him. He also sounds like he's too smart to fall for tricks."

This is frustrating. "Yeah. He's prepared himself for this situation. Or at least something like it."

"How are you feeling? Captain Martin says you took a major hit to the face."

I'd only given him the rough outline of what happened, not the gory details. "I'm fine. A little bruised. I'll be okay." If Martin's wife set my nose right, hopefully it'll be good as new when the swelling goes down.

"I'm not what you'd call superstitious, McPherson, but in your case, I'm beginning to wonder. Did you do something in a past life that you're paying a price for?"

"I'm pretty sure I was a bloodthirsty pirate or something. I'll have you know, I was extra careful this time and kept my distance. I also didn't ask to go on the raid at Copley's house. I let the local police do their job," I tell him defensively.

"You followed the man underwater."

"That's my version of you following a suspect into Home Depot. The water is the safest place in the world for me. In fact, I only got hurt coming *out* of the water."

Solar doesn't even bother to sigh. I just get a long-ass pause from him. "What did they find in his house?"

"Lots of fancy dive gear. He loves his toys. Two laptops. Three burner cell phones. All encrypted."

"Any weapons?"

"No. Not at the other place either. Nothing to charge him with. We're still trying to find his actual identity. Copley is definitely a pseudonym. He's got an odd way of speaking. Or at least people who know him here say so. Like he's covering up an accent. We're going to try to get him on tape and have an FBI linguist figure it out."

"That's interesting. So he might be an international."

"Yeah. People say he likes to watch soccer. So I'm putting the odds that he's not American at close to a hundred percent. I'm also positive he has military training. But not ours."

"How does the FBI feel about the encrypted phones and computers?" asks Solar.

"Not confident. Copley was smart enough to use good encryption. All passcodes, no thumbprints or face scanning, so we can't compel him. That may be a dead end."

"Maybe not completely. We might not be able to get what's on the phones, but we might be able to find out who he talked to," says Solar.

"Noyes said that the cell phone tower logs wouldn't be useful without being able to access the phones. Plus, this place has thousands of tourists coming through here, making it impossible to tell a burner phone from a visiting phone."

"Have you looked at a map of the island?" asks Solar.

"Yes, why?"

"Did you ever notice the large islands to the south and to the west?" he replies.

"You mean San Clemente and San Nicolas?"

"Yeah. Naval bases with all the nuclear missiles, early-warning systems, and antennas. Those are kind of important parts of our national defense. You think naval intelligence might have an interest in any cell phone traffic on the closest island with civilians?"

"Sure . . . but that's naval intelligence and . . . oh." The severity of the attack on *The Sea of Dreams* is dawning on me. It's being investigated as an act of terrorism, which means that different laws regarding surveillance and interrogation might apply.

"Does this mean we can threaten Copley with being sent to a black site? I know one in South Florida where he can stay," I reply. I had my own unpleasant experience two years ago when some intelligence contractors decided to overstep their bounds and try to intimidate me. It didn't work. It only made me more pissed.

"Let's focus on the phone records first. In this case, it's an advantage that Olmo and the others are barking up the wrong tree," says Solar.

"I just wish I knew what tree we're supposed to be barking at."

"If Copley talks, that would make a big difference."

"He seems pretty committed to not talking. And . . ." I stop as I think something over. "If these people were willing to kill Howell and Schrulcraft to keep their mouths shut, let alone bomb a cruise ship, do they trust Copley?"

"He might have as much to lose by talking as they do," replies Solar.

"Yeah . . . but playing devil's advocate, which in this case might mean the actual devil, Copley is dead in the water and a major risk for the others. Can they risk him taking a plea bargain and telling us what he knows? While time may be on Copley's side, it's not on his accomplices'."

"Damn it, McPherson, I'm afraid you may be right. Where's he being held?"

"At the Avalon police station."

"Is it secure?"

"We've got armed deputies on the lookout in case his friends from the boat he was talking to decide to make a rescue."

"If anyone shows up for him, I wouldn't bet on it being a rescue. It'll be an assassination. Probably by a hit team with no connection to Copley's employers."

We're a hundred yards from the waterfront. A speedboat of masked men in body armor could enter the harbor, make it to the station, enter with guns blazing, and kill Copley in minutes. They could then disperse, unmask, and blend in with the tourists.

We've been so worried about keeping Copley from escaping, we haven't considered who might come here to kill him.

The lights of the boats in the harbor are making me uneasy. "I'm going to go talk to them. Tell 'em we need to move Copley."

CHAPTER 37
TARGET

I walk back into the lobby of the police station. Captain Martin is on the phone with someone via speakerphone while the other deputies listen in.

"Could you spell the name for me?" asks the person on the other end.

"C . . . O . . . P . . . L. Hold on. Do you have the right police station? This is Avalon. Uh-huh. Let me put you on hold." Martin sits on the desk and stares at the phone. "Let's see how long we can keep him waiting."

"What's going on?" I ask Miko.

"A man called saying he's Copley's lawyer and asking to speak to him."

"Ask him for a number to call back," I blurt out.

"What?" asks Martin.

I point my thumb at the break room. "That could be his employers calling to make sure that he's here."

"We can still hold him for another day," says Martin.

"You don't understand. They won't be sending a lawyer. They'll be sending gunmen."

"Hit men? *Here?*"

"They already attacked a cruise ship with four thousand people aboard."

The deputies' eyes widen at this. This is the first time most of them have heard about the connection to *The Sea of Dreams*.

"We've been watching for people leaving," I explain. "We haven't seen who's arrived on ferries. There's been plenty of time since he attacked me for his accomplices to send people here."

Martin thinks this over, then starts issuing commands to his deputies. "Musil, call Harbor Patrol, make sure they're looking at boats coming into the harbor. Rothko, Miko, get the others and start checking for anyone who looks out of place. And everyone, vest up. Noyes, if you have any other FBI agents lurking around, have them get their asses down here."

Everyone starts moving. Martin glances down at the phone and thinks for a moment. He can only stall the caller for so long before they know he's trying to play them. As far as we know, hit men could be across the street at this moment. Or only inside my fevered imagination.

He picks up the phone and takes the caller off hold. "Can you give me a number to have someone call you right back?"

Martin sets the receiver back down and looks at me. "They hung up. Time for a new tactic." He checks his watch.

The emergency dispatcher runs in from the other room, breathing hard. "There's gunfire at the Seawind Breezes!"

"Damn it," groans Martin. He reaches for his radio. "Why there? It's clear across . . . Those *bastards*. They're trying to divide us." He grabs the phone instead. "I'm going to call Island Helicopter and have them land a chopper across the street. The sooner we get him out of here, the better."

"Or they could be waiting for us to move him," I suggest.

Martin's eyes roll. He's in a hell of a position. We're trying to outguess phantoms we're not even certain are real. Are they about to attack? Or are they waiting for us to move?

"McPherson, you've dealt with these people the most. What's their next step?"

"I doubt these are the actual people. Just hired guns. But either way, they won't be stupid. They're not going to come running in here without—"

The door opens, and a young Hispanic woman carrying a little dog in her purse enters the police station. She looks around the lobby, then at Martin.

She's attractive, well dressed, and has a bit of a princess vibe to her.

"Is there a bathroom I can use here?" she asks sweetly.

Exasperated, Martin shakes his head. "Across the street by the tour-ticketing booth."

"Thank you," she says and heads for the door.

I get in her way, hold the door shut with one hand while I draw my gun with the other and point it at her head. "Back away from the door. Do anything else, and I put your brains on the wall," I say coldly.

She freezes; her hands go into the air. She also waits too long to respond. "What's this—"

"No talking," I interrupt as I back her out of view from the glass door. "Noyes, cuff her."

Noyes takes a pair of handcuffs from her bag, slides the woman's dog-purse off her shoulder and sets it on the counter, then handcuffs her.

"McPherson . . . ?" asks Martin, trying to figure out what's going on.

"She's their scout. They sent her in here to check the layout and see how many people are inside."

"How do you know that?"

"Because it's what I would do. And that." I point to her purse. "Women who carry Hermès handbags don't use public toilets."

"You're so fucked," whispers the woman.

"How many friends do you have here?" I ask.

"Go fuck yourself, you raccoon-looking cunt."

I push her face against the wall, hard.

"McPherson!" says Martin. "This is my station!"

He's a good man and a good cop. He also has no idea what kind of hell we're about to have unleashed on us. I'll gladly take the fall for this if it means saving lives.

"You heard the man," says the woman.

"Are you supposed to call them or speak face-to-face?"

"You're such a dumb bitch," she replies with fake laughter.

"Noyes, get her purse and look for a phone. Then take her dog in the back room."

"What?" The woman tries to pull away from my grasp.

I shove her against the wall even harder and push the muzzle of my gun so hard against the back of her skull that it's going to leave a bruise.

"If I so much as hear someone knock at that door, I'm squeezing this trigger. Then my friend'll kill your dog," I whisper into her ear.

If she knew anything about me, she'd know my first threat is probably a bluff and my second one a complete and total lie.

"You wouldn't," she says, starting to sob.

"Where *are* they?" I squeeze the back of her neck, letting my nails claw into her skin.

"I don't know. I'm just supposed to text them."

"And say what?"

"Tell them how many people and the layout of the place. They're expecting my text right now," she whimpers.

"I'll ask you again: Where are they?"

"I don't know."

"How many?"

"Six," she says.

"Including you?"

"No. Six plus me."

I have to think fast. This place is filled with tourists. We have to end this before anyone gets hurt.

"Hand me her phone," I tell Martin.

Martin picks it up off the counter and places it into my outstretched hand. "I'm not sure . . ."

"Yell at me later," I tell him.

The phone has a passcode.

"What's the passcode?"

"I . . ."

I put my mouth right up to her ear so only she can hear me. "If your friends don't hear from you, they're going to come in here and kill us all. Including you."

"8721," she says, trembling.

I unlock the phone. It opens to a text message conversation in which someone's asking What's taking so long? in Spanish.

I holster my gun and type a message back.

"Take her." I push the woman toward Martin. "I need one of your SUVs from out back. The one with the tinted windows."

"Why?"

"I texted her buddies that you're taking Copley down to Casino Point to be transferred to a boat."

Martin gets it immediately. That would draw them away from the main part of the town. It would also make the SUV a sitting duck.

Martin hands the woman off to one of the FBI agents who'd been talking to Copley. "Take her. Shoot anyone who comes into the station . . . within reason."

He tosses a radio to me. "Explain it to my deputies. I'll drive the vehicle."

"You don't need to," I tell him as we walk through the station to the back exit.

"This is my beat." He stops at a rack and grabs another vest and a helmet.

"They'll try to shoot the driver first," I explain.

"If I get there fast enough, there doesn't have to be a driver."

We race out the back door and make sure there's no hit team on the street. He gets into the police vehicle, and I climb into the passenger side.

"Damn it, McPherson," says Martin, reminding me a lot of Solar.

"Just get us there."

I start issuing commands to his deputies via his radio, hoping the hit team isn't on the police channel. Martin rolls through the exit and down the street to the road that takes us to Casino Point.

In the rearview mirror, I see the shadow of a moped with its lights off following us. Another one joins from a side street.

"Are you seeing them?"

"Yes," says Martin. "Our plan to get there first isn't turning out so well."

"Your plan," I reply.

He continues on, taking us down the narrow road leading to the point. I spot several other mopeds joining the ones that were already following us.

"This is a cartel-style hit. Any moment now, they're going to speed up and fire on us from both sides."

"Any suggestions?" asks Martin.

"If you want to survive this, you're going to have to let me drive."

"McPherson . . ."

"Trust me," I tell him. "I'm capable of things you wouldn't even think of."

CHAPTER 38

RAMPAGE

There's no time to pull over or try to race ahead and stop so we can switch places. Martin puts the SUV on cruise control, pulls his seat back, and I crawl over as he slides under. It's undignified, but it gets the job done.

We've been rolling slowly down the road with only our headlights on. As far as the hit men know, we haven't a clue that they're following us. They think we're going to turn into the point, park, then wait for the boat—leaving us wide open to a drive-by.

We're a hundred feet from the turn. I glance back at the rearview mirror and see the outlines of the men on mopeds backlit by Avalon. They're spread out in a loose line down the center of the road.

Perfect.

"So what's the plan?" asks Martin as he checks his gun.

"Your plan is to duck. Mine too."

I slow down at the turn that leads to Casino Point, giving me a better view of the men on mopeds and a view of the clear road behind them. Any pedestrians would be on the footpath next to the road. I just hope there's nobody on a golf cart that I'm missing.

I make the turn, but keep turning. Instead of exiting, I accelerate into a one-eighty, putting us head-on with the men on the mopeds.

"McPherson?" says Martin.

"Get on the PA and duck!"

I flip on the high beams and the police lights, throwing in the sirens for good measure.

The men on the mopeds are caught by surprise. One of them pulls out a pistol and starts to fire wildly at the SUV. The others raise their guns.

CRACK! A bullet hits the edge of the windshield on the passenger side but doesn't penetrate. The glass is bulletproof laminate, which means it can take some shots. But not a lot.

There's no way to outgun them by ourselves. So instead, I've drawn them away from the populated part of town. Onto a narrow road with a choke point where they can pin us down and shoot at us.

But having our SUV face the other way enables me to line them all up.

"Hold on!" I yell as I floor the gas pedal.

BAM! The metal bumper slams into the first moped and sends both it and its driver into the air.

I don't bother to stop and exchange insurance information.

I swerve into the next one as he aims his pistol at us.

BAM! He gets thrown against the hillside.

I swerve again.

BAM! There goes another.

I hit two more and drive over their mopeds, crushing them under the tires.

The last rider spins his moped around and heads back toward Avalon. When he sees another police unit coming his way, he turns into the guardrail and catapults onto the walkway below.

I slam the SUV into park, exit, and run back toward the men I just ran into and over, kicking their weapons away as I spot them.

Martin gets on the loudspeaker. "Stay down and lock your fingers behind the backs of your heads. If you move, we will use lethal force."

From the looks of the men with broken legs and smashed faces, I don't think we're going to get much resistance. I check the first one I hit to see if he has a pulse. His moan confirms that he's alive.

Captain Martin and his deputies catch up to us and start handcuffing the men, even though some of them probably need to be in intensive care instead. But it's better than taking a chance. These are killers who came to murder us all.

Martin catches up with me as I check the pulse of another man. Still alive.

"Jesus, McPherson. Jesus," he mutters. The captain's still in shock and trying to assess what just happened.

"You saw that they all fired on us?" I ask.

"Uh, yeah. A minute ago, I thought we were about to die."

I kneel to look at one of the unconscious hit men. "Assuming none of these assholes dies, I think it turned out as well as we could have hoped."

"Yeah. That's one way to look at it." He turns around and surveys all the broken men and mopeds. "I . . . don't know what to say."

"Just tell me that you have my back on this."

While this was obviously self-defense to anyone present, time and distance have a way of distorting events. I don't want Martin to have second thoughts because of political pressure and claim that he wasn't sure the men were armed or a clear threat.

I don't want him to lie for me. I just don't want to get thrown under the bus.

Miko holds up one of the guns. "Five-sevens. All of them." She points to the first man being loaded onto a stretcher. "Gang tattoos. How much do you want to bet all these douchebags are already in the database?" She nods at me. "You're my new life model. Except for the face thing."

I walk over to the railing overlooking the ocean, take a deep breath, and think about how I'm going to explain this to Solar and Run.

A breeze chills the part of my face that's not covered with a bandage and snaps me back to my senses. In that moment, I have a realization.

I respect Solar and I love Run, but neither of them is my father. If I know something is right, I don't need their permission to feel good about myself, or their forgiveness when I do something wrong.

That burning I felt deep down earlier today when my face got smashed . . . it wasn't just rage, and it wasn't only my fear of mortality; it was also the fear of what Solar or Run would say when they found out that I got myself into another stupid situation.

It was the fear of their disapproval because I hold their opinions of me so far above my own.

It's not anything they've forced on me. And maybe they don't know how I internalize it, but I have to start accepting that I'm an adult, not some kind of second-class person who needs my self-opinion validated.

They can tell me I did something stupid—chances are they'll be right in most situations—but that doesn't mean that I'm a stupid person.

I have to pay more attention to what Sloan thinks about Sloan than what they think.

I turn back to the road and the scattered bodies of the killers and feel something I've been trying to suppress. I suppress it because I've conditioned myself to feel guilty whenever I feel this way.

Screw it.

I'm not reckless . . . well, not always. I'm *brave*.

And how do I feel right now? Other than the aching face and body?

How do I feel when I hear the moans and cries of these killers and see their twisted bodies?

Proud.

I. Feel. Mother. Effing. Proud.

Lives were saved. Nobody got killed.

It was a good day.

Except for my meth-raccoon face. That sucks.

CHAPTER 39
ROOM SERVICE

I take the lid off my room service plate and get a whiff of my late-night cheeseburger. Even after passing through my swollen nasal passages, it's the best smell in the world. The meal arrived just as I got off the phone with Run after a much longer conversation with Solar.

Events have been nonstop since I followed Copley into the water. After the "incident" at Casino Point with the hit squad, I flew back to Los Angeles on an FBI helicopter and checked in to a hotel near LAX with an armed guard sitting outside my room. This is my first chance to catch my breath and relax. It's also the first time I realize that my nose isn't as swollen as before.

I'm already in the hotel bathrobe, ready to eat my dinner, devour the strawberry ice cream, and then drink a glass of wine in the tub before heading for the airport in four hours.

Primal instincts take over, and I start shoving fries into my mouth between sharklike chomps at the burger. My attempt to savor this is overridden by the cavewoman part of my brain that always seems to be in fight-or-flight mode.

I catch a glimpse of the giant feasting raccoon in the mirror and flip it the bird. No judging. I'm hungry, and the aspirin's starting to wear off.

My phone buzzes on the nightstand where I've plugged it in to charge. I glare at the glowing display as if it's a predator looking to swoop in on my kill.

Just one more bite before I fall back into chaos?

"Mhello?" I say, my mouth filled with fries.

"McPherson?"

"Yah. Eating."

"It's Noyes. Are you at the hotel?"

"No. I'm at Nobu partying with friends."

"Oh."

"Yes, I'm at the hotel." I swallow a mouthful of water to wash down the food. "What's up?"

"Everything's hectic, of course. We have Copley here at the FBI building. We thought he'd be more talkative after we told him what happened with the hit squad. But that didn't work."

"That's because you don't have anything he wants. Ethically speaking, you can't dangle protective custody in front of someone who you know is liable to get killed without it. Especially when you know and he knows he's your best witness. He's playing for time."

"Yes. That's become clear. There's just one thing."

"What's that?"

"He says he'll talk to you. Unrecorded and just to you."

"Me? Why?"

"We don't know. We've been talking about it here, trying to weigh the risks. I know it's a lot to ask, but would you be willing to come down tonight and see what he has to say?"

I glance down at my unfinished hamburger and my melting ice cream. I haven't even touched my wine, and I smell like seaweed and sweat.

Terrence Copley has to be playing some kind of game. He's too smart and has too much experience working the other side of the law not to have an angle.

Is this an attempt to lure me out of my hotel and make me vulnerable?

That doesn't make sense. I'll have an armed escort, and how does hurting me help him? I stopped the people who were trying to kill him. Copley doesn't have anything to gain by having me murdered.

Is there some other angle? Does he think I can get him a better deal? We handed him over to the FBI because he was tied to *The Sea of Dreams* investigation, and that's officially an FBI matter.

I'm not sure what Solar or I can do to get the FBI to consider leveling a lesser charge. Even if I could . . . Given that Copley dropped his tank on my face—and likely shot at Hughes and me on *The Sea of Dreams*—I'm not sure how personally invested I am in that proposition.

What Copley knows could solve everything for us, or at the very least tell us what we're dealing with. The more I try to solve that puzzle, the more frustrating it gets. It's sad but true: we have no idea who we're up against.

Anything could have been inside those smuggler's compartments. Drugs, money, weapons, bioweapons . . . people. That's what's so infuriating. Knowing one of those factors would at least enable us to move in a direction.

"Can you do it?" asks Noyes.

The fact that I already have my shoes on tells me that I've made my decision. The fact that I'm still in my underwear under the bathrobe also tells me that part of me hasn't thought everything through all that well.

"Yeah," I reply.

"Thank you. We already have a car waiting for you downstairs."

CHAPTER 40

TRICKERY

The ability to talk to a suspect and get them to tell you something they hadn't planned on revealing is an art. You can study it, watch hundreds of hours of trained interrogators conducting interviews, even have them break things down for you, and still not be an expert at it.

One factor is chemistry. Large departments choose the interrogator based upon the suspect. Often the choice seems counterintuitive. For Capricia Boleda, the young woman with the dog and the ten-thousand-dollar purse, the LA Sheriff's Department might assign a Hispanic woman slightly older than Capricia to develop a kind of simpatico, or they might instead send in an older, domineering father figure to berate her into confessing.

In special cases, suspects might initially be questioned by several people asking benign questions, not to break them, but to see which one they respond to the most. Does this cop remind them of their brother? Is there a rapport with the officer who has a similar accent?

The type of suspect makes a big difference. It's not hard to get a confession out of someone who's never been interrogated before. Serial killers will often spill their guts a few hours after being caught, once they realize that everything is real. The interrogation offers a means of unburdening themselves.

Oddly, there are suspects with criminal records who can't wait to talk. They'll tell you everything, even though they know it will send them to jail. This is frequently the case with criminals who've been to prison multiple times and understand it as a way of life. They can be shockingly honest and sincere when they're not carjacking you or punching you to the ground.

The hardest suspect is the one who understands the procedure and knows what to expect. If you've never been arrested before, you might have no idea how long police can hold you before you can talk to a lawyer. Arraignments . . . the difference between jail and prison . . . what a bail bondsman does. Those things are a mystery to most.

From the moment the bracelets are put around your wrists, you are in a state of helplessness with almost zero control. There's the humiliating part where you're "processed." That's when you have to strip naked in front of a complete stranger and get searched more intimately than most people have even been probed by a medical professional. Then there are all the firm voices that tell you where to stand, where to sit, when you can go to the bathroom or speak.

That's one of the hardest parts for a first-time suspect to understand. You're dealing with people with guns and batons who have complete control over your body.

Then there are the other suspects. A city or county jail is nothing like prison. Sure, some fighting and intimidation might take place, but most inmates are trying to get out as quickly as possible. The social order is constantly changing, and the more experienced suspects know this is where you *don't* cause problems.

For some first-timers, the moment they break is when they realize they have to use the toilet in full view of a stranger. Desperation hits. Can they talk their way out of this? Can they say the right thing and go free?

None of that would faze someone like Copley. For starters, if he's ex-military, the lack of control and the toilet situation means nothing to him. If he's smart, he understands the game the interrogators are playing—the Hollywood good-cop/bad-cop scenarios, or making him wait in a room alone, endlessly.

Some departments have their own little tricks, like sending someone in with the wrong case file and asking unrelated questions, so the suspect thinks there's been a mix-up and attempts to clarify himself.

I once read a transcript of a suspect wanted for doing smash-and-grabs at jewelry stores with two other people:

"How well did you know Jeff Takimoto?"

"Who?"

"The victim who was killed last Tuesday in Las Vegas?"

"I didn't. I was in Long Beach."

"Oh, what were you doing?"

"Out with some friends."

"Can I get their names to verify your story?"

"Sure . . ."

It took only two minutes to get the names of his accomplices, who turned on the suspect the moment investigators told them they'd been given up by their compatriot.

Copley doesn't have to know all the tricks. He just has to know there *are* tricks. The smartest thing he can do is wait for his attorney. Any deal the police try to offer before then won't be in his favor.

So why does he want to talk to me?

Noyes meets me at the elevator in the parking garage with a cup of coffee and takes me to the floor where Copley's being held.

"Thanks for coming, Sloan."

"What, and miss another chance to talk to this gentleman?"

"Oddly, he's been surprisingly polite. All, 'Yes, sir' and 'No, ma'am.' He hasn't told us anything, but otherwise he's been cooperative."

I shrug. "He's a pro."

"Definitely. Which is why, when he asked to speak to you, we were so surprised. One of our agents explained what happened with the hit team. We were hoping it would scare him, put him on our side. It didn't. But it made him curious."

"How exactly did it come up?"

"He asked if the woman with the broken nose was involved in taking them down. We didn't tell him. But that's when he told us he'd talk to you if it was true."

"Did you confirm it?" Telling him flat out that I was the one would be a serious breach of trust between me and the FBI.

"No," says Noyes as the elevator opens. "Absolutely not. That's why I wanted to talk to you. We're not friends . . . but friend-to-friend, anyway. This is up to you. He doesn't know that was you until you show up. You don't have to go in. I think you understand the risk."

I appreciate her honesty. If I back out now, I don't get to hear what he has to say, but I get to protect myself and my family.

Except not talking to him could put Run and Jackie at a greater risk.

Ugh. I hate these choices because the impulsive part of me often decides without contemplating the consequences.

"Let me speak to him."

Noyes leads me into a room where two other agents are waiting.

On a video screen I can see Terrence Copley, real name still unknown, sitting at the end of a conference table in the adjacent room with his hands cuffed and resting in his lap. Noyes is showing me the setup before I enter.

"We have his legs cuffed under the table," says Agent Vogler, the older man handling the interrogation.

"He's requested no recording. But he asked for a piece of paper and a pen," says Noyes.

"We gave him paper and a crayon," adds Vogler. "If you're okay with that."

I shrug. "What's he going to do? Draw a picture of a gun and try to shoot his way out yelling, 'Pew pew pew'?"

"Why does everyone in your generation think they're a comedian?" groans Vogler.

"Because we're all crying on the inside."

"You're all soft."

"Hey, Old Man Winter," says Noyes, "tell me the last time you took down an armed suspect by yourself, let alone five?"

"Bah. Beginner's luck."

"Ignore him," Noyes tells me. "We use Vogler to wear down suspects with stories from his childhood hanging out with Fred Flintstone."

"Another comedian," he mutters. "So, are you ready? From the look of your face, you know not to go near him. Don't tell him anything personal. Blah, blah. You're going to do whatever you're going to do. I'm not a fan of any of this."

I get his point. This is unusual and unorthodox. There's little chance anything Copley tells me would be admissible. Vogler's right to be irritated, and I'm not far behind him on that. I'm too tired and cranky to deal with any bullshit from Copley at this point. I'll be the one needing restraints if Copley's brought me here to play mind games.

I take a deep breath. "All right, let's see what he has to say."

CHAPTER 41

INTERROGATION

Special Agent Vogler unlocks the interrogation room door and holds it open for me. Copley watches me as I enter, take the seat at the other side of the table, and set my coffee down.

There's a camera above him facing my side of the room and another behind me trained on him. On the middle of the table lies a tape recorder that looks a hundred years old.

The room is filled with microphones connected to digital recorders, so I don't know if this is a backup or included for dramatic effect.

Although Copley resembles the man I saw filled with fury as he lay handcuffed on his floor, he's completely composed now, attentive and acting as if I've entered a boardroom meeting.

He looks at my face and says, "I'd hate to see the other guy."

"Did you think that one up while you were waiting for me?"

"Not much else to do until my lawyer arrives."

He's not trying to be overly cordial, nor is he trying to intimidate me. I don't see his angle . . . yet.

"I'm here. Let's hear what you have to say."

"First things first. Is this being recorded?"

"No."

Copley glances up at the camera facing him. "I'm only talking under the agreement this will not be recorded. Understood?"

"They can cut the sound, but not the video. We can't have you bang your head against the table and say it was me." Especially when I'd be happy to do it myself.

"I understand. No sound. That's the condition."

Strangely, he's not concerned about the others hearing what he has to say. He just doesn't want there to be any official recording of it. He also hasn't brought up this conversation being used to incriminate him in court. He's more concerned with a physical record of it. Why?

Recordings leak.

I look at my camera and say, "No sound recording, and I want someone to confirm it."

A moment later Noyes opens the door and tells us, "No sound recording."

"Happy now?" I ask Copley.

He holds up his shackled wrists. "Clearly, no. But I'll deal with it." He leans back, and his eyes drift to the floor as he thinks about what he'll say next. "I'm sorry for what happened to you at Casino Point."

"You mean when you threw an air tank at my face and tried to kill me?"

Again, Copley takes a moment to respond. "I have no recollection of such an event. But however it happened, I'm sure the person did it for a good reason. Maybe they thought you were someone else. Maybe they thought their life was in danger. Had they known you were a cop, that wouldn't have happened."

Interesting. Who did he think I was? It seems like he wants to tell me something, but he's too afraid.

"Understood. You'll have an opportunity to explain that to a judge."

"We'll see," he says cryptically. "Anyway, the other thing. I heard what happened when the gang came to kill me. It would have been easy for you to walk away from that. You're the reason I'm alive. Think what you want, but you don't know me. I don't double-deal. I don't stab people in the back."

"Convince me I made the right decision," I tell him.

"That's why I asked to talk to you. Once I realized it was you in the morning and you this evening, I knew I had . . . an obligation." He nods to the paper and black crayon. "May I?"

I push them toward him. Copley tears off half the paper and writes something, then slides it back to the middle of the table.

I pick it up. It's a phone number.

"That's the number for my ex-wife. She lives with my daughter. I need to know they're going to be protected."

For the first time, I see vulnerability in the man's eyes.

"Give me a second." I step out into the hallway, where Noyes is waiting with a senior FBI agent I haven't spoken to before.

"Tell him we'll do it," says the agent.

"Will you?" I ask.

"Yes. Until we find out who sent the hit men after him, we have to."

"Also, this woman might help us learn more about him," adds Noyes.

She's right. Copley knows this too. By giving us her contact information, he's put himself at greater legal risk.

I walk back inside and sit. "They'll do it."

"Thank you."

"Now that we've helped you, what do you have for us? *Who* do you have?"

Copley nods. "Here's the deal. I'm going to write something down. You get to look at it, but then you have to promise me you'll tear it up."

"But I'll have seen it."

"Yes. No audio recording. No showing it to the camera. These are the rules. I'm asking you on your honor to do that."

This is a weird game he's playing. He knows everyone in the other room will learn what he's written. We'll have the name. Why is he being so coy? The only thing he'd get out of this is a lack of an evidentiary trail connecting him to whoever he's about to give up.

"Okay."

"Promise?"

"Promise."

Copley writes something on the paper, shielding it from the camera. When he's done, he folds it in half and pushes it toward me like a restaurant check. I open the note in my lap so the camera can't see what he's written.

It's a name. A name I recognize.

"This is bullshit."

"Tear it up," says Copley.

I don't need the paper to remember the name, so I tear the paper into small pieces and drop them on the table.

"Could you put them in the coffee cup?"

"I was going to drink that," I tell him. "Fine."

I take off the lid and drop them inside and even give the cup a stir for good measure. I doubt a forensic expert would have much trouble assembling the pieces, so it's more of a symbolic gesture.

"And could you not say the name aloud?" asks Copley.

"He's not Voldemort," I point out. Not to mention that this is bullshit.

"Please."

Right now, the agents in the other room have no idea what name I just read. The context of the conversation will be completely lost on them. I could go out and inform them, but I suspect that would stop Copley from talking.

Not that it makes any difference, because it's all a stupid game at this point. Copley walked me through all these steps simply to say "screw you" to my face.

I tap my coffee cup holding the torn pieces. "Is this a joke? He's behind all this? He's the mastermind?"

"He's not who you think he is."

I don't know the man personally, but everything I've ever heard about Ethan Granth is positive. The hedge fund billionaire has been investing heavily in South Florida, spending millions on environmental issues, including *The Sea of Dreams* cleanup. There's been talk of a run for governor and maybe even the presidency at some point.

And now a man who tried to kill me, not once, but possibly twice, is trying to tell me that Granth is some kind of Bond villain plotting something we can't even comprehend?

"Ecoterrorism? Is that it? Trying to ruin the cruise industry?"

Copley looks confused for a moment, then shakes his head. "No. Of course not. Money. Power. The same as it always is."

"This is a bridge too far," I tell him.

"Okay. Answer this: How does he make his money?"

"Hedge fund. That's common knowledge."

"Who are his clients? What does he invest in?" asks Copley.

"I don't know. But I'm sure somebody knows." As I say it, I realize how stupid I sound. That's exactly what people said about Bernie Madoff and Jeffrey Epstein.

"You should look into it."

"It sounds like a job for the SEC. Was he trying to manipulate the market?"

Copley raises his cuffed hands and makes an "I don't know" gesture. "You're the cop. I'm just a guy who was hired to do one little job."

"Which was . . . ?"

"Nice try. I don't have all the pieces. But I know who was controlling them all. There's a reason he tried to have me killed."

"Then why not help us now?"

Copley makes a laugh that sounds more like a sneer. "Do you know how many friends he has? Judges and prosecutors and cops that owe the man favors."

I almost blurt the name out loud. "*This* guy?"

"That guy. You know I was searched thoroughly in my house, at the police station, and here."

"Yes." I'd hope so.

Copley leans back, slides his fingertip into the pocket of his jeans, pulls out something small and metallic, and drops it on the table.

Noyes bursts into the room with her gun drawn.

Copley raises his hands. "It's not mine. I found it on me an hour ago."

Noyes holsters her gun, then calls through the open door, "Can we get forensics in here?"

I get up from my chair and walk over to have a closer look at what Copley claims he found planted on him.

"I've had a dozen people put their hands on me. I couldn't tell you which one did this," Copley says. "Now do you get my point?"

I don't know if Granth is really behind all this, but if Copley isn't lying, the billionaire arranged a cartel-style hit on American soil within only a few hours' notice. If he pulled that off, then it would be a simple matter to get someone to plant this object on Copley even while he was in protective custody.

It's a razor blade. Written across it in black ink are the words *Loose lips sink ships.*

CHAPTER 42
OCEAN VIEW

Solar and Hughes listen to me reiterate in person what I told them in the email I sent before taking the red-eye back to Fort Lauderdale. This is our first chance to talk in person about what happened—and Copley's implication of Granth.

I finish the last detail, then gulp my coffee down, trying to find the energy to keep my still-swollen eyes open. It's been a long day that keeps on going.

At the end of my story, Solar just looks to Hughes, and they exchange nods. No follow-up questions, no requests for added details.

"That's it?" I ask. "Do you take any of it seriously?"

"All of it," replies Solar. "Hughes and I have been spending the last two days trying to figure out what fits into an extremely elaborate web. Who had the capability to pull something like this off and the brazenness to think that it would never come back to them? Granth makes sense."

"So you'd already narrowed it down to him?"

"No. Not at all. We've been scratching our heads. He fits. Not in an obvious way, but it works. There's been some rumors about Granth that I've heard and didn't know what to make of. Things that sounded like lies to cover up other lies."

"Like what?"

"I've heard that he became wealthy in part by acting as a middleman for the CIA. One of the companies he owns is a bank that transfers money in third-world countries. Ostensibly, it assists in economic development, but it's also one of the banks the CIA uses to transfer money to rebels or coalition partners.

"Three years ago, an offshoot of the Houthi movement tried to rob one of the banks Granth controls in Yemen. That night, a drone strike took out the top floor of the building where they were hiding. It sent a very clear message about not messing with the flow of money."

"That's pretty extreme," I say. "So, he's playing both sides?"

"We don't know that. He might just be doing what the government needs to get done and then running that as a cover for other profitable endeavors that don't conflict," says Solar. "The CIA used shady pilots to fly guns to rebels and then looked the other way when those planes came back with cocaine."

"And then there's IM Banco," adds Hughes. "It's a South American bank that Granth effectively controls."

"Money laundering?"

"No. More like influence. Let's say you're a company that wants a more favorable lease on a port. Instead of outright bribery, which can get you in trouble with US law, you loan the money to IM Banco, which then makes a loan to the politician you want to sway. If the candidate gets elected and decides in your favor, the loan is forgiven or renegotiated with extremely generous terms. It's all technically legal."

"So why is he blowing up cruise ships?" I ask. "It sounds like he has a good thing going. Why end up on a terrorist list?"

"He's a gambler," replies Solar. "A guy like him doesn't just want a percentage of the transaction. He wants the whole thing. Our best guess is that he may have overextended himself. He might have dipped into the money that was moving through his channels and created a kind of Ponzi scheme. Whatever he did, maybe he's desperate."

"What about the FBI or the CIA?" I ask.

"Almost all the hinky stuff happens outside the United States, which makes an FBI investigation less likely. As far as the CIA is concerned, he hasn't done anything wrong."

"Have you brought Granth up with Olmo?"

"No. Hughes and I have been going over your notes and researching Granth. To be honest, I'm not sure we want to go to Olmo just yet. What did you tell the FBI back in Los Angeles?"

"I asked them to sit on it while I checked it out. I'm sure it will make its way to Olmo soon."

Solar nods. "On the surface, Granth is such an unlikely suspect, I don't know how seriously Olmo will take it. We might need to build the case first if we want his help."

"How do we even begin to build a case?" The whole idea seems hopeless to me. Granth's a powerful man with more lawyers than I can count, and he's potentially being protected by the CIA. To get anywhere, we'd need wiretaps, surveillance, witnesses, and a thousand other resources we simply don't have.

"I have a suggestion," says Hughes. "We confront him directly. See what he does. If he panics and starts to lawyer up, then we know to push. If he's confused by it, then it's not him or he's a lot smoother than I anticipate."

"Do we show up at his office and spring this on him?"

Solar shakes his head. "You need to get him off guard. He talks to angry lawyers all day long. He's been involved in countless civil actions. He won't be afraid of someone coming through the front door."

"Okay, so we put on Freddy Krueger masks, break into his house, and force him to tell us everything."

"I'm not sure if I can get a warrant for that," replies Solar. "Right spirit. Now give me the legal version of that."

"We only get one shot before he starts claiming harassment," notes Hughes.

Solar shakes his head. "Actually, I don't think so. He won't do that. Granth doesn't want his name and the word 'investigation' to ever appear next to each other. He's not a mobster. His most valuable asset is his reputation. Think of a way to use that."

"Approach him at one of the restaurants he owns?" asks Hughes.

"No. Not that. We need to intimidate him, not humiliate him," says Solar.

"Approach him in a restaurant *while* wearing Freddy Krueger masks?" I suggest.

"Don't make me create another McPherson policy . . ."

Current McPherson policies include a prohibition on doing outboard engine repair on the conference room table and leaving eggplant parmesan in a desk drawer over the weekend.

Hughes pulls up a profile of Granth on his computer from a South Florida lifestyle magazine. "He has a mega-yacht, the *Itanic* . . ."

"Guilty," I declare. "Anyone who takes out the *T* so he can put *I* first doesn't need a trial."

Hughes ignores me as he reads the article. "Hmm. He owns several restaurants, as well as the nightclub Limitless. I haven't heard of that one."

"Would you have gone otherwise?" I joke.

"Probably not my scene."

"Well, I know it. It's a three-story, high-end club with three restaurants and a wine cellar that has vintages older than the US Constitution," I tell them. "Some of Run's wealthier, more degenerate friends have been there."

"According to the article," says Hughes, "Granth spends time at the club. There are photos of him with celebrities who are so famous I have no idea who they are. Getting in there and confronting him would probably rattle him."

I turn to Solar. "Would this be covered by the department expense account?"

"If you can get in there and promise not to order anything bottled before Thomas Jefferson died, I think I can make it work. You plan on asking one of Run's friends to get you inside?"

"No. There's a McPherson policy on that too. What I plan to do is get Granth to invite us into the club."

"How does that work?" asks Hughes.

"A place like this caters to high rollers. People who blow a million in a casino and laugh about it. They'll come to a club like this and waste a hundred thousand dollars in one night, or get so coked up they stay for days." I look to Solar, then Hughes. "You know why the club is called Limitless? Because they promise you literally anything in the world. They'll fly in chefs from Paris. Dancers from Vegas. I heard some Middle Eastern oil billionaire had Chris Rock flown in to do a comedy routine at his table. I didn't know Granth was the owner, but it makes sense."

"That's great," says Hughes. "But you haven't explained how we get Granth to invite us into this bacchanalian paradise."

"All these clubs and casinos talk to each other. If you just spent half a million dollars in Las Vegas and decide to go to Macau to play some more, the casino in Vegas calls a casino in Macau and arranges to have a car waiting for you when you land, as well as a private table and a room. Limitless is part of that circuit. If someone calls them from Monte Carlo and says a Russian billionaire is flying into South Florida on a private jet and wants to party, they'll send a car."

"It's that easy?" asks Hughes.

"It only costs them gas."

"As long as we're not renting a jet . . . ," says Solar.

"No. But we do have to spend enough money to make Hughes pass for a Russian oligarch. That Tommy Bahama look won't cut it."

CHAPTER 43
METHOD

Hughes just snorted a rail of cocaine off the back of his hand in the Rolls-Royce as our concierge watched him from the corner of her eye. If I didn't know it was crushed aspirin and that we'd borrowed the TOM FORD suit he's wearing from Run's closet, I'd swear my partner was the Russian party boy we're pretending he is.

Marta, the concierge, was waiting for us at the executive airport by the time the flight I pretended we were on landed. She's a pretty twenty-two-year-old sent to escort us back to the club.

She asked if we needed hotel arrangements or someone to handle our luggage. The answer was no because Hughes's valet (actually Solar, waiting with empty luggage) would take care of that.

It was a more elaborate ruse than we needed, but we decided to take the precaution when it dawned on us that Limitless was probably more than a fun side venture for Granth. A man who works with different intelligence agencies is probably as interested in gathering as much intel as he can. From any source.

Russians with money to blow in Miami are a dime a dozen, and neither Hughes, aka Alex, nor I, aka Siona, his assistant, will be particularly interesting to the billionaire. Other people, like Prince Mohammed bin Salman's business partner and childhood friend, would likely get more attention. Probably a helicopter ride to the club, not a spin in this five-year-old Rolls-Royce.

Maybe.

I've already spotted two lipstick cameras in the car's interior woodwork, including one directly overhead that can read our cell phone screens. The entire vehicle is wired for surveillance.

I'm not sure if anyone is watching from the other end, but Granth's people have had every opportunity to observe us and, if we're not careful, every text message or passcode we type.

Granth's setup is clever and makes sense, given what we've learned about him. I can only imagine what those hidden cameras have seen.

Uh-oh. I assumed Hughes noticed the same cameras I did when we got in; he's normally extremely attentive to things like that. But following his fake coke-snorting, he's gotten on his phone.

Doesn't he realize they can see our screens?

Should I text him and tell him to get off his phone? Should I take it from him?

Pretending to be a Russian cokehead isn't going to fool Granth if Hughes is texting his wife that he won't be home too late . . . in English.

Damn it. He's still on his phone, texting!

I could speak to him in English and subtly mention something. His cover is that he understands English but is more comfortable with me doing his speaking.

My cover is that I'm an American who's wearing too much makeup and a pair of sunglasses because I just had a nose job. The dark-red wig is one I've used before for undercover work. It also hides the fact that right now my hair is hideous and still contains flakes of my own blood.

Jackie offered to wash it for me tomorrow at her "salon," which happens to be in my master bathroom, and I am looking forward to nothing more than that right now.

Hughes is still on his phone, swiping away at something. I'm about to start talking to Marta to distract her as I push his phone away, if it's not already too late. But then I catch a glimpse of his screen in the window's reflection.

He's on a dating app.

What the . . . ?

Oh my. Those are photos of guys . . .

He's not on a dating app . . . he's on a *hookup* app.

While Marta isn't looking, Hughes makes a small gesture with his thumb toward the hidden camera that's mounted over his head.

Holy hell.

Far from being oblivious, my partner is fully aware of the surveillance and has decided to add another layer to his fake persona.

Our car takes the off-ramp into an industrial part of Miami that looks like it was permanently shut down in the 1980s. We turn a corner and enter an entire block filled with light. Limitless is a beacon in the night, complete with moving searchlights and miles of neon. A line of people waits behind a red rope while valets park Lamborghinis.

The driver takes us around the back to a VIP entrance, then steps out to open our door. A chiseled young man about Marta's age is waiting at the entrance.

"This is Eric; he'll be taking over for me here," says Marta.

"Hello, welcome to Limitless." Eric greets us with a smile, revealing perfect white teeth.

In all likelihood, Granth's people were not watching us in the car because they were suspicious. They were probably trying to figure out what would make Hughes, aka Alex, spend the most money here. While on the surface, traveling with an attractive—I hope—young woman would indicate that he's straight, for a man from a place like Russia, it could be a front.

Eric leads us, or rather leads Hughes, down a tunnel. He's already decided that I'm just an accessory and is directing all his attention at Hughes. Not because he's trying to pick him up, but because the concierge's real job is sales.

The tunnel emerges into the middle of the club, which has several layers of dance floors. The effect is something like being inside an aquarium. Lights splash around, and different-colored lasers paint pictures in the fog. There are people above and below us. Dancers in G-strings swing from trapezes overhead, while bartenders create concoctions out of smoke and fire below. The music is loud but not overpowering.

The experience, however, is overwhelming.

"We've got you set up in a VIP booth. Is there something we can have sent to you right now?"

"A bottle of Suntory and a bottle of Château Lafite Rothschild to start," I reply.

Eric calls this into his earpiece, then tells us, "Good news, we have the Nemo booth open. It's a little more private, if you'd like that. It's next to the elevator to the dance floor."

I have a feeling it's not the best booth they have to offer, but suitable enough for someone willing to start a five-thousand-dollar bar tab after only a minute inside the club.

Eric takes us up a flight of stairs, through a door, and into a small room with a booth that overlooks the dance floor through a window. He walks over to the table and picks up a tablet with a control screen.

"If you want privacy, you can touch this button here." He demonstrates, and the entire window darkens. The music from outside also lowers in volume.

In a booth directly across the dance floor, I see two women wearing little more than a smile dancing on the table for four men in suits. *Yikes.* I can only hope they clean these booths between seatings.

Hughes and I slide into the seats. Eric hands us each a menu. "We'll have someone here to take a food order and another drink order. In the meantime, have a look and tell us what you want."

The menu is completely blank.

I can't help myself. "What if I ask for panda meat?"

Eric holds up a finger and laughs. "You're not the first person to ask me that. Only they weren't joking. Anything within reason. If your culinary tastes are that extreme, we do have a sister establishment in Hong Kong. But that might be a little extreme even for them."

He turns his attention back to Hughes. *"Yest' chto-nibud', chto vam nuzhno?"* he says in what I assume is Russian.

Hughes leans over and whispers, *"Tabletki dlya erektsii."*

"Ne problema," replies Eric. "Anything else?"

"He'd also like to meet Ethan Granth," I reply.

"I don't know if Mr. Granth is in the club tonight."

"Could you tell us where he is so we can go there? Mr. Granth is the only reason Alex came here tonight," I explain.

"It would help if I could tell him what this is about," replies Eric as he tries to figure out how important we actually are.

"It's about something off the menu," I reply. "Or more precisely, on a much bigger menu."

"I'll see what I can do." Eric leaves us alone in the booth, closing the door behind him.

I scan our surroundings for cameras but can't see any—which makes me even more suspicious. I also want to know where Hughes learned enough Russian to respond—and exactly what he told Eric. But I'll save that for later.

Hughes takes out his phone again and dials a number with a foreign area code. *"Da, da,"* he says, then hangs up. A moment later, he calls another foreign number, then clicks off and throws his phone on the table in frustration.

When the server brings us our drinks, Hughes tosses back five hundred dollars' worth of Japanese whiskey like it's water.

My partner's going full method actor, and it's driving me nuts. I feel like an impostor. To be more precise, an impostor at being an impostor. I can only hope that good ol' "Alex" is doing enough to sell this act for the both of us.

CHAPTER 44
VIPs

When we arranged to have a call placed from the casino in Monte Carlo asking if Limitless could accommodate two guests flying into Miami, we used a Russian patronymic that was easily searchable and belonged to a prominent family in Russia with a lot of relatives and a lot of money. Getting into the club was one thing; having Granth decide we were worth talking to was a different matter.

That's why we chose the name of a man who's the younger brother of a high-ranking Russian security official. It's not a name a criminal would ever use.

A few minutes after we asked for Granth, the door to our private booth opens.

"Alex!" says a short, fit man in his early fifties standing in the entrance. He's dressed in a casual, long-sleeve dark-blue shirt that makes him look underdressed for the club. He comes in and warmly shakes Hughes's hand, giving me a polite smile.

So, this is Ethan Granth in person. I've seen interviews with him, but I've never been this close.

"I'm glad you could make it. What do you think of it?" he asks.

"It's wonderful," I reply, even though the question was directed at Hughes.

"Thank you. Where did I see you two last?" Granth pretends to try to remember where we could have met before.

"I believe this is our first time," I reply again, speaking for Hughes.

Granth is now studying me, trying to figure out the dynamic. A minute ago, he thought the closeted younger brother of an important Russian intelligence official was in his club with a woman acting as his beard.

Now he's dealing with a woman who keeps speaking for the man without having to ask for permission.

I can see the calculus running in Granth's head. "Are you American?" he asks me.

This is interesting. Granth probably wonders if I'm with the Russian Foreign Intelligence Service. I'm tempted to respond, "*Nyet*," just to see what he says.

"I'm his business associate," I reply, not answering the question.

Granth looks a little uneasy. He's used to having the upper hand. Also, the possibility that I'm a Russian agent might be troubling him.

"We're interested in some beachfront property," I add.

"Oh." Granth relaxes and leans against the glass window. "I can get someone to help you out. What ballpark are we talking about?"

"That depends." I take off my sunglasses. Granth studies my face and can see where I've covered up the bruising.

"Where did you get your work done?" he asks, pointing to his own nose. "I got a guy that does it without any bruising."

"Catalina," I reply. "He was actually your guy."

Granth's face freezes. He looks at Hughes, then back to me. It takes a moment for him to regain his composure. But it's too late.

"Catalina? Huh. Well, if you figure out what you're looking for, let me know."

Granth starts to move toward the door, but Hughes steps in his way and shuts it. "Don't leave yet, we were just talking," he says with no trace of a Russian accent.

The fact that he's been played dawns on Granth. "I have no idea what you're talking about." He gestures around our booth. "We have cameras. My people will be here any second."

"And then what? You'll throw us out?" I ask. "We haven't even paid our tab yet."

"It's on me." He fakes a smile, still trying to understand exactly what's going on.

Although he's probably never been confronted like this, I'm sure he's run through different scenarios in which the police show up. He still can't be sure who we really are, but I bet he's worried he's already come across as too suspicious. Now he wants to unwind all that.

He leans back against the window and forces another grin. "What's this all about? You have me at a loss here."

"How much money do you need to owe before you decide that committing acts of terrorism against innocent people is the smart way out?" I ask.

"Are you cops?"

"Are you a crook?" I fire back.

He crosses his arms and shakes his head. "Okay, this just went into bonkers territory. I'm going to have to ask you to leave."

"We could refuse and create an incident," says Hughes. "I could call you out right now for the attack on *The Sea of Dreams* as part of a smuggling operation. And then when your people come in and create a ruckus, giving us a reason to subpoena this video recording, you'll have to explain to your friends why law enforcement is investigating you for acts of terror."

Granth sucks in a deep breath and regains his composure. "No one's ever going to see this video, and by tomorrow you won't have jobs.

You'll be nobodies without badges, without friends. You have no idea who my friends are or what they can do."

"I'm sure Jeffrey Epstein felt the same way," I reply.

"He didn't know the people I know," says Granth.

There's a loud knock on the door. "Is everything okay in there, Mr. Granth?"

Granth glares at us. "You flat-footed pieces of trash. How did you even get in here? I should let my guys come in here and kick your asses."

"Is that a threat?" I say with a smile.

"Everything's fine!" Granth calls to Eric through the closed door. "I'm leaving now."

Hughes steps away from the door to let him pass.

Granth reaches for the doorknob, then stops. "Remember what I said. Tomorrow I'll have your badges."

"We'll see about that," says Hughes.

Granth leaves us and takes his security guards with him. I'm sure he's on his way to a room with a lot of computers and people who know how to use them to figure out who the hell we are.

I would have told him if he'd asked, but the man was so rattled that he never thought to. He was good at making threats, though, and I believe he *thinks* he has that much power. Even so, he lost his head.

Hughes picks his phone up from the table.

"Checking to see if you have a date tonight?" I ask.

"Nope. Calling us an Uber, because I'm pretty sure Granth won't be letting us go home in the Rolls."

CHAPTER 45
SKUNK WORKS

When I walk into the office the next morning, Solar and Hughes are sitting at the conference room table with two men in suits and lanyards around their necks bearing Florida Department of Law Enforcement badges. I don't recognize either of them.

Solar introduces them. "McPherson, this is Detective Minguella and Detective Charlton. Would you gentlemen care to explain to my investigator why you're here?"

The older, balder man speaks up. "We're from the Florida Department of Law Enforcement anticorruption unit. Your department"—he checks his notes—"the Underwater Investigation Unit, is being suspended, and you two are on immediate leave pending an investigation."

Holy crap.

"And what are the charges?" asks Solar.

"We're not at liberty to discuss those at this point. We're here for your badges and your service weapons," replies Charlton, the less bald of the two.

"Okay, so let me get this straight: I have two men in my office that I've never met telling me they have the authority to disband my department?"

"That is correct," replies Charlton.

"You don't have a warrant, an affidavit, so much as a slip of paper?" says Solar. "And I'm supposed to believe that? Hughes, would you and McPherson arrest these two men for impersonating police officers."

I think he's bluffing, but Hughes gets up anyway.

"Hold up," says Minguella. "No paperwork's been sent through yet. I only just got the call."

Solar motions for Hughes to sit.

"You only just got the call? So this isn't some long-standing investigation you buffoons have been conducting? As far as I know, last I checked the chain of command, I answer to the governor and the attorney general." Solar leans in and squints. "Nope. Neither of you."

"We have an emergency authorization," says Minguella.

"From who?" asks Solar.

"I can't disclose that."

The veins pop out in Solar's neck. "Then you can go fuck yourselves, to put it politely. We're in the middle of a public corruption investigation, and you two dimwits pop out of nowhere telling us we have to shut down. Doesn't this feel a bit banana republic for you?"

"Those are the orders," says Charlton.

"Well, we're going to ignore them until you prove they're legal," replies Solar.

Minguella takes out his phone, dials a number, and starts talking into it. "He refuses to accept the order. He says we need a writ and a name of a judge with authority. Okay. Hold on." He hands the phone to Solar.

"George Solar speaking. To what idiot do I have the pleasure of speaking? Uh-huh . . . So you're the idiot, Your Honor . . . Yes. I see . . . No, I understand perfectly. Right away. I hope you understand the implications of this . . . No, that wasn't a threat." Solar slides the phone back to Minguella. "Okay, then. McPherson, Hughes, please hand these men your service weapons and your badges."

"What the hell?" I protest.

Solar raises a finger, signaling for me to shut up. "Badge. Gun."

Hughes's face is flushed. I've never seen him this angry. He throws his badge on the table in front of the FDLE detectives, then makes a show of field-stripping his gun and pushing the pieces over to them.

I simply empty my chamber, pull out the clip, and set the gun down next to my badge. Charlton gathers them up and places them into an evidence bag.

"This isn't easy for us either," he lets us know.

"You ever hear of slow-walking? Procedural delay?" Solar asks, then decides it's not worth pursuing.

Minguella and Charlton take our guns and badges and walk out the door.

"That was *Granth*?" I ask Solar. "We only left his club ten hours ago."

"Early bird gets the worm," he replies. "It seems you agitated him."

"Lot of good that did," says Hughes.

"Are you sure?" Solar goes over to his desk and pulls out a bottle of whiskey. "Get three cups, Hughes, and set them on the table."

"Is this the time . . . ?" Hughes begins, then shuts himself up and takes three glasses down from the cupboard by the sink.

Solar pours us each a finger and pushes the glasses into our hands. "Congratulations. This is graduation day."

"Graduation from what?" I ask.

"You both know I did time as an undercover police officer. Real time. Real prison. I met some mean people in there. You ever ask yourself why I did that?"

"It was the right thing?" I suggest.

"There's the right thing and then there's agreeing to be locked up with people who want to kill you and violate you. Some might say it was a suicide wish," replies Solar. "The truth is, things were getting so corrupt in my unit I felt like I was drowning. I'd have walked through hell rather than sit still. Better to get killed trying to fix what's wrong with the world than die believing it was meant to be broken. Anyway, speech over. Now you have to decide to sit still or keep walking."

Hughes and I look at each other.

"Don't be so glum. You rattled Granth so hard he pulled out his big guns, a Florida Supreme Court judge he had in his back pocket. That was his mistake. He just told us the rules of the game *and* what cards he's holding."

"How does that help us now? No badge, no gun. Do we start a podcast?"

"Well, McPherson, that depends. Do you both want to see this through, now that you know what kind of games he's going to play?"

"Of course."

"I'm all in on the podcast," says Hughes. "Even the Freddy Krueger thing's looking good."

Solar points to our whiskey. "Okay, then. Drink up."

Hughes and I take reluctant sips.

"I said drink up." Solar checks his watch. "You only have five more minutes."

"Five more minutes until what?" asks Hughes.

"Just drink."

I gulp back my whiskey and slam the glass on the table. "Happy?"

"Couldn't be prouder."

Solar fumbles with the intercom on the table, placing a call.

A man's voice answers from the other end of the line. "Deputy Director Aldiss's office."

"This is Solar. Tell Katherine they're here."

Click. "Hey, George. Have them raise their right hands."

"McPherson, Hughes," Solar says, gesturing for us to raise our hands. "Okay, they're doing it," he says before we actually do it.

"All right: I, Katherine Aldiss, Deputy Director of the United States Marshals Service, hereby deputize you as US Marshals, etcetera. Please sign the paperwork and send it back to my office at your convenience."

Click.

"Wait? What?" I ask, confused.

"You're US Marshals now. At least until I get that idiot judge overturned or, better yet, in jail."

"Wait, how did this happen?" replies Hughes. "Did you set all this up this morning?"

Solar walks over to his desk and puts the whiskey bottle back. He then takes out a lockbox and places it on the table.

"This morning? No. I planned for something like this a long time ago. Katherine and I go back ages." He unlocks the box and pulls out two badges and two pistols. "They're not loaded, so you'll need ammo."

Hughes and I are still dumbfounded. It's as if we just watched a baffling magic trick.

"You have to see these things coming. You have to be paranoid. You have to be prepared for them to try to take everything from you." Solar leans in and lowers his voice. "Now, the gloves are off."

"Okay. So we rattled him. He rattled us back. Now what?" I ask.

"It's a different kind of game now. I'm not worried about process so much as exposing him. You understand?"

"I think so."

"There's someone I want you to talk to. Actually, two people. But one of them in particular should be helpful. All of this is off the record. You never met them. You never talked to them. Understand?"

"Not at all," replies Hughes.

"Right now, they're on a yacht in Aventura Harbor." Solar suppresses a smile. "The boat is called *The Sorceress.*"

CHAPTER 46
POWER COUPLE

The Sorceress is a sixty-foot yacht with a graphite-gray hull and a tower loaded with equipment I've only seen on spy ships. It's sleeker and even more futuristic than some of the vessels I've seen at Run's boatyard.

What impresses me most is the woman standing at the end of the gangway. Tall and lithe with jet-black hair just above her shoulders, she looks like a fashion model playing the role of a spy or vice versa.

She's how I want to look when I slip on a fancy dress, or in this case, denim shorts and a T-shirt she somehow manages to make look elegant. I know she's at least ten years older than me. The difference makes me feel like an awkward tween. She's a *woman*.

"Is that . . . ?" whispers Hughes behind me.

"Hello, I'm Jessica," she says, gesturing for us to join her on deck.

She doesn't need to say her last name. Anyone who has watched a true-crime show or read a newspaper knows who she is. Every woman with a badge has paid attention to her career. The fact that she's a recluse and doesn't do talk shows or write books about her exploits only deepens the mystery surrounding her.

I'm shaking hands with Jessica Blackwood.

"It's an honor to meet you," she says.

Me? Honor?

"The Bonaventure case was fascinating." She nods to Hughes. "And the Swamp Killer case. That was some incredible investigative work."

I feel like saying, "Aw shucks," but instead I simply smile.

"Here. Let's sit inside. Theo will be up in a moment."

Theo. Theo Cray? Cray's work was mandatory reading when we were trying to find the Swamp Killer.

Hughes and I take a seat in the lounge. We're like two kids who don't know what to say.

"Nice boat," I manage.

"We're borrowing it. I understand you spend quite a lot of time on ships," she replies.

"I basically grew up on one."

"George Solar put us together because I reached out to him about something Theo and I are looking into. He mentioned Ethan Granth, and I thought we might compare notes."

"How do you know George?"

"I was a Miami-Dade police officer before I joined the FBI. George was one of my training officers," she tells us. "We kept in touch."

"Sorry. It's just . . ." *Like finding out your mother is best friends with Wonder Woman.* "Interesting."

"We've been tracking down part of the network created by Michael Heywood, the Warlock. He was able to move a lot of money and influence around. We know he didn't do it alone and that he helped set up other people in positions of power. Ethan Granth popped up on our radar as one of those people. We think he's trying to build a kind of syndicate," she explains.

"A syndicate?" asks Hughes. "How do you mean?"

"Think of it as a power cartel. Or an underworld United Nations. Or another United Nations, if you ask Theo. He's a bit more cynical than I am. Which is saying a lot."

"I'm still not following you," I tell Jessica.

"Okay. If you need something, say mineral rights in Afghanistan, a deep-water port in the Baltic Sea, they name a price. If they deliver, you pay it."

I see Hughes nodding dumbly as I do the same.

"They pull it off by using a network of bureaucrats, bribed officials, and even intelligence agencies. The key is knowing who controls what and what they want. Granth is very good at finding vulnerable points and figuring out how to exploit them. Take what happened in Catalina. The FBI's going to announce that it's connected to an LA gang working for the Sinaloan cartel. What won't be announced is that the gang's actually controlled by the brother of Sinaloa's governor. The brother was also his campaign manager."

"IM Banco," Hughes murmurs.

"Actually, no. Another bank controlled by Granth that's less well known. One that functions only in Mexico but has a two-way line of credit with a major bank in the United States that had a cash crunch recently and doesn't care where money comes from as long as it's not directly tied to drugs. These are the kinds of deals Granth makes," explains Jessica. "And in your case in Catalina, the cartel didn't know who was ordering the hit or why. Trying to kill Copley was a way of paying off interest."

"So, is this about money laundering?" I ask.

"We don't know what's going on with Granth. We're focused on another suspect. But it looks like Granth's been buying up assets and businesses using companies that he controls outright. The numbers don't add up. He's either getting the money from somewhere else or he's stealing from his clients, which will only go on for so long before they come to collect."

"Is he taking money from another country?" asks Hughes.

"It's possible he's being funneled money from the Chinese or a Middle Eastern country. What concerns us is the attack on *The Sea of Dreams*."

"Do you think he'll do that again?" I ask.

"Not likely," says a voice from down a set of stairs.

A man dressed in a T-shirt and shorts comes walking up the steps, holding a laptop. He has a rugged, tan face and short, almost-blond hair.

"I'm Theo," says Professor Theo Cray.

He drops down onto the couch opposite us and puts his feet on the table. There's an almost comedic contrast between Theo and Jessica. Although Theo is well built and taller than she is, he reminds me of a dwarf sitting next to an elven princess.

Theo continues, "Now that Granth has committed an act like this on US citizens in the US, whatever psychological barriers he had against killing civilians are gone. His attack on you and the law enforcement agents in Catalina proves it. But the real danger with Granth is that he's a ticking time bomb. He would pull off a 9/11-level event if it benefited him. The ship attack wasn't an intentional act of terrorism; it only looked that way, which shows you how high the stakes are for him."

"We're more worried about what happens next than what he did," adds Jessica.

"So how do we stop him?" asks Hughes.

"Stop thinking like cops and start thinking like soldiers. This isn't policing anymore. This is war," says Theo.

"So, we get sniper rifles and take him out?" replies Hughes.

Theo shrugs. "I wouldn't leave that off the table."

"Yes, you would leave that off the table," Jessica snaps, correcting him. "We're not saying that. You have to be strategic. You don't need a bullet to stop him."

"Poison would work," mutters Theo. "Snakebite . . ."

Jessica rolls her eyes. "You'll have to excuse the mad professor. He spent a little too much time in the jungle and still hasn't adjusted to normal life. Think about it this way: What's the most valuable thing in the world for Granth?"

"His reputation," I reply. "His whole brand's based on being clean and above it all."

"Then that's where you attack him. You don't need to go after him for everything. You have to nail him in a way that there's no escape from. Something that will make people see him in a new light. And I don't mean public opinion. The people who control his money," she clarifies.

"All right. But we're still trying to figure out how to even start."

"Blue Parrot Key," says Theo. "After you left his club last night, he made a call to a small island in the Upper Keys. There's a former oceanographic research center there that he owns."

"I never saw that in his holdings," says Hughes.

Theo smiles. "You're young. You'll learn."

Jessica turns to me. "I wish we could help you more, but we have our own crisis to deal with."

"Bigger than this?" asks Hughes.

Theo nods. "Oh yeah."

"If you need anything, George knows how to reach me," says Jessica. "And when we're done with our thing and you're done with yours, maybe we'll all have dinner sometime."

"I'd like that," I manage.

"Assuming the world is still inhabitable," says Theo.

CHAPTER 47

TOURISTS

It's a two-hour trip from our headquarters in Fort Lauderdale to Blue Parrot Key via our boat. Solar and Hughes are checking our weapons and making sure we'll be well armed and protected for whatever we find there.

The tricky part was coming up with an excuse to set foot on the island. Solar searched through the history of the property and found out that Granth's people built an antenna tower on the island but had failed to maintain the proper FCC license. This gives us probable cause to search the island for any electronic devices that may be making use of the antenna—which broadly includes anything connected to a Wi-Fi network . . . phones . . . computers.

If we find evidence of lawbreaking, will it be admissible in court? Probably not a chance in hell. But that's not our purpose. We're going to Blue Parrot Key to find dirty laundry. We'll decide what to do with it later.

"We're ten minutes out," I call down to Solar and Hughes in the cabin below.

Solar comes up and hands me a vest and a tactical helmet. I let him take the controls and start suiting up. The vest is heavier than normal because of the metal plate inserts we've added for extra protection.

Storming a remote location like this should be at least a twenty-person operation. Unfortunately, we lack the people or the clout to get that much support.

If we'd brought our claims and flimsy warrant to Special Agent Olmo, he would have kicked us out of the office and possibly made a phone call or two that would have tipped off Granth. And while we're US Marshals on paper, it's really more of a technicality. To get even the Marshals' full support, we'd need more evidence than we have now.

We're a rogue operation. If we can't find what we need on the island and Granth raises hell about it, we might be risking more than our badges.

I pull the chinstrap tight on my helmet, kill the boat lights, then pick up the long-range night-vision goggles. I see that a two-hundred-foot dock protruding from the island is deserted except for a small rowboat.

"No large boats on the dock," I call out to Solar and Hughes.

I scan the small island for people but don't see any movement. The entire key is the size of four football fields, so it's not hard to search. The south end has mangroves and a marsh, while the north, where we're headed, has the dock and buildings.

There's a boathouse near the dock, two metal warehouses, and what appears to be a main building. The main structure has two stories, a deck that wraps all the way around it, and a four-story-high observation deck on its roof.

In the '80s and early '90s, the island hosted oceanographic research for several universities and agencies. When a much larger facility opened north of here on the mainland, this one was shut down and lay dormant until Granth acquired it.

We found an old announcement that claimed it would be developed into a new environmental research center, but nothing ever came of that. At least in the news. I don't know if the plan was sincere or simply a cover that Granth used for his own purposes here—purposes that we still haven't determined.

Given its location and relative remoteness, it wouldn't be a bad place to run drugs or weapons through. The Sinaloan-cartel connection supports such a scenario. While the island is too small for a runway, it does host a helicopter pad.

You could dock a vessel, then move the cargo onto another boat or straight to a helicopter, and land it just about anywhere in South Florida.

While you couldn't completely avoid scrutiny here, a man like Granth could access enough federal intel to track the locations of coast guard and DEA aircraft.

One of the most understated developments of the drug war is how much traffickers have improved their game. Some cartels even hire former air traffic controllers to track DEA spotter planes and plan routes to avoid detection.

Hughes is on deck using a thermal-imaging camera to make his own sweep of the island. The device picks up heat signatures of people, vehicles, and anything else that runs hot.

"No movement. Nothing standing out . . . Huh."

"What is it?" I ask.

"The smaller of the two warehouses. It looks a little warm, but I'm not seeing any smoke."

"Do you think anyone's home?"

"That call Blackwood and Cray intercepted might have been Granth telling them to clear out," says Solar.

"Damn it," I mutter.

"Don't get worked up, McPherson. They could be hiding out. They could be gone. Either way, we forced Granth to react and put him on his back foot. I'd rather we were the ones throwing the punches."

Solar kills the engines, and we slowly drift toward the dock. I push my HK416 rifle to the side, grab the docking line, and leap out of the boat and onto the weathered boards.

Hughes does the same, and we tie the boat in place. I'd wanted to assault the island by swimming in, but Solar put the kibosh on that, reminding me that we were serving a warrant, not acting as an assassination squad.

Solar picks up the microphone to our loudspeaker. "US Marshals serving a search warrant. Come out with your hands up."

The only response is the sound of waves lapping the shore.

Solar repeats the message. Still no response.

I get a sense of déjà vu, recalling Maxim Schrulcraft's sailboat and my attempt to find out if anyone was home.

"Okay, time to have a look around," says Solar.

He joins us on the dock, and we fall into a tactical line with Solar in front, then Hughes, and me in the back. The goal is to provide the smallest target possible, using the first person in line as a shield for the rest.

Even though Solar is in his late fifties, the man is agile and moves quickly. As he aims his light at the buildings ahead, Hughes and I search our left and right flanks.

The purpose of small-unit tactics is to function as a single machine. You maintain a low profile and can cover all your blind spots by remaining tightly together.

The downside is that your small group composes one easy target, and if your enemy fires at you from a blind spot, a bullet that goes a little wild still has a chance of hitting someone.

We keep in our line until we reach the wall of the small boathouse. Solar calls out my name, and I sidle over to the door. There's a padlock on it, so I take out the bolt cutters and snap it off.

"Door!" I shout as I slide it open and press my back to the wall.

Hughes races around Solar and enters with his light illuminating the dark interior. Solar follows him, and the pair searches while I keep an eye on the rest of the compound. I mostly watch the observation tower, afraid someone will pop up with a sniper rifle and start picking us off. Something about that structure unnerves me.

"Clear," says Solar, and they exit.

The doors to the large warehouse are open, and we can see that it's empty without having to enter but perform a quick check anyway. We then move to the smaller warehouse, where Hughes spotted warmth, and follow the same procedure. This time the locks are already open. I wait outside here as well, watching the compound and the tower as they search the interior.

"Clear," Solar says again. "Generator's in there, but nothing else of interest."

We move to the main building. I use my mini pry bar to pop open the door. Large men have been impressed by how I'm able to use this to defeat dead bolts, steel hinges, and other barriers. The key is that it's a lot like throwing a punch. They're watching my hands and elbows, while the real work is in my legs and shoulders. It's something my dad taught me. He's a great improviser when it comes to tools. I never could have imagined that I'd be using my family's methods to pry open doors for law enforcement.

We enter the main building and spread through the first floor, which is lined with windows overlooking the ocean. There are rows of tables and chairs and nothing else. The back section has wet labs and a room with a large aquarium that has been drained.

We climb to the second floor and find offices and a large observation lounge. Hughes aims his rifle-mounted flashlight at the floor and tells us to hold back.

He kneels and picks something up. It's a bottle cap. Hughes gives it a sniff.

"Fresh," he replies.

I aim my light on the floor and start searching for clues. There's a line in the dust where someone pushed a broom recently enough to still leave a trail.

"It would appear that they left in a hurry and quite recently," says Solar.

I take a seat on a table and rest my arms over my assault rifle. "Now can I say 'damn'?"

Hughes uses the thermal imager to scan the island below us. "They shut the power down. Everything. This building wasn't even locked."

"That tells you that whatever they were concerned about isn't here anymore," replies Solar.

"Clearly," I add.

"And," he continues, "it also tells us they had to leave in a hurry and may not have been as thorough as they'd normally be. There's something on this island that Granth doesn't want us to find."

"Like his dead cat buried in the backyard?" I grumble.

"If it comes to us digging up every square inch, I'm prepared to do that," Solar replies.

"Yeah, me too," I say. "I mean, I'll whine a bit, but hand me a shovel."

CHAPTER 48

BEACHCOMBERS

"Do we need to do this search in the dark?" I ask Solar.

"I don't see any reason to," he replies.

I flip a light switch and, predictably, nothing happens. The entire island seems to be powered by the generator in the other building we searched. "I'll go see if I can get the power back up."

"Be careful," says Solar.

"Of what? Blackbeard's ghost?" I tell him. "Yes, I'll be careful."

Despite my snark, I follow Solar's advice and check every room as I exit the main building. I also give the compound a good look before crossing back to the generator building.

It's a small shedlike structure mostly filled by the large generator and benches with tools. The diesel fuel for the generator sits outside in drums on the opposite end of the building. Thankfully, there's enough fuel already inside the tank that I don't have to drag one of them inside.

I set my rifle down and pump the fuel line, then press the button to get things started. The motor purrs to life, and the overhead light switches on.

It took all of ten seconds. The generator is brand new and still has an instruction manual attached to an intake hose. *Interesting*.

One thing's certain: Granth made sure there'd be plenty of reliable power on this remote island. Despite the lack of clues we've found so far, I'm convinced there's more to be found here. Nobody leaves this quickly without screwing up.

I sling my rifle over my shoulder and head to the main building, which is now lit up. I use my flashlight to search the ground outside the front entrance for any kind of clue.

If dirt, gravel, and grass are important clues, then I've hit the jackpot. Otherwise, I'm out of luck. I decide to walk the perimeter of the building. Other than an amazing view, the island has no obvious secrets to reveal. Despite that, I still feel a sense of foreboding, but I can't quite place what's causing it.

Back in the main building, Solar and Hughes are searching desk drawers.

"See anything interesting?" asks Hughes.

"Brand-new generator," I reply. "How about here?"

"Nothing. I'm sure a forensic team could tell us more, but that's not a luxury we have. Although I did find this." Hughes walks over to a corner of the office and pulls a blue cable down from a shelf. "Ethernet."

"So, this place had Wi-Fi."

"Yes. They must have ripped out the routers in case there was something we could get from them."

"Granth sure was thorough. I'm going to take a look from the observation deck. If you hear a loud thump, that's me jumping off."

Solar's kneeling on a section of carpet he's pulled back. "Just make sure you jump on the ocean side so we don't have to step over your splattered body."

"Will do."

I find the staircase that leads to the roof of the building and follow it up to the top. A set of open stairs takes me to the top of the observation deck, giving me a 360-degree view of the ocean on one side and Biscayne Bay on the other.

This would have been one heck of a place to do research from. Hell, it would be a great place to live. Close enough to civilization that you can see the sparkling lights of Miami, but far enough away to ignore it all.

I lean over the railing and survey the island. What was Granth doing here? Assuming it wasn't drugs or gun-running, what else would an isolated island be useful for? Raves? Orgies? Island of Dr. Moreau animal experiments? Bioweapon research?

I shake my head in frustration and glance upward. A small piece of blue cable is sticking out from the roof of the observation tower above me.

I climb up on the railing to get a better look. It's an ethernet cable that leads down through the main building's roof below.

Why does he need ethernet up here? Normally a satellite antenna would have a coaxial cable going to a modem and then to ethernet.

I try to lean out and get a better view of the top of the roof, but I can't see anything from this angle. Now I'm super curious.

I hop off the rail and run down the stairs to get a look from the ground.

"Everything okay?" asks Hughes as I hustle through the floor he's on.

"Yep. Just checking something."

I move well away from the building and look back up at the observation tower's roof. There's a wind gauge and a flattened, oval-shaped device I hadn't noticed before. At the north end of the building, I see the satellite dish that provided internet service.

I run back up the stairs, passing Hughes again. Solar says something like, "Check on her."

I bolt up to the top of the observation platform and take off my rifle and my vest. I then climb back onto the railing and hold on to a support with one hand and the edge of the tower's roof with the other.

If I swing out, I might be able to make it up onto the roof. As I get ready to make my move, something grabs me by my belt and yanks me back onto the observation deck. Hughes is glowering at me when I turn around.

"I almost made it," I reply.

"You almost broke your neck."

"There's something on the roof," I explain.

"Great. Then let's use the ladder behind the warehouse to have a look."

"Ladder?"

"Yes, the tall thing you climb on?" Hughes gives me a slow shake of the head.

"Um, yeah. Good call."

❦

We bring the ladder to the main building's roof, then extend it all the way to the roof of the observation platform. From the condition we found the ladder in, covered in branches and salty brine, it's pretty clear that it had been long forgotten.

As Hughes holds the base, I climb up onto the roof and get a better look at what I saw from the ground. There are two instruments mounted on arms sticking out from a central post.

The wind gauge is the easiest one to recognize because of the spinning cups measuring wind speed. The other instrument is a mystery. The oval object seems too small to be a radar dish; it has a black band around the center and several vents. I've seen a ton of marine electronics, but this is alien to me.

When I aim my flashlight at the black band, the beam reflects off an array of lenses that go all the way around the device. From this angle, I also notice a faded decal.

"What's EarthWise?" I shout down to Hughes.

"It's an environmental sensor. Wind, temperature, that kind of thing. There's a whole global network of them," he shouts back.

From below the device runs the ethernet cable that was cut off on the other side of the tower's roof.

"Do they all have to use ethernet?" I ask.

"No. They're supposed to be able to talk to each other in a mesh network. But out here I guess they needed internet access because they're spread too far apart."

Well, this has been educational and completely useless. I almost broke my neck for some grad student's science project. I start back down the ladder.

"Want to hear the interesting part?" asks Hughes.

"What's that?"

"Guess who controls the foundation that builds the devices?"

"Granth?"

"Yep."

I stare up at the device in disbelief. "So, our maniac controls a worldwide network of environment-sensing instruments that have cameras, microphones, and who knows what else built in?"

"Who needs spy satellites when businesses and government agencies will let you install your surveillance gear for free?" replies Hughes.

"That little bastard . . ." I look down at Hughes and notice something well beyond him. "Remember when you saw the heat signature on thermal vision from the boat?"

"Yeah?"

"Coming down!" I finish descending the ladder.

"I assumed it was the generator. Is it something about the EarthWise?" asks Hughes.

"No. Something else. You shouldn't have seen any heat coming from the generator. It was cold when I got there. But I noticed another vent." I run for the stairs.

"What about the EarthWise?" asks Hughes, following me.

"We'll get it later. I'm sure you'll figure out how to Vulcan mind-meld with it or something."

I race down the stairs with Hughes a step behind me.

Solar, inspecting ceiling tiles, mutters, "It's contagious," as we pass.

I run around the generator building to a spot in back, where I find a concrete pad. Tucked away behind the mangrove trees, it was easy to miss. A large cylinder lies on its side with a ten-foot chimney sticking out the top of it.

"An incinerator," says Hughes.

I put my hand on the surface. "Still warm."

I open the door and find a smoldering mound of ash. Hughes grabs a shovel, and we start piling the debris onto the ground.

Orange embers flicker in the breeze. I find a bucket and fill it with water so we can stop the fire from consuming the rest.

We take handfuls of the smoking ashes and douse them, then set them on the concrete pad. Solar finds us and uses his flashlight to help us see.

"This feels like paper," says Hughes. "Were they trying to get rid of documents?"

My fingers feel something inside the water bucket, and I hold it up to the light. Solar kneels for a closer look. I don't have anything to say because I'm still processing what I'm seeing.

If this is what I think it is, the implications are big. *Real* big. The need for the remote island . . . The coverup . . . The lengths to which Granth was trying to protect himself . . .

I'm holding on to the charred corner of a hundred-dollar bill.

There are only two reasons you burn money like this: you're either shooting a rap video, or you're counterfeiting and covering your tracks.

Last I checked, of all Ethan Granth's businesses, rap artist wasn't one of them.

CHAPTER 49

INTAGLIO

Secret Service Agent Stephanie Uhlan examines the fragment under her microscope as Hughes and I watch from the other side of the lab bench. We'd already performed our own inspection of the bill based on what we understood about anticounterfeiting measures, but we couldn't tell the difference between what we found and a real bill. She agreed to meet with us first thing in the morning to give us her professional opinion.

Given the amount of time Uhlan has spent scrutinizing the fragment, we're not the only ones baffled. While it's possible this is a genuine bill, burning real legal tender wouldn't make any sense.

Solar brought up the possibility that we shouldn't put it past Granth to burn a few hundred thousand dollars of real money to make us look like idiots.

"Magnetic inks, holographic ribbons, iridescent inks, embedded fibers, even the things Treasury doesn't talk about . . . they're all here," Uhlan says as she stares into the microscope. "I'd need to see the whole bill, but this is pretty compelling."

"Is it real, then?" asks Hughes.

Uhlan leans back from her microscope and slips her glasses back down from her dark-brown hair. "Short answer, I don't know. In a case like this, if we had the whole bill, we'd compare it to one that came from the same print run and look for clues in the paper grain and ink compositions." She points to a zoomed-in view of the bill fragment on a monitor. "There are things you see in a bill, and there are also things that are hidden. Chemical tags need to match up with a given print run. I'm sure if I put this under the electron microscope, I could find manufacturing differences. Warping of the fibers, that kind of thing. I find it suspicious enough to compare it to the Reserve data. But that's only because I'm generally paranoid."

"Let's say the rest of the bill is as good as this part. If I walked into my bank tomorrow with a million of these, what would they say?" I ask.

"They'd run a random sampling through their machines. Which this bill would probably pass. They'd then check the serial numbers in a database to make sure this bill isn't actually supposed to be sitting in a Federal Reserve somewhere, or hasn't even been printed yet. If all that checks out, they're probably going to ask you where you got a million dollars, and that will flag a call to us and to the FBI. We might send someone out to do a test if there's any suspicion. At that point, they'd be more concerned with your credibility than the money," she explains.

"And if Jeff Bezos walked in with these bills?"

"Same check, but he'd end up with a hundred million dollars added to his balance," replies Uhlan.

"What about a bank in South America?" asks Hughes.

"They'd use the same measures and probably have a banking official verify it. If the person has a legitimate reason for having it—which at some of those banks can include illegitimate means of *acquiring* it— then the deposit would be accepted," she explains.

"What happens to the money after that?" I ask.

"That's where it gets interesting. Sometimes nothing. After it's been counted and placed onto a pallet, the money may never go into circulation. The bank counts it as an asset, and it might get moved around from one point to another like gold bars. But that's it. At some point they may exchange the money for newer currency, in which case Treasury would do an inspection and then destroy the bills. Of course, bringing counterfeit money directly to a bank is only slightly dumber than bringing it to us. No sensible counterfeiter would try that."

Unless you were so far above scrutiny that you weren't worried about raising red flags.

"How was it made?" asks Hughes.

"Good question. The superdollars the North Koreans manufactured used very similar methods to how we make our money. They had artists create their own plates and were able to manufacture paper almost exactly like the kind we use. We created countermeasures for that, but the newer supernotes are almost impossible to detect outside a lab." Uhlan sighs. "And *now* we've seen samples of *hypernotes*, which we think use an entirely new method of production. Instead of traditional methods, they're made using a kind of 3D printing process. A machine that can control the texture and the inks basically clones another bill. What's also concerning is these machines can make just about any other currency. Allegedly, they were invented by a foreign country as a way to destabilize other countries' money supplies."

"Who would that be?" asks Hughes.

"China wouldn't want anything that could trace back to them, but they're not above helping an ally along. Of course, the same can be said for us. We may have tried to manufacture counterfeits of other currencies to destabilize them. In World War II, we made fake stamps that had a caricature of Hitler with a skull for a face and put them into circulation in Germany. That amount of effort suggests that the US was also making counterfeit German currency. They tried the same with us."

"So you're saying the hard part is putting that much money into circulation?"

"Yes. You could run a hypernote machine all day and all night long, but your biggest problem is moving all that money. On the other hand, once you moved the money and it passed through a bank as legitimate, no bank or country would be eager to find out their money was fake. There are probably billions of suspect notes sitting in reserves around the world that banks are treating as real, because the moment someone declares them counterfeit, the bank is on the hook for the full amount. It's better to squint and look away than find out your money is imaginary.

"Now that I've answered your questions, maybe you could answer one for me. One of my colleagues got a wild call two weeks ago. We sent it over to the FBI, but nobody ever got back to us. I was wondering if you had any thoughts on this." Uhlan goes over to her computer, pulls up an email, and opens a sound file. "This came through our tip line. When someone tried to call back, there was no answer. We assumed it was a crank. And then . . . well, just random chance."

She plays the audio. A man's voice plays out over the speaker, sounding a little drunk: *Hello. I, uh, wanted to know if I could talk to someone. I wanted to know if there was some kind of reward for um . . . well . . . I don't want to get into it . . . but it involves a cruise ship and money. Hah, a lot of money.*

"A week later *The Sea of Dreams* incident happened," says Uhlan. "We didn't know what to make of it. But we sent this on to the FBI. Like I said, we never heard back."

"Can we see the number the call came from?" I ask.

"Sure. But it was a prepaid phone. We couldn't trace it." She pulls up the number. "Here you go."

Hughes already has his phone out and is checking it against his notes. "Whoa," he breathes.

"Robert Howell?" I guess.

Hughes holds his screen so I can see. "Same number."

"We'd love to talk to this person," says Uhlan.

"It would be a one-sided conversation," I reply. "We found his body shoved into a drainage culvert. On a related note: How big would this hypernote machine be?"

"I don't know. I've never seen one. I'd guess you could fit all the parts into something the size of a small refrigerator."

Hughes and I exchange glances. A small refrigerator . . . or a *mini-fridge-size* compartment hidden on a cruise ship. Since Granth's goons were empty-handed when we chased them off *The Sea of Dreams*, this bill would seem to be proof that he already got his hands on one machine . . . and may have another counterfeit device still hidden aboard the ship.

CHAPTER 50
HARDBALL

Mom's car is in the driveway when I get home, and so is Dad's truck. Run didn't say anything about inviting them over tonight. I guess this was a last-minute surprise. My mind is a million miles away, thinking about counterfeiting machines and cruise ships. Maybe a little family drama will help clear my mind.

When I walk through the front door, the one Jackie and I call the "King Kong door" because of its size, Jackie runs from the living room into the foyer and throws her arms around me.

We haven't been spending as much time together lately, but Jackie compensates with extra hugs. I'd prefer the time plus the extra hugs, but it's something.

"How's it going?"

"They're out on the patio. Daddy's bartending," she replies.

Run at the bar without music playing? This is odd.

I make my way to the backyard bar, where Dad is sitting next to Mom and Hank. Run is nodding, listening to something Dad is saying. From everyone's body language, it doesn't look like a joyful occasion.

I give Mom a hug, then take the empty chair between Hank and Dad. "What's with the long faces?"

"Nothing, darling. Just commiserating on the state of the world," says Dad.

Run slides me a glass of wine. "Drink up, soldier."

"Not until I know the occasion."

"Drink your wine, dear," says my mother.

"You used to say it would ruin my complexion."

"I told you a lot of lies to keep you on the straight and narrow."

"It didn't work," Run observes.

"Did That Bastard Run Jacobs just say something?" Mom shoots back. "Just keep our glasses full, and we'll think about your penance."

"You've been working on that for fourteen years," he says.

"How are things, Hank?" I ask Mom's boyfriend.

"Great. Never better," he replies.

This is too weird. "Now I *know* everyone is full of crap. Hank, you never waste a chance to complain about something."

Hank simply stares at his beer bottle. I look at Run. I can read his body language. He'd tell me what's up, but my parents have sworn him to silence.

I take a sip of wine. "Cool. This is going well. Dad, how's the salvage support going?"

Salvage work on *The Sea of Dreams* has turned into his biggest payday in a long while.

"It's . . . going," Dad replies.

"Going?" I can tell when Dad is holding something back. "That's a bit noncommittal. Going good? Going bad?"

"Going gone." Dad sighs.

"Gone? What happened?"

"It's nothing, darling. Nothing to worry about."

I put my glass down. "Hold up. What happened?"

"Things change. Everything will be okay." Dad tries to form a wry smile to reassure me.

"Run?"

He holds his hands up in the air. I could push him, but I don't want to overstep boundaries. He has a good relationship with my parents, despite the nicknames.

"Dad. Tell me. Don't make me get the stun gun."

"Everything's okay," says Mom.

Jackie speaks up from a deck chair by the pool, where she's sprawled out. "Grandpa's contract thingy got canceled, and Uncle Hank just lost the lease on one of his print shops and has to move. Also, I think Dad is getting sued by someone for a zillion dollars."

"Hey, Mouth," says Run. "Upstairs. Homework."

"I don't have any homework," she replies.

"You do now. Go look up the word 'quisling.'"

"Ugh. I live in a house of lies," Jackie murmurs as she heads inside.

I turn back to the adults. "So now that it's out in the open, when did all this happen?"

I've been away for a while and not paying as close attention to what's been going on in my family as I should be. That's one of the downsides of my work.

"Today," says Mom. "A day that will forever live in infamy."

"Today?" It couldn't be . . .

I step away and take out my phone to call Hughes.

"What's up, partner?"

"I just wanted to check in and see how you and Cathy are doing."

"We're managing . . . why you asking?"

"This may sound odd, but have you had any bad news today?" I ask cryptically.

"Hold on. Let me go in my office." A minute later he continues. "Well, yes. Cathy has been on leave from the school where she teaches. She just got notified that they won't be renewing her contract. Which came out of nowhere."

Oh lord. I look at the faces of my family and the pain they're trying to hold back.

236

"This is Granth," I tell Hughes. "My dad just lost a cleanup contract, and a lease got pulled from Hank, my mom's boyfriend."

"Granth had his fingers all over the salvage operation," says Hughes. "Now it makes sense. Another way to keep a close eye on the investigation."

"And now he's using that and his other connections to mess with us. Let me get Solar on the line."

"Hello," says Solar a minute later.

"I've got Hughes on with us. Dumb question: Have you or Cynthia had any bad news?"

"Word gets around fast. She and her paper just got hit by a hundred-million-dollar defamation lawsuit from a former state senator she ran a critical piece on last year. One of her sources recanted and claimed Cynthia made the quote up."

"Oh man . . ."

"No need to worry. She's used to this. Her paper is standing by her. If they don't, she can go indie. I've been telling her to do that for years."

"Listen, George: it's Granth. He's messing with us. He killed a contract for my dad and also for my mom's boyfriend. He got Cathy fired from her job at the school. All of this happened today. Barely a day after we went to his club." Not to mention his island last night.

Solar is quiet. Hughes and I wait for him to respond. Finally, he breaks the silence.

"I think he underestimated who he's dealing with. But it doesn't make sense."

"He's an asshole. Of course it makes sense."

"No. Now he has three angry people willing to tell everyone exactly what kind of an asshole he is. Unemployed, angry people with nothing to lose. He's too smart for that. Even when rattled. No, it's a message. Granth wants us to know we're puppets on a string," says Solar. "Another shoe will drop soon."

"What'll it be? A criminal investigation? Planting drugs?"

"We're law enforcement. He knows we know people. He doesn't want that risk. It'll probably be something else. A reason for us to drop everything."

"Like a job offer doing security for a tech company in Atlanta that's willing to pay me three times what I'm making, plus stock options?" asks Hughes.

"Maybe. I don't know if it would be that specific," says Solar.

"The email that just arrived is very specific about the offer."

I pull open my email app. "Let me check my inbox."

"Anything?" asks Hughes.

"Macy's is having a sale. Nope." I don't know if I should be hurt or flattered that Granth hasn't tried to buy me off.

I look over at my father sitting at the bar. "Hey, Dad. Check your email."

He pulls out his phone and taps through to wherever he accidentally moved his email app the last time he used it.

"Huh. I just got offered a contract in Tampa." He shows the screen to Run and shrugs happily. "See: when one door closes, another opens."

Hank holds up his phone, showing us a text message. "They changed their mind about the lease."

I return to my conversation with Hughes and Solar. "What're the odds Cathy gets an offer from a school in Atlanta next?"

"I don't understand his game," replies Hughes.

"It's a game meant for people who he thinks he can corrupt," Solar explains. "It's also a show of force. Stick and carrot. He took something away from us, then offered something else in exchange. It's not meant to be subtle. Next time, he'll take something even bigger and not offer anything in return."

"What a dick!" I blurt out, earning stares from my family at the bar.

"This is Granth's soft touch," says Solar. "I'm sure he's already planning his next move if we don't take the hint. That's what worries me most. Next time, it won't be lost contracts and lawsuits. It will be more like Catalina."

"What do we do now?" asks Hughes.

"Remember the first time they took our badges and I asked if you were all in? This is where we have to follow through on that. We need to strike back at him fast. Hit him in a way he's not expecting."

CHAPTER 51

Snare

Hughes and I are sitting in my SUV, staring at *The Sea of Dreams* as the morning crew of workers on a nearby barge drag hoses, move equipment on cranes, and do all the other things required to repair and keep the injured ship afloat. Tourists sit on blankets, enjoying the sun and the beach. The occasional curiosity seeker on a Jet Ski who strays too close to the ship is warned off by one of the coast guard crafts patrolling the vessel's perimeter.

The news has leaked that Maxim Schrulcraft is the sole suspect in the attack: stories about his ecoterrorist days, and acquaintances giving their accounts on talk shows about the quiet, angry young man he once was.

Looking at it from the perspective we have now, it seems apparent that some of the leaking and story creation came from Ethan Granth. He needs everyone to believe that Schrulcraft was a lone wolf, and the attack on *The Sea of Dreams* purely an act of ecoterror.

The million-dollar question, or rather billion-dollar one, which Hughes and I are trying to answer, is whether Granth got everything off the ship. While the illicit compartment and burned bill might indicate that he already has a hypernote machine back in his possession, the armed search team he sent onto the crippled ship indicates that Granth didn't get everything he wanted the first time.

There's also the report we got from a contact inside the coast guard: three men tried to board *The Sea of Dreams* yesterday at the end of shift. They claimed they were contractors hired to fix leaking internal hydraulics, but the salvage operator couldn't verify their contract.

Mix-ups like that happen all the time, so the men were sent on their way back to shore. Thankfully, someone at the coast guard thought to tell us.

"So you're a super villain who has your money-making machine stuck on that ship. And despite all your connections, you can't get a crew aboard to retrieve it. What's your next move?" I ask.

"Wait it out? At some point, security will loosen up," Hughes says. "That's probably what the three goons were hoping last night. Maybe send another team today?"

"Let's say we find it first. Then what?"

"We have to connect it to Granth."

"How? He has so many layers between himself and what he's doing, I'm not sure we'll be able to do that. There's also the fact that he almost surely has another machine," I explain, "which he very recently removed from the island."

"He might try to destroy the one on the ship instead of letting it be discovered. 'Cause if we got a look at one, it might make it easier to spot fake bills created by the other," suggests Hughes.

"Huh. You might be onto something. What would he do if he heard we found his other machine?" I ask.

"Panic. Move the other one again. Too bad we can't track it somehow," says Hughes.

"Maybe we can," I reply.

"I'd like to know how the hell you'd pull that off."

I think my idea over carefully. It sounds like it would work. I'm just afraid it will be obviously stupid once I say it out loud.

"We're not just talking about a machine; we're also talking about a group of people who run it. This would have to be a small team that Granth trusts. They'd be the ones moving the machine and setting it up again," I tell them.

"Like Copley?" asks Hughes.

"No. I think he was just a contractor Granth used in an emergency, like the Sinaloans, except he was a dive expert. This would be a core group," I explain.

"Okay, so we have a team and a machine. That doesn't narrow it down much."

"I think it does. If you have people, it's a sure thing that they have cell phones. If we could get their phones' IMSI IDs, we could track them from the air and find out where the machine's being kept."

"So we use our Crossbow cell phone sniffer to get their IDs . . . but how do we know where to look? Unfortunately, we only know where they've been, not where they are now," says Hughes.

I point to the ship. "Three of them may have tried to board *The Sea of Dreams* last night. At least two of Granth's people plus someone to cut through the bulkhead. I don't think he's trusting any third-party contractors at this point."

"So we put a sniffer out there and wait for the team to return?" asks Hughes.

"Maybe. But Granth is paranoid. These guys would have their phones off, if even on them at all. We'd need to catch them when they're more relaxed and not surrounded by the coast guard."

"He is paranoid. Cameras everywhere. I bet he's even . . ."

"Watching the ship right now," I finish.

I get out of the truck and look for the tallest hotel. It's the Commodore, next door to where we had our briefing about *The Sea of Dreams* when it first ran aground.

Hughes and I dart across the street and hurry up the block to the lobby. We take the elevator to the top floor, then enter the stairwell and climb to the roof.

Air conditioners roar as the ocean breeze blows at us. The roof is divided into three sections with small walls separating them and a higher wall to keep anyone from walking off the edge.

Hughes goes to one end while I search the other. I find a satellite antenna and a cell phone repeater, but nothing like what I saw on the island.

"Here!" Hughes is pointing to something over the wall below him.

I race to his side. On the next building, five stories shorter than the one we're on, hangs the familiar, oval-shaped device. The big decal isn't worn off this one and clearly says "EarthWise."

"That's where we had our meetings," I reply. "He had a camera there watching the boat the whole time."

"I wouldn't be surprised if he had the conference room bugged too," adds Hughes.

"That's what we get when we hold secret meetings in banquet halls."

From the vantage point between the buildings, there's also a clear view of the section of the beach and parking lot where the salvage teams are moving equipment back and forth to and from the cruise liner.

"He's watching everything that's happening . . . Maybe there's some way we can use that to our advantage?"

"How?" asks Hughes.

"Let me get back to you on that."

CHAPTER 52
PINPOINT

It's late, and the wall of our meeting room is covered with a projection of a map showing all the flights Ethan Granth's private planes made in the last year. There are the familiar destinations you'd expect for a man like him: Aspen, Los Angeles, New York City, London, Ibiza. There are also a number of Latin American flights, as well as trips to various places in the Caribbean.

Solar, Hughes, and I are trying to map out how he moves money. We're pretty convinced that he doesn't move currency on his own plane—that would be too much of a security risk—but instead uses one of the commercial services that transfers cash to and from banks and reserves around the world.

These specialized courier services facilitate transfers when companies want to move assets or make large transactions that require the banks involved to have the cash on hand.

Heavily regulated, they're not the kind of thing a drug lord would want to use. But if you're handling a transaction between a CIA operation and some friendly group in another country, this is how you would move money.

While Granth himself controls a firm that handles transactions like this, he doesn't own any of the companies that do the physical transfer.

We've been able to match up flights Granth's airplanes have made with flights made by AirSecure, one of the more popular companies that physically transfer cash.

Flight manifests show two passengers, Hilary Mire and Aran Lopez, on Granth's plane. They don't show up anywhere in his official organization records but apparently work for an unlisted part of his company.

Mire has a background in international law and worked for several large law firms before joining Granth. Lopez has a military background and worked private security in Iraq and Yemen.

Mire appears to represent Granth's business interests and Lopez his security.

"What about Lopez as a witness?" I ask.

"Maybe," says Hughes. "But a guy like that is hard to turn. He either knows who he's working for and accepts it or doesn't and can't cough up the real details."

"He knows people and places. That would be enough to make Granth nervous," I reply.

"Maybe," says Hughes. "We could talk to him. Once we do, the cat's out of the bag. We should be ready with the right questions."

I examine the crisscrossing flight paths. "Mire has to know what's up. She'd be our best chance at nailing Granth. I bet if we showed up and interviewed her, Granth'd piss himself."

"Not if *we* did it. Granth would assume we're chasing anything we can out of desperation," says Solar. "Now, Mire suddenly disappearing and not contacting him . . . *that* would make Granth nervous."

"Can we arrange a kidnapping with TaskRabbit?" I joke.

"That wouldn't be my first choice," Solar deadpans.

I study the flight times of Granth's planes. "It's interesting that they almost always leave an hour after the AirSecure plane arrives."

Hughes taps on his laptop. "That's a recent thing. Started three months ago."

A thought hits me. "Do we believe the hypernote machine he got off *The Sea of Dreams* is the first one he used? I've been assuming the bill we found on the island came from there. What if it came from an older machine?"

"Are you suggesting that Granth was already circulating forged currency?" asks Solar.

"Why not? What if he's been replacing one out of ten bills in the money he's moving with hypernotes? The Secret Service agent told us a bank wouldn't be able to tell the difference. If they came upon a pallet that's supposed to have come straight from the Federal Reserve or a trusted source, then they'd apply less scrutiny. We assumed that was his plan going forward, but what if he's already been doing it?"

Hughes sits back and looks at the photos of Mire and Lopez on the wall. "And his people leave as soon as the bills are accepted at the airport in case there's a problem later at the bank?"

I think through the scenario. "Would you rather be inside or outside Colombia when a bank in Bogotá realizes you just passed them fakes? As the trusted point of contact, Granth is who they would talk to first. He could even explain it away and replace the notes with real ones if things were about to go south. Especially since these transactions involve bureaucrats who are more concerned about the money than the ethics of it all."

"And that's assuming a bank ever notices. But a guy like Granth probably has a contingency plan. Maybe even an excuse, like his funds got accidentally mixed up with some seized assets at the money vault, or whatever."

"That might work with a foreign bank," says Solar. "I'm not sure how well that excuse would work here."

"That's my point. That's why he's able to get away with it. If they notice some funny notes after they accept the money, then they either have to eat it, like the agent told us, or hope he makes good on it. In that case, maybe that's where it ends. He replaces the money and says he'll take it up with the US Secret Service and never does. The bank doesn't care because the hot potato leaves their hands."

"How do we use that to our advantage?" asks Solar.

I stare at the wall but imagine a Scrooge McDuck vault filled with money. "We could call the last several banks he's made transfers to and tell them to check their bills."

"And they likely won't find anything suspicious with them," Solar replies.

"True. Nor would they want to . . . Okay, let me think about it. Hughes, how far in advance do they file their flight plans?"

He checks his laptop. "Usually a day in advance. Huh, he's got an upcoming flight plan that matches an AirSecure flight to Bolivia tomorrow. The plane then goes to Paraguay and Peru."

"Someone's rattled," says Solar. "I think Granth is trying to move as much currency out of the country as possible. The way he's spreading it around is extra suspicious. But those foreign banks may not know whether it's his money or money he's moving for some US government operation."

"Okay . . . so what would happen if those banks got a call to be on the lookout for counterfeit money being passed on to them in large bundles?"

Solar scratches his chin and thinks it over. "If they're smart, they'll refuse to accept the shipment and have their own officials verify the money with the sending bank and the US Treasury Department. And if Treasury's taking the hypernote we found seriously enough, we might be able to get the Secret Service to send out a bulletin. It'll only be good for a few days, but if Granth finds out his money is no good in one of the banks, it'll panic him."

"Would he send it back on AirSecure?" I ask.

"I don't think AirSecure would let him. He'd have to put it on his plane and find some other place that'd take it," says Solar.

"What if nobody will?"

"He'll have a plane full of money, much of it counterfeit. If he's smart, he knows where in the stacks the fake bills are located. That's assuming it's not all fake. Which it might be. Either way, he'll have tens of millions of dollars of fake money he'll need to get rid of before he brings the plane and the real money back to the United States."

"We can call Customs officials in every country he heads to and tell them to search the plane," suggests Hughes.

"We want to do more than harass him," says Solar. "We want to nail him here in the United States with the money on his plane, or else in a friendly country where they'll hold Mire and Lopez. And we'd still have to prove that it's counterfeit."

I answer my buzzing phone.

"McPherson."

"I have one small favor," says the voice of Coast Guard Warrant Officer Kevin Mason. "Could you have your friends at the DEA do their searches in normal business hours? I'm stretched thin and don't have the manpower to watch everything."

"Wait, what? Who?"

"DEA out of Tampa. Not the guys we work with. Two of them just came aboard with two technicians to search *The Sea of Dreams*," he explains.

"Are you sure they're *real* DEA?"

"Yes. Badges and everything. We checked them out. They have a search warrant for narcotics on the ship."

I'm confused. "Why didn't they go through the Miami office?"

"Hell if I know. I thought you would. I'm guessing the other office got a tip."

"How long ago did they board?"

"Ten minutes ago. Is something wrong?"

"Maybe. Don't do anything. Just go about whatever you're normally doing. We'll be out there soon."

"What's going on?" asks Solar.

"Some DEA agents out of Tampa are serving a search warrant on *The Sea of Dreams* and looking for drugs."

"Granth isn't moving drugs," says Hughes.

"Correct. Wanna bet they're working for Granth and will find a way to get the remaining machine off the ship and out from underneath the coast guard's nose?"

"Should we tell Mason to stop them if they start cutting into a bulkhead and find something?" asks Hughes.

"That could get dangerous. Just tell him to keep an eye on them."

CHAPTER 53

PURSUIT

Hughes has the throttle all the way down as the three of us race toward *The Sea of Dreams*. I called Mason, but he didn't pick up.

If we can catch Granth's people in the act of trying to retrieve the second machine, that might give us more leverage. Also, as Uhlan said, if the machine has a signature, like a certain indentation pattern or a slight defect, it could help Treasury spot Granth's fake bills in circulation.

We exit the port and make the wide turn around the jetty toward the crippled cruise ship. It's raining, and there's a mist that makes it hard to see. *The Sea of Dreams* and its attending vessels are mere blurs from here.

Our biggest concern at the moment is that those weren't actual DEA agents. Granth might be desperate enough to have hired hit men to pose as DEA agents so they could make their way on board. If Mason or any of the other coast guard crew confront them, there's a chance of an armed conflict. That's why we want to get there first.

"Ten minutes," says Hughes.

Solar and I strap our bulletproof vests on, then I take the wheel so Hughes can gear up.

The salvage lights on the ship grow brighter, and a coast guard boat starts running parallel with us. Solar hails it on the radio and identifies us. The pilot waves to us and veers back onto their patrol route.

Solar starts talking to someone else on the radio, but I can't make out his voice over the roar of the engines.

Hughes is taking us straight to the salvage barge. There's a tugboat docked next to it and two smaller coast guard craft.

I grab the bow line and leap aboard the barge, tying us off on a giant cleat. Mason comes running down the stairs from *The Sea of Dreams*. I look around but can't spot the boat the DEA agents used to get here.

"Are they still here?" I shout.

"No. They just left to take one of the technicians to the hospital. Apparently, they had an accident with one of the welding tanks and had to clear the deck until the gas dissipated. They're taking him to get checked out," he explains over the wind.

"How long ago?" I look to the shore, seeking any sign of their boat.

"About fifteen minutes ago."

"What's going on?" asks Solar as he and Hughes catch up.

"It seems they had their exit plan all worked out," I reply. "What deck were they on?"

"Deck four, port side," says Mason.

I start heading for the stairs. Hughes and Solar follow.

"Where are you going?" yells Mason.

Solar turns back. "Try to find that boat. Stop it if you can. Those technicians were hired thieves. The DEA agents probably had no idea."

"I don't understand," says Mason.

"Just stop that damned boat!" Solar shouts.

I reach the top of the stairs and race inside the ship. Electrical cable and hoses run up and down the decks, and work lights are positioned in the main junctions. The rest of the ship is dark, so I have to use my flashlight to avoid tripping over anything.

"This way," says Hughes, pointing to the stairwell.

We run up the steps two floors to deck four. We're in the middle of the ship, so the corridor runs in two directions, both completely dark.

"I'll take the bow," I say as I start running down the corridor.

I hear Solar's footsteps behind me as he follows. Thankfully, the furniture and luggage that blocked the corridors last time have been removed, making it easier to run despite the angle of the ship.

I swivel the beam of my flashlight back and forth across the cabin doors and walls of the ship. Two-thirds of the way down, we come to an opening cut into the wall. The smell of burning metal is still in the air.

The technician's welding tanks are resting on the ground, along with tools used for cutting. The metal plate cut from the opening leans against the opposite wall.

Solar catches up with me as I aim my light into the hidden compartment. To no one's surprise, it's empty.

"We were close," says Solar.

I step inside the space and inspect it more closely, subconsciously hoping that it's some kind of mirage that will vanish and reveal the hidden counterfeit machine.

Solar flicks his flashlight on and off at Hughes, who's all the way at the other end of the ship. He comes running back toward us.

"I hope they catch the boat," says Solar. "But I'm doubtful. Actually, at this point, I hope the DEA agents are okay."

"You think they were duped?" I ask.

"We saw how easy it was for Granth to get a judge to disband our merry little agency. Planting a tip-off about hidden contraband on here to get two of his people aboard would have been a lot easier."

"How did he arrange for the guys who cut through this to be his own?"

"He's got someone in the Tampa DEA office that he's compromised sufficiently to ask for favors. It probably seemed innocuous."

Hughes is on the phone when he catches up with us. "Mason says the boat docked and the technicians already went to the hospital, according to the DEA agents."

"That seems sloppy," says Solar.

"Mason's getting descriptions. There might be something we can do with that," replies Hughes.

I stare into the compartment, thinking about what must have just happened. Something doesn't make sense. Wind from an open door blows through the passage, chilling my face.

I think out loud: "Granth's guys got aboard with the DEA agents. They cut open this part of the boat to get to the machine. Then what? Did the DEA guys see the machine? Why the 'accident' with the acetylene tank? What purpose did that serve?"

"Maybe to clear the agents out before they finished cutting it open?" offers Hughes.

"Or, one of them had a mask on and had the two DEA agents take his partner out of here so he could try to close the tank but actually retrieve the machine?" I suggest.

"That's one hypothesis," says Solar. "Of course, that leaves one obvious question."

"Where's the machine?" I supply.

Hughes aims his flashlight around the open cabin doors of the ship. There are several hundred on this deck alone. Not to mention all the other hiding places that exist on a vessel like this.

"He could have moved it anywhere. Someone else could come pick it up tomorrow or another day and never arouse any suspicion because he's not using a cutting torch—the one thing we told the coast guard to watch out for," Hughes observes.

"Yeah . . . it still seems risky, though," I say. "I'd want to get that machine out of here as soon as possible."

The breeze in the corridor picks up. I turn toward the end of the ship where it's coming from and aim my flashlight into the darkness.

There's a passageway fifty feet from here leading to the outer deck. I run down the corridor through the open doors and reach the railing. City lights stretch in either direction through the mist. One of the coast guard boats patrolling the waters near *The Sea of Dreams* is anchored between the ship and the shore.

I hurry toward the aft section and the ship's back railing. My feet slide on the wet deck, and I have to grab a support to keep from sliding into the rail like an extra in *Titanic*.

Hughes and Solar, both holding on to the railing like smart people do, reach me as I'm pulling myself back up.

I lean over the edge and stare down at the water below. "What if they didn't stash it on the ship, but down there instead?"

Hughes points to the lights of several unidentifiable boats in the distance. They're outside the coast guard perimeter, but close enough to send divers to retrieve something that was dumped overboard.

They could already be down there . . .

I slip-slide over to a bright-orange box and pull off the lid. Inside is a rescue float attached to a very long rope.

"McPherson!" shouts Solar.

"It's ten yards down. I can do this in my sleep," I say as I slip off my shoes.

"More like fifteen. And then what?"

"I free dive to the bottom and find it. There has to be a glowstick or some kind of marker."

"Take the boat and use your scuba gear," he replies.

"George . . ."

"Now! That's an order. You and Hughes go get the boat. I'll keep an eye out here and have the coast guard stop anyone that comes close."

I start to protest but realize that he's being rational. We're higher up than I first thought. There's a nonzero chance that I hit the water wrong and knock myself out. That would force Hughes to enter the water after me.

"Fine!" I race down the deck, taking the fastest path to our boat.

Hughes is already running ahead of me, having correctly anticipated who would win that argument.

CHAPTER 54

PLUNGE

I've already got my tank strapped on by the time Hughes has pulled away from the barge and started piloting us to the back of the cruise ship. The plan is for him to stay on the surface and communicate with me while I search for the machine on the seafloor. Solar's standing on the edge of the stern above us, watching everything like a hawk.

Seeing how far up he is and where I was about to jump from, I feel a little embarrassed. My impulsive nature has been even more impulsive lately. Hopefully I can make up for my attempted suicide plunge by finding the machine.

Presumably it's sealed inside one or more oversize, watertight diving bags.

"Here we are," says Hughes. "Let's do a—"

I plunge into the water and start swimming for the bottom, which is only about thirty feet from the surface. While I descend, I flip the switch on my mask that controls my radio.

"As I was saying . . . let's do a radio check," says Hughes's voice inside my helmet.

"Um, check," I reply.

I take out my light and switch it on. The beam cuts through the murk, revealing an ocean floor with large stone blocks strewn about.

I remember something about a plan to drive pylons into the seafloor near the ship to help stabilize it in case another storm approached. The blocks might be part of that effort. Some of them are stacked on top of each other, nearly high enough to reach the surface.

"There's a lot of concrete blocks down here," I tell Hughes. "It might take me a little while to search the area. Plus, it's pretty murky."

"Blocks of concrete? I'd hate to be some idiot who tried to high-dive into these waters," he replies.

"Point taken. For the record, I have a very shallow recovery. I once had an offer to be a cliff diver."

"That's a lie, McPherson."

"Well, I thought about it. How do things look up there?"

"Still got several boats just outside the perimeter. I'm watching them on night vision. They look like they're fishing, but that's what I expect a boat with secret divers to look like they're doing. Be careful. If I can see them, they can see me."

And they can radio their divers that I'm in the water . . .

I slide through a gap in the blocks and move my light back and forth, trying to find the machine. It would be easier if I knew exactly what the waterproof casing looked like. What I'm really hoping for is a light stick to show me the location like a neon sign.

I push myself through the crevices, trying to make my way closer to the back of the boat, where I'd expect the machine to have landed. As I swim to the spot directly underneath where I was about to jump from, my flashlight catches the glimmer of a propeller taller than I am. It's mounted to a massive shaft that allows it to swivel in either direction, making it easier to steer *The Sea of Dreams* into port.

I train my light back on the seafloor and start searching in a more orderly pattern. It would be easy to miss something only a few feet away on the other side of a block.

"I see movement on sonar. Two shapes," Hughes says calmly. "Heading in your direction."

It could be schools of fish or a shark chasing a school of fish. It could also be two divers . . .

I cut my light and move to my left a few yards. If they saw my light, I don't want them knowing where I am. I also belatedly realize that if I'm looking for a glowing light stick, working in the dark might make it easier.

I adjust the air in my vest so I can pull myself around the concrete block with minimal effort. This allows me to glide without having to flap my fins too much. It also keeps me closer to the stones for protection.

"Where are they now?" I ask.

"Passing directly below me," says Hughes.

"So they know you're here."

"And they know you're down there. I'm going to suit up."

"Wait. No. Turn on the underwater lights," I reply.

"Won't that expose you?"

"No. I'm hidden."

Suddenly, a bright glow shines from overhead as the lights from the *Cobia Kai* illuminate the sea below. Even in this murk, the cone of light is easy to make out.

I see a shadow pass by at the opposite end as a diver is caught in the glare. He's swimming without his light on, just like me, which may mean the hidden machine does indeed bear some sort of luminescent marker.

I slide between two blocks and into a small clearing. I'm still within throwing distance of the back of the ship, but I'm also close to where the divers should be right now. I start doing longer breath holds to limit my bubbles. At the same time, I keep an eye on the glow of our boat lights in case a diver passes in front of it. This is a known technique that predators with limited night vision use. If you can't see well in the dark, put yourself in a position where your prey will come between you and a source of light.

Two shadows move past, only a few yards from where I am. I push myself lower, toward a large black rock at the bottom. I reach out to cling to the stone and feel an unexpectedly smooth, slick surface.

This is no rock . . .

My heart skips a beat as I imagine myself grabbing a bull shark that's sitting on the sea bottom. Thankfully, the object doesn't move, and it feels rather flat. Unless there's some new species of cube shark in South Florida, I may have found Granth's machine.

I reach around the front, which is wedged next to a stone, and touch a strap. I also feel a small plastic cylinder, which is probably the light stick. I couldn't see it from above because the container landed facing the wrong direction.

"I've got good news and bad news," I say into my radio. "Good news, I found it. Bad news, the bad guys are right on top of me. Shutting up now so I don't give off bubbles."

Okay, so how do I haul a container that's almost as big as me from the seafloor to the surface?

A shape moves past the light again, this time heading in my direction. They seem to have narrowed down the possible locations for the machine. Which also means they've narrowed down the possible locations for me.

I pull my knife from the sheath on my leg and bring it up in front of me. If they do find it, I'm putting up a fight.

"Where are you in relation to our boat?" asks Hughes.

"Fifteen yards west," I reply.

"Stay low."

The boat starts to move, and the cone of light heads in my direction, catching the silhouettes of two divers in the glow.

One of them spots light reflecting from my mask and starts to swim toward me.

He's holding a speargun.

Now he's aiming it at me.

As I push myself behind the machine, my last thought is, *What the hell is Hughes's plan?*

I hear a loud *clank*, and the diver with the speargun jerks violently, then releases his weapon. His body starts to descend and slip away as a boat anchor slides off his back and onto the seafloor.

The other diver turns to see what happened to his companion and reaches out to grab him. I kick against the rock behind me and launch myself at him like a torpedo.

Before he has a chance to look up and see me coming, I've ripped his mask off and started slashing his hoses.

He's disoriented, surrounded by a cloud of bubbles. Likely panicked too. His only choice is to surface. Either saving his friend along the way, or not.

He chooses to save his friend and begins to ascend to a spot near the back of our boat.

"He's coming to you," I tell Hughes.

"On it."

I wait for the all clear.

Boom!

The sound of a shotgun is distinct, even all the way down here.

"Hughes?" I ask over the radio.

"All good. Had to make a point. Coast guard's coming in now. We'll get you and the machine up in a second."

"No hurry," I reply.

CHAPTER 55
THE MACHINE

Stephanie Uhlan stares at the device in awe. Two other Secret Service agents, including the district supervisor, are with us in the lab with our find. They're realizing the urgency of our request for a late-night meeting. Faye Padros, the more technically inclined expert, has disassembled the machine on the lab table and is examining each section.

She holds up a flat metal plate about the size of an old-fashioned mechanical credit card machine. "This is used in microchip foundries to emboss chips. It's a newer method, and the precision is laughable for a modern microprocessor, but by printing standards, it's incredibly precise."

She slides a metal component back and forth. "This etches the pattern into the metal like a laser cutter, but the difference is that the laser can cut at an angle and create a recess inside the plate that the paper gets pulled up into." She picks up another component like the first one. "They can do multiple passes on the bill with different inks. And this . . ." She holds up a device that looks like a small version of a 3D printer from Jackie's school. "This controls an impression point that can add texture and even create a watermark inside the bill."

She sets it down and stares at the device with admiration. "There's a USB port for controlling the device and getting updates on currency runs from the Reserves. The final section over here is actually a commercial counterfeit detector. That's how they spot the rejects."

"How long before these are for sale on Alibaba?" I ask.

Gately, the district supervisor, gives me a sickened look. "That's not even funny."

"But it's a possibility," says Solar. "The important question now is, Can you spot fakes made by this machine?"

"That's difficult to answer," says Uhlan. "We'd need to see actual print runs."

"I could spot one," replies Padros.

"How?" asks Uhlan.

"They made a mistake. I don't know if they even realized it. You have to see the machine this close to realize what it is." Padros places a digital caliper next to a metal-impression block. "In a normal print run, there's going to be a little variance in every bill because of its placement on the sheet, drying time, and other conditions. That means that the tolerance will be within a few microns. Let's say 7.2 to 7.5 microns for the width of one of the wavy lines in a thread of hair. On a real bill, it will always fall between those numbers with a margin of error of several decimal points. Like 7.253. Rarely ever the exact number. And the chance of every line being the same exact width on a single note is astronomical. It would be like every hair on your head being the exact same length. The average might be one inch, but it's essentially impossible for all of them to literally be one inch in length."

"Our optical scanners can pick up variations," says Gately.

"They look for notes that are outside the tolerance range. They don't look for notes that are too precise. But that's an easy fix, now that we know what to look for. If a bill gets flagged at a bank as suspect, we can check the chemical composition with the serial number," Padros explains.

"So you're saying you can spot them and tell other banks how to do it as well?" I ask.

"With a software update, banks that use the new detectors with the high-resolution optical scanners could," says Padros. "We also have a system where they can send us images of the bills and we do a visual check. That doesn't tell us conclusively, but it helps flag suspect notes."

"Can we talk about where this came from?" asks Gately.

Hughes and I shut up and let Solar handle this. We never discussed next steps after pulling this out of the water and sending the rogue divers away with the FBI.

"I need this sat on for forty-eight hours," says Solar.

"I don't think that's realistic," replies Gately. "If there are more of these out there . . ."

"We're sure there are. If you want to get them all, then you have to trust us. We're dealing with somebody who has his nose in a lot of places."

"I can promise you we don't leak," Gately says, a little put off.

"I'm not worried about you. Or anyone else here. My concern is the judge or the clerks we have to go through to get a warrant," Solar replies.

"We've never had a problem before."

"You've never dealt with this person before. He managed to get my entire department shut down by a state judge with one phone call. He'll have ears in places we never thought about."

This isn't sitting well with Gately. And understandably so. This is like walking into the Department of Homeland Security with a nuclear bomb you found and asking them to chill for a while.

"I'll make you a deal," says Solar. "You can have the collar when it's time. This can even be your case. We just want to see this guy go down. And go down fast."

"We can work with that," replies Gately. "Now, what precisely are you asking us to do?"

CHAPTER 56
ENEMY OF THE STATE

United States Federal Judge Steve Torrell, the on-call judge we have for warrant approval, yawns as he reads the paperwork spread across his kitchen table. We hastily put together everything we had so far and even tried to get the divers we pulled from the water to talk, but they haven't said a word. Lacking their testimony, our best bet was to follow the chain of events that led the DEA to get the "technicians" aboard *The Sea of Dreams*.

Solar's suspicion is that Granth got to one of the DEA's trusted informants, paid him off to tip the DEA, then managed to get someone in the Tampa DEA office to use the divers we caught. Figuring out exactly how that happened is a problem for the DEA to solve now.

What we do know is that the DEA is now extremely pissed at someone pulling their strings, much like the Secret Service's feelings about the hypernote machine. We also have the FBI's support now, since Olmo desperately wants his agency to be part of the takedown of whoever is behind this.

We haven't named anyone yet because we're trying to build up as much support as possible so that when we go after Ethan Granth, we can hit him hard and he won't be able to swat us away.

Granth knows we got the machine. He may not know yet that *we* know what it is.

In a bit of subterfuge, we had a large container taken to the Broward Sheriff's Office and locked in an evidence locker. We traveled to the Secret Service building via Uber, in case Granth had people watching our homes or headquarters and tracking our vehicles.

Judge Torrell finishes going through the paperwork and slowly shakes his head. "George, if this was homework, I'd give you a D-minus."

"If I weren't dealing with someone who could easily buy off one of your idiot friends to have my entire department shut down, I'd have been a little more thorough. As it stands, we don't know if he's going to come at us with lawsuits or cruise missiles."

"Let's not exaggerate," says Torrell.

"Is a cruise ship crippled by bomb blasts an exaggeration? How about McPherson's face? Is someone who'd do that to a cop a person you'd take lightly?"

Um, why is my face part of this?

"The case is still thin," says Torrell.

"That's why I came to you. If his name was Mohamed Al Mohamed, you'd have signed it already. If I told you he lived on a farm in Central Florida and had been mumbling to friends that Hitler had a few good ideas, you'd be giving us blank warrants with your signature," argues Solar. "You're the judge that signs terrorism warrants. You have the power to grant us what we need."

"And if you're wrong?" asks Torrell.

"I go to jail and you get mean things said about you that nobody will remember a year from now. People already say mean things about you, so what's the difference?"

"And you think it's likely he's planning another terrorist attack?"

"Without a doubt." Solar doesn't articulate that by "terrorist attack" he means counterfeiting—which, under current US law, counts as terrorism if it's meant to or could potentially destabilize an economy. It's a distinction that Torrell himself has made, so it's not like he gets to cry about it later.

We're asking for a warrant to search all Ethan Granth's properties. His homes, his businesses, his yacht, everything. Even undisclosed assets.

"Fine," says Torrell. "I'll probably make more money on the speaking circuit if I get removed and disbarred." He signs the warrant and hands the papers back to Solar. "Or I'll say you made me sign it at gunpoint."

"We can arrange that if it will ease your conscience," says Solar.

"Get out of my house," growls Torrell, "and take your zealots with you."

CHAPTER 57
IMPOSTOR SYNDROME

Back at our office, we're guzzling coffee to stay alert as we stare at maps of South Florida spread across the conference table, trying to figure out how to execute a pincer move on Granth. We want to push him hard enough that he moves his counterfeiting operation and we catch him in the act.

With Torrell's warrant, we can use an array of methods to tap his phones and track him that we didn't have before. Tools that Granth would never expect us to have access to.

The key is to track the people he works with and map their movements. We're hoping that we can monitor outbound and inbound calls and learn where the machines are being kept by analyzing the movement and communications of his people.

Granth keeps a layer between himself and his illicit operations. But every time we rattle him, he has to shift things around or else run the risk of being exposed.

On the map, we've circled all the different properties we think he has access to and ones that we suspect he controls. I'm staring at those circles, trying to see some kind of pattern that isn't there.

A buzz comes from the intercom on our front gate. One of the disadvantages of being based out of a defunct marine repair shop in an old marina is you don't have a conventional office.

"Who the hell is that?" asks Solar, checking his watch.

Hughes views the security feed. "Florida Department of Law Enforcement vehicles."

"Now what? Get rid of them. I'm going to the john," says Solar as he gets up.

I roll up the maps and our notes and shove them into a metal storage unit. Hughes buzzes our visitors through the outer gate, and two SUVs pull into our parking lot.

"They have on body armor," says Hughes as he looks at the feed.

"Hurry up and open the door so they don't knock it down."

I sit back down to watch this latest development as Hughes pulls the door open.

"Florida Department of Law Enforcement!" shouts a uniformed man as the door swings open.

"Can I offer you a beverage?" Hughes asks as he gestures to our refrigerator.

"Up against the wall!" replies the officer. "Hands in the air!"

I'm about to kick over the table and draw my pistol, fearing these are impostors, until I spot Minguella and Charlton following the tactical unit.

I raise my hands to prevent any itchy fingers from shooting me on the spot.

"Where's Solar?" asks Charlton.

"Not here," I reply. "Mind if I ask why you're holding two law enforcement officers at gunpoint in our own goddamn office?"

"I think we clarified that the last time. You're no longer law enforcement. You've been acting without authorization and illegally presenting yourself as police officers," says Minguella.

"Marshals," says Hughes. "We're deputized US Marshals. I've got a badge and everything. Her too. Looks like you guys screwed up big-time."

Minguella pulls a piece of paper from his pocket. "Are you sure about that? It says here that the head of the US Marshals Service revoked your status this afternoon. Nice try, though. We'll need your badges and your weapons."

"Technically, the badges belong to the Marshals Service, and the guns are personal weapons. You can, however, eat a dick," I tell him.

"McPherson . . . ," warns Hughes, trying to keep me from getting shot.

I keep my hands in the air as I let loose. "*No.* I'm sick of this. Who the fuck do you think's pulling your strings, you buffoons? What game do you think you're playing? Do you go home at night thinking, 'Man, I was a good cop today'? How the hell did you even end up with the FDLE?"

"Cuff her," says Minguella to one of the uniformed officers.

"You touch my detective, and I'll have you so buried in shit you'll forget what sunlight looked like," Solar's voice booms from the back of the room.

"Stay out of this," says Minguella. "We only have warrants for these two. Don't make me arrest you too."

Solar's hands are at his sides. "You come near me or touch her, someone's going to have a lot of explaining to do. It'll probably be me because I'll take you down first, Minguella. I know whoever rescinded our deputization didn't ask for it this way."

Minguella seems to realize that this could quickly escalate. "Everybody relax."

"I'm relaxed as could be. It should frighten you how relaxed I am," says Solar.

"As I explained, your US Marshals authorization has been revoked."

"This afternoon. I heard you. Last I checked, we weren't notified. Consider us notified. Now you can leave."

"I still have a warrant," argues Minguella.

"Let me see it."

Minguella hands him the document. Solar flips back and forth through the document, then tosses it back to Minguella.

"Did you read it?" Solar asks.

"Clearly," replies Minguella.

"Then explain to me how a warrant for impersonating law enforcement could be issued *before* the US Marshals Service revoked their deputization? It looks like someone got a little excited and jumped the gun."

"You're welcome to contact an attorney on your subordinates' behalf after we process them," replies Minguella.

"This warrant's invalid. I won't be calling an attorney; I'll be waking up a judge, and then I'm going to call the governor."

Minguella's sweating now. "It's more complicated than you realize."

"Take our badges and leave," says Solar. He looks at the men in tactical armor. "You fellas have no idea what bullshit this clown dragged you into."

"I don't think you understand either, Mr. Solar," says a woman in a business suit who quietly enters the office. She's in her early forties, has short blonde hair, and holds a briefcase. "I'm Dr. Emily Fuller. I work with the State Department."

CIA spook, I think. I've dealt with people like her, and it wasn't a fun experience.

"Mr. Minguella, I think everyone would be satisfied if we took their badges. Mr. Solar is correct about the warrant, and I don't think it really serves any purpose anymore."

"I'm not sure if that's—" Minguella starts but is cut off.

"I have this now. Why don't you collect their badges and leave," she suggests forcefully.

I look to Solar. He nods, so I set my badge on the table. Charlton picks it up and takes Hughes's badge as well.

Minguella and Charlton leave with their FDLE agents, and Hughes shuts the door behind them.

Fuller takes a seat at the conference table. "Please sit down," she says, as if it's her table.

We all comply and stare at Fuller, waiting for this new development to unfold.

"Ethan Granth is secretly working with the United States government on an important operation you're about to ruin."

CHAPTER 58
TRIPLE AGENTS

Dr. Emily Fuller waits for our reactions to this revelation. None of us says anything. Solar waits to see what she says next, and Hughes and I are happy to let him do all the talking, or not-talking.

"His work is vital to US interests, and that's all I can say on the matter," she tells us, then looks at each of us for a response.

Solar gets up and walks over to the refrigerator. "I'm grabbing a tea. You want anything, Dr. . . . Fuller? Water? McPherson, Diet Dr Pepper? Hughes, same?"

I follow Solar's cue. "Sounds good."

He places drinks on the table and makes a big show of popping the top of his can of tea, then taking a slow sip.

"I'm sorry, Ethan who?" Solar finally replies.

"We were talking about Ethan Granth," Fuller says, clearly annoyed.

"Hughes, McPherson, were we talking about him?" asks Solar.

I shrug and pop my top, then take a sip. I'm tempted to let out a belch. I don't know what game Solar's playing, so I stay mum.

"I'm sorry, Dr. . . . Fuller." Solar pauses on her name again, clearly making fun of her use of the title outside of a hospital or university. "We have no idea who you're talking about."

"You were at his nightclub, harassing him," she says.

"I can swear to you on a stack of Bibles that I was not," Solar assures her. "Either way, we haven't established who you are or why the heck you're in our office."

"I think I made it clear that I work for the State Department. I think you understand the implication," she snaps back.

"Do you do physicals? I'm sorry, I'm not tracking any of this."

Fuller's getting seriously agitated. "You think this is a game? What just happened with the officers in body armor and weapons? That was a friendly warning. Back off Granth, or you'll do serious damage to national security."

"A friendly warning? That's not how it works. A friendly warning would be your boss calling my boss, and then my boss calling me. Which, last I checked, he hasn't. Not that it matters. You have our badges. We're no longer US Marshals," says Solar.

Fuller stands up. "Then I think we understand each other. I would like any documents or casework you have on Ethan Granth turned over to me."

Solar just stares at her.

"Now," she says. "I believe I've made myself clear. I can return with a subpoena and make things even more difficult . . ."

"That would be great, actually. I'd love to see the name of the judge you get to sign that subpoena. That would be very interesting and telling. But don't bother bringing it here, because we'll be on vacation or looking for other jobs."

"That's the smartest thing I've heard you say," says Fuller.

Solar waves goodbye.

We sit in silence as she gathers her briefcase and leaves. After the door closes, I look under the table.

"Searching for a bug?" asks Hughes.

"Yeah. Nothing there, though. Can never be too careful . . ."

"I wish he tried that," says Solar. "It'd be easy to get a full FBI wiretap on Granth if he had his flunky pull a trick like that. Anyway, I hope that was a teaching moment for you all."

"I guess? She was CIA, right?" I ask.

"CIA adjacent. Some State Department hack who thinks up a brilliant plan, then lets it blow up in other people's faces while she moves on to some new fiasco and a higher pay grade."

"How serious should we take her?" asks Hughes.

"Very," Solar responds. "She's like a child with a gun. Only this gun shoots Navy SEALs and Predator drones at you. The big question is, Does she know what Granth is really up to? Is she in on it? Or is she too dumb to see what's happening?"

"Which is worse?" asks Hughes.

"Probably the latter, because then she can actually follow through on her threats."

"So Granth's not really a secret agent man, just to be clear?" I ask Solar.

"I'm sure he's neck-deep with the CIA and other agencies. I think we established that with the money transfers. She might have been here because of that," says Solar.

"The CIA wouldn't be stupid enough to be involved with the counterfeiting operation," I reply.

"There's nothing too stupid for some of them. But no. And if they were, it's still a crime."

"But we're no longer cops." I motion toward the safe where Solar has the warrant. "And that isn't much good without law enforcement officers to enforce it."

"This is true," says Solar. "I'd get the whiskey, but we have a long night ahead of us."

He takes his phone out of his pocket and dials a number on speaker.

"Hello?" says a tired voice.

"It's Solar. I need you to do the thing we talked about a few minutes ago."

"This is rather unorthodox, you know," replies the man.

"Time is ticking."

"Fine . . . it's McPherson and Huey, right?"

"Close enough," says Solar.

"I, Special Agent in Charge Jefferson Gately, deputize you as agents of the United States Secret Service. Congratulations. Fill out the paperwork and send it to my office. Good night."

Now I know what Solar was doing in the bathroom while the FDLE agents were marching in here.

"So, how does this affect our pension plan?" I ask.

"We can't collect if we go to prison," says Solar. "We need to end this tonight."

Hughes taps away at his laptop. "What's the over/under on Fuller being in on it with Granth? Like, knowing about the machines?"

"She probably knows. She's sticking her neck way out for him. If he's calling in *that* kind of favor, then he knows the risk of it backfiring. Better if she's equally culpable," says Solar.

"Second question: Does she have the power to pull evidence from the Broward County Sheriff's Office?" asks Hughes.

"Possibly," says Solar.

Hughes nods as he watches something on his computer screen. "The tracking device we put inside the fake container—it's moving."

"Really?" I reply. We wanted to see what would happen if we put what could be Granth's seized hypernote machine into an evidence locker. Would it panic him? It looks like the answer is yes. "Where's it heading?"

"Best guess, the executive airport," says Hughes. "The one where Granth has a plane."

"Go!" shouts Solar. "I'll lock up!"

Hughes and I bolt for our SUV.

"I'll drive," I tell him, then climb into the driver's seat. "Find out if there's a flight plan filed."

Hughes has his laptop open next to me. "Already on it."

I put the pedal to the floorboard and almost clip the gate on our way out.

CHAPTER 59
TARMAC

Hilary Mire is handcuffed and sitting in the back of a Broward Sheriff's Office patrol car parked on the airport tarmac when we pull through the gate. She's yelling at the BSO officer, who knows nothing other than everyone boarding the private jet was to be detained.

Ironically, I had to flash the FDLE badge I was originally given back when we launched the UIU as a satellite agency. I've long kept it in the glove compartment because it's so easy to lose track of a badge when slipping in and out of wet suits.

"Mind if I try this first?" I ask Hughes as we get out.

He nods and sets his laptop on the hood of our SUV.

"What the hell's the meaning of this?" asks Mire as I walk up to the police car.

The case from the container is sitting on a cart near the back of the jet, ready to be loaded. Apparently, Mire was in such a hurry that she never bothered to have it opened. This will work to our advantage as long as she doesn't realize it's a dummy case.

I search around for Aran Lopez, but he isn't here. He might not have any idea what Granth was transporting. Or he's elsewhere, doing his dirty work.

"Is that your case?" I ask Mire.

"I'm not talking to you," she fires back.

"You're at an airport. You're an attorney, and you understand that means you've waived certain rights."

"I demand to know why I'm being detained!" she shouts.

"Is that your case?" I repeat slowly.

She falls silent.

"If it's not your case, we're going to seize it and open it up. We're also going to look at the security footage to see if you arrived with it," I tell her.

"I have nothing to say," says Mire. Which is the smartest thing for her to say.

She knows she's between a rock and a hard place. Or at least thinks she is.

"Deputy, would you give me a moment to talk to her?" I ask. "My partner can help clarify the situation."

"Be my guest," he replies as he walks over to our SUV to talk to Hughes.

I fold my arms and try to channel a less threatening demeanor. "We both know what's inside that case. What we don't know is what Granth's going to do when we arrest you and take it into custody. Will he let you take the fall? Will he cut and run? Will he do you like he tried to do Terrence Copley in Catalina? One thing's for sure: this time, I won't be there to save you."

"You're not scaring me," replies Mire, who, by breaking her silence, reveals that she's scared.

"I don't need to. When the other Secret Service agents show up and verify what's in there"—I gesture toward our fake case—"how will that look for you? What's in your future?"

"You're not Secret Service," she says in a half-questioning tone.

"Don't worry about that, honey; you have bigger problems right now. What kind of guy is Granth?"

"Like I said, I'm not talking."

"That'd be a smart move if this was a normal situation. If I were you, I wouldn't want to be the only person going to jail tonight. Now, is that case yours, or is it his?"

Still no response.

"You know how this works. First one to point the finger gets the better deal. I'll make it even easier on you. You don't have to admit any wrongdoing." I take my phone from my pocket and turn on the recorder.

She stares at it, thinking things through. As a lawyer, she knows she should shut up. As someone who works with Granth, she knows he'll make her take the fall . . . or worse.

"All you have to say is that Granth is the owner of the machine that was hidden aboard *The Sea of Dreams*. We then go arrest him tonight and charge him with possession of said machine," I explain.

"Do I still go to jail tonight?" she asks.

"Of course. That's happening either way."

She shakes her head. "I need to talk to my lawyer."

"That's fine. But we're going to arrest you for possession of the machine inside the case. You understand that, right? If you tell us it belongs to Granth, we arrest him tonight and charge him."

Mire's rocking back and forth. If I'm reading her right, she's on the verge of breaking down.

I lower my head so we're eye to eye. "It comes down to a simple question: Who are you more afraid of? An Ethan Granth behind bars, without all his influence? Or an Ethan Granth running free?"

Tears start to well. Her chin's trembling. I find myself starting to feel sorry for her.

"He's a bad man who makes good people do the wrong thing," I tell her, prompting her to unburden herself.

"He wasn't always like that," Mire says, then glances at the phone in my hand and nods.

CHAPTER 60
PARTY BOY

Ethan Granth is sitting at a full table in the steakhouse on the upper floor of Limitless. I recognize the deputy mayor of Miami and at least one local newscaster sitting with him, laughing as a chef serves them seared fillets from a tableside grill.

The big man sees us enter and freezes midstory, then continues as if we were figments of his imagination.

We entered through the front door and used a radio jammer so his staff couldn't warn him. The bouncers quickly made room for us when they caught sight of the four Miami-Dade police officers we brought along as backup.

As we approach the table, Granth can see the Secret Service badges and lanyards that Gately gave us in the parking lot. He keeps looking from our badges to our faces, trying to process this development.

The last text Granth got from Mire was actually sent by me. It simply said:

I have the machine. Airborne.

As he was breathing a sigh of relief, Secret Service agents were quietly closing in on the locations of the six other machines Mire told us about.

Six.

They were kept in locations so disconnected from his legitimate businesses that it would have taken us months to find them, if we ever did.

Our appearance in his club, when Granth thought he'd just sent us to jail, must be a shock to his system. As we near the table, he looks like a man trying to wake himself up from a nightmare.

Hughes and I walk around either side of the table. His guests are so fixated on their food and conversation that they don't even notice us.

"Remember us?" Hughes greets Granth. "What did you call us? Flatfoots?"

Now that his guests see us, their side conversations have stopped.

Granth stands confidently from the table and makes a dramatic gesture. "Is everything okay? Should we step outside?" he asks, pretending this is a friendly visit.

His security people try to enter the room but are held back by the police officers we brought along.

Granth eyes his guests and realizes this is a really poor choice of company when you're facing federal indictments.

"Agent McPherson, why don't you read the charges?" says Hughes.

"Where do I begin?" I then proceed to rattle off the long list of charges, from counterfeiting to terrorism.

His guests can't be sure whether this is a joke until we push Granth against the wall and handcuff him. He starts yelling threats and demanding we let him go—all the things you'd expect a man in his position to do if he was completely guilty.

"You dumb bitch," Granth mutters close to my ear. "I'll be out by tomorrow."

"Are you sure this time? Mire wasn't so sure. That's why she talked to us."

At that, Granth goes quiet and still. Reality's hitting him hard.

"Want to take him out the back way?" asks one of the Miami-Dade police officers.

"Oh, hell no," I reply. "We're taking him straight across the dance floor and out the front door. I want this asshole going viral on Twitter."

EPILOGUE

I can see the bubbles from Jackie's and her cousin Robbie's scuba gear as they swim around the other side of the reef ahead of me. The sun is shimmering through the water above us in perfect rays that illuminate the reef fish and coral like a glowing underwater cathedral. Run is a few yards away from me and gives me a sideways glance through his mask. I nod back to him. My blood pressure has dropped, and I don't feel like screaming about what happened with the Granth case anymore.

Two hours ago, we got the news that Granth cut a major deal with the federal prosecutors. No terrorism charges. No federal attempted-murder charges for trying to have his hit men kill me when we had Copley. No charges for a number of other serious crimes.

The counterfeiting charges stuck, however. He'll spend the better part of the next decade in jail, but that's small consolation for the magnitude of the harm he's done. People died, and he put thousands more on *The Sea of Dreams* in jeopardy.

Solar was on the call when his contact in the US Attorney's office broke the news. She tried to make the point that it was a hard case to prove.

"Why is it always a hard case when it's somebody so politically connected?" growled Solar. "It's like you don't even want to try."

"Well, cases like this are complicated," she replied.

"I think the word you're looking for is 'compromised.' Who made the deal? What else was at stake?"

The long pause was all we needed to hear to know that Solar's instincts were right. Somewhere, somebody had applied pressure for leniency. Maybe some intelligence agency that was worried about Granth using what he knew as leverage. Maybe some politician who was complicit.

I don't know if we'll ever know. All I do know is that roughly around the time I finally finish my PhD, Granth could be a free man.

The counterfeiting conviction may rob him of the prestige he had. Any chance of a political career is probably gone. Probably, because who knows what the future holds in our crazy world. But it's not enough for me.

Granth still has money, and he still has influence. We're already seeing stories being pitched about how he was wrongly made the fall guy in some convoluted government operation. His PR agency—yes, he has a PR agency—has been working behind the scenes trying to get a movie with a leading star to play him in some bullshit spin on the truth.

That's what angers me the most. It's not the minimal amount of time he'll spend behind bars; it's the idea that the media will fall in love with this version of events and help him rehabilitate his image.

Run didn't have to ask me how the call went after it ended. He saw the look on my face. "Gear up! We're going diving," he announced to Jackie and Robbie, who were spending this Saturday afternoon working on a school project.

Run knew the best place for me right now was in the water with the people I love.

We'll probably have a little gathering tonight with friends and family, and I'll be able to commiserate over beers with Solar and Hughes. I can throw my middle finger in the direction of the federal detention center and Granth and gain some solace in the knowledge that, no matter how much money he has, how many people are reposting Instagram selfies with him or using the #GranthWasFramed hashtag created by his social media team, he's alone right now.

He was a lonely man before.

He'll be an even lonelier man when he realizes, hashtags or not, that he's nothing more than a joke meme and no one truly cares whether he lives or dies.

About the Author

Andrew Mayne is the *Wall Street Journal* bestselling author of *The Naturalist, Looking Glass, Murder Theory, Dark Pattern,* and *Angel Killer,* as well as an Edgar Award nominee for *Black Fall* in his Jessica Blackwood series. *Sea Storm* is the third book in his Underwater Investigation Unit series, following *Black Coral* and *The Girl Beneath the Sea.* The star of Discovery Channel's Shark Week special *Andrew Mayne: Ghost Diver* and A&E's *Don't Trust Andrew Mayne,* he is also a magician who started his first world tour as an illusionist when he was a teenager and went on to work behind the scenes for Penn & Teller, David Blaine, and David Copperfield. Ranked as the fifth-bestselling independent author of the year by Amazon UK, Andrew currently hosts the *Weird Things* podcast. For more on him and his work, visit www.AndrewMayne.com.